A new volley of fire struck the hill

Then more bullets scattered leaves five feet away. What the gunmen were doing was obvious. Since they could no longer see their target, they intended to shoot holes through every inch of the pile until they got him. Using his arms, Bolan burrowed deeper into the hill. Through the tangled mess he could see the damp earth below, two feet away. Twisting his head, he looked up and saw that the leaves and limbs had closed over the hole he'd made when he dived into the pile. A burst of fire shot over his head, through the cut foliage where he had hidden only seconds before.

The next burst had moved past him, to his right. For the time being he was safe. The men were shooting over him into the mound. But they would change their angle of trajectory sooner or later. He would have to move again.

Where he'd go next, he wasn't sure. He felt like an animal suddenly trapped in its own den.

MACK BOLAN ®

The Executioner

DON PENDLETON'S
EXECUTIONER®
THE
JUNGLE CONFLICT

A GOLD EAGLE BOOK FROM
WORLDWIDE®

TORONTO • NEW YORK • LONDON
AMSTERDAM • PARIS • SYDNEY • HAMBURG
STOCKHOLM • ATHENS • TOKYO • MILAN
MADRID • WARSAW • BUDAPEST • AUCKLAND

First edition May 2002
ISBN 0-373-64282-2

Special thanks and acknowledgment to
Jerry VanCook for his contribution to this work.

JUNGLE CONFLICT

Bread of deceit is sweet to a man, but afterwards his mouth shall be filled with gravel.

—*Proverbs* 20:17

Dost thou hate to be deceived? Do not deceive another.

—St. John Chrysostom:
Homily XIII, c. 388

Drugs and dishonesty have many things in common. At first people find them a lot of fun—if they didn't, no one would do them. But eventually it all catches up to both the doper and the deceiver. And I catch up to him, too.

—Mack Bolan

To James A. Keating

Prologue

Steady streams of automatic rifle fire shot through the jungle, clipping the dense foliage and sending a storm of torn green vegetation jetting through the air. Kenji Rivas dived facedown onto the soggy ground, hiding himself in the thick undergrowth.

Rising slowly to a sitting position, Rivas flipped the selector switch of his AK-47 to full-auto. The explosions continued, with some of the 7.62 mm lead projectiles flying past him to the sides while others embedded themselves in the trees in front of him. He turned slightly, his eyes scanning the area to his rear. None of the eight men he had brought with him were visible. They might be hiding as he was. Or they might be dead on the jungle floor. He had no way of knowing.

Turning back toward the direction of the assault, Rivas raised his rifle and jammed the wooden stock into his shoulder. His fingers tightened on the pistol grip as his index finger snaked into the trigger guard. He was about to return fire, shoot blindly into the thick green leaves ahead, when he heard a voice whisper through the trees.

"Renaldo," the voice breathed softly, "you and Freire move to the right. Circle around them."

Rivas's finger lifted off the trigger and moved up to push against the front of the guard. A frown of both confusion and concern crossed his face. He hadn't known who had suddenly

opened fire against him and his New and Free Peru brethren in
the jungle. This close to the Ecuadoran border, it could have been
the hated Peruvian army or any of the various NATO troops that
were currently stationed along the border between the two nations. It could even have been Ecuadoran soldiers who had
sneaked past the NATO guards and crossed the border on a raid-
ing trip. He wouldn't have been surprised to have heard the
words just spoken whispered in Spanish, English, French or any
of a half-dozen other languages.

But he had certainly not expected to hear what he had just
heard in Quechua.

The ancient language was still used by some of the tribes in
Peru and Ecuador, tribes that had once been part of the Inca empire. Rivas's father had been of Inca heritage, and Rivas spoke
the language as fluently as he did the Japanese of his mother, as
well as the Spanish of the ancient conquistadors, and the English
of the modern conquistadors—the Americans. But the fact that
he was hearing Quechua now, from the mouth of some unseen
enemy in the jungle, could mean only one thing.

These weren't the government troops of any recognized nation shooting at him and his men. They were Indians. Like him.
Half of him, anyway.

Rising slightly, Rivas let the AK-47 fall to his side. In the same
language he had just heard, he shouted, "Renaldo and Freire. My
friends, there is no need to circle around men who are your
brothers."

For several seconds, the jungle was silent. The only sounds
Rivas heard were the buzz of insects and the ringing that was still
in his ears from the rounds fired a few moments earlier.

Finally, the same voice he had heard whisper earlier spoke
again, louder this time. "You speak our language. Who are you?"

"Kenji Rivas." He paused, wondering just how much he
should give away at that point. A moment later, he decided to go
for broke. "We are the army of the New and Free Peru. And as I
said before, you and I are brothers."

Again silence fell over the jungle. Rivas started to ask the other man who they were, then stopped. He already knew. There could be but one answer to that question. "And you are of the Quechua tribe," he stated instead of asked. "Let me come forward for we are, indeed, of the same fathers."

"Drop your weapons first," the voice warned in the ancient language.

Rivas stood and stepped from behind the tree trunk. He shrugged out of the rifle sling and used it to lower the AK-47 gently to the jungle floor. Slowly, he drew the blue-worn Argentinean-made copy of the .45-caliber American Colt 1911 Government Model from the weathered leather holster pressed against his tiger-striped fatigue pants, and dropped it to the leaves next to the other weapon. A Ka-bar fighting knife was sheathed on his other hip. He had taken it, and a tiny .32-caliber North American Arms semiautomatic pistol, from an Australian mercenary he had killed only a few days before. The knife, he suspected, wouldn't be cause for alarm. And the .32-caliber pistol was buttoned under one of the flap pockets of his camo blouse. He would leave them where they were. Just in case.

Ahead of Rivas, a tall, slender man with a long nose stepped into view. He was clean-shaven, and wore a black rag tied around his forehead and knotted in the back to keep his shoulder-length hair out of his eyes. He had the high cheekbones and other sharp features of an Inca. They hadn't been softened, as Rivas's own face had been, by the inclusion of Japanese blood in his heritage.

The Indian held his own AK-47 against his shoulder, the barrel pointed at Rivas's belly. The New and Free Peru leader saw the tall man glance past him into the dense jungle, then return his eyes to the front sight of his rifle. "How many men are with you?" he asked bluntly.

"Eight," Rivas answered truthfully.

"Tell them to show themselves."

Rivas knew his men had heard the words and waited. When nothing happened, he called over his shoulder, "Do it, friends."

Slowly, one by one, the men rose from their hiding places and walked forward to stand next to their leader. At the same time, perhaps two dozen men joined the tall man with the AK-47.

"New and Free Peru," the Indian said, lowering his weapon only slightly. "The NFP. We know of you. But what are you doing this far north?"

Rivas shrugged. The situation was still out of his control, but the fact that he and his men hadn't been shot yet was a good sign. "Looking for the enemy," he said. "And while we may have come farther north than usual, we are still in Peru."

The Indian dropped his rifle to the end of the sling but kept his hand on the pistol grip. "No, you are not," he said. "You have crossed over into Ecuador."

Rivas was mildly surprised. But he hadn't taken a compass reading for several hours. "If we have trespassed on your land, you have my apology, my brother," he said. "You speak Quechua, as I do. Now, let me ask you the same question you asked me. Who are you?"

"CONAIE," the Indian said.

Rivas felt his face tighten. He had expected these men to be nothing more than a violent ragtag offshoot splinter group of one of the Quechua-speaking tribes. But CONAIE was an acronym for the Confederation of Indigenous Nations of Ecuador, a political pressure group made up of the various tribes within the country. Recently, they had occupied the parliament building in Quito and demanded constitutional recognition of Ecuador as a multiethnic nation. They also wanted amnesty for roughly one thousand peasants charged with offenses under the penal code. CONAIE's president warned that if the Indians' demands weren't met, they would form their own parliament and create a "state within the state."

"I've heard your president speak on TV."

The tall Indian in front of him let a sneer curl his lips, then turned to the side and spit on the ground. Looking back, he said, "He is an idiot. There are occasions when we must act on our own."

A light bulb suddenly flickered in Rivas's head. Yes, he knew who these men were. A splinter group as he'd first suspected, yes, but a splinter group of the CONAIE rather than just an offshoot of a local tribe.

"You are the Lightning Bolts," he said, his voice barely above a whisper.

The tall Indian nodded. "Some have called us that."

Rivas stared the man in the eye, knowing the answer to his next question before he even asked. "And what do they call *you?*"

The Ecuadoran met the Peruvian's gaze, his eyes unwavering. "The name given me by the conquistador bloodsuckers was Carillo. Alejandro Carillo. But I am now called Relámpago."

Rivas's frown became a thin smile. *Relámpago.* Lightning. This was the man after which the violent faction of CONAIE had been named. He had made a reputation for himself by attacking oil fields, mines and government installations throughout his country. The Lightning Bolts had kidnapped dozens of American oil field executives and American and Ecuadoran dignitaries over the past few years, holding them for ransom from their families, their companies, and the Ecuadoran and United States government. In spite of the fact that few of those kidnapped were ever released alive, both governments—governments who publicly proclaimed they would never deal with terrorists—continued to pay behind the scenes. Relámpago and his men had earned a reputation that was destined to live long after they were rotting and burning in hell. They not only had a propensity for violence but for cruelty and torture of their kidnap victims.

Yes, Rivas thought as he continued to study the man in front of him, Relámpago was known as a man to fear. But he was also as a man who got things done.

In other words, he was just the kind of man Rivas had been looking for. Here was the final piece to the puzzle that made up the plan he had been working on since leaving the cocaine trade a few months earlier.

But that piece would have to be added to the puzzle skillfully to ensure it fit.

The thin smile on the NFP leader's lips broadened into a friendly grin. He took a step forward and extended his hand. "I am pleased to meet you and your men, Relámpago," he said. "My name is Kenji Rivas and, as I said before, we are from the New and Free Peru liberation army." He watched in satisfaction as the tall Indian finally released his grip on the AK-47 and took his hand.

Rivas gripped the other man's fingers in his. "I think there are things we should discuss," he said. "Things which are of mutual interest to both of us." He let the other man's hand drop but continued to stare into the cold black eyes. "My men and I were just about to build a fire for dinner. Won't you join us?"

1

Mack Bolan carried his duffel bag and two shoulder bags across the tarmac to the terminal in Iquitos, Peru. From the corner of his eye, he could see his pilot taxiing off toward the hangar where he would await any emergency transportation Bolan's mission would require.

The man known as the Executioner smiled to himself as he neared the terminal. Jack Grimaldi was not only Stony Man Farm's top flyboy, he was one of Bolan's oldest friends. Together, they had fought more wars over the years than either of them could remember.

Bolan's jaw set firmly as he thought of the mission ahead. Another war was about to commence.

The steady beat of lively Latino music drifted out the doorway of the terminal as Bolan approached. Through the opening, he could see the colorfully costumed members of a string and brass band. A woman, dressed in the costume of an ancient Inca princess, stood at the microphone singing the eerie, chanting words of an equally ancient song. She was surrounded by dark-skinned, long-haired men wearing silver medallions, armbands and other primitive South American warrior armor. But rather than spears, bows and short swords, their hands held acoustic guitars and Andes flutes.

Which was just as well, the soldier thought as he stepped into the terminal. The ancient weapons of the indigenous people of South America would be of little use in the war about to come. Even the more modern weapons of war such as assault rifles, high-capacity pistols and explosives were not likely to play a very big part in the outcome of the hostilities that had once again arisen between Peru and her old enemy to the north, Ecuador. The fact was, both countries were rumored to be in possession of modern means of mass destruction.

And it was for that reason that Mack Bolan had come to Peru. To find and destroy those weapons before the two nations used them to destroy each other.

Bolan entered the terminal. Like everyone else around him, a light film of sweat covered his skin in the tropical heat and humidity. The band played on, the music lending to the adventurous charm of an antediluvian people and land. Across the terminal Bolan saw a sign which read Immigration and threaded his way through people toward it. A line had already formed, and he took a place at its end, dropping his bags next to him on the scuffed tile floor.

Not wanting to draw attention to himself once he reached Iquitos, Bolan had asked Grimaldi to first set the plane down in Peru's capital city, Lima. He had gone inside the airport long enough to get his passport stamped and receive documentation that the aircraft had cleared Peruvian customs. Which, considering all of the items hidden inside the canvas and nylon bags that Bolan now carried, would not have been possible without the help of Hal Brognola.

The Big Fed had assured him there would be no actual inspection. Due to a combination of diplomacy and outright bribery, the Executioner's weapons and other equipment had been overlooked. As director of the Sensitive Operations Group, located at Stony Man Farm—America's top secret counterterrorist installation—Brognola answered directly to the President of the United States. All it had taken was one well-placed phone call from the Oval Office, and things had been set up for entry.

Leaving Lima, Grimaldi had then whisked the soldier back into the sky and over the Amazon jungle before landing in Iquitos. Since he was arriving by private aircraft, Bolan now needed only to present his passport and customs tag before going on about his business.

Bolan thought of that business now as he waited in line in front of the counter. Relations between Peru and Ecuador—never good—had at least calmed for a while after the fighting in the 1980s and 1990s. But the situation was threatening to heat up again. Both countries were claiming land northwest of Iquitos, between the Amazon River and the Ecuadoran border. A reopening of hostilities between the two old enemies seemed imminent, and in a last ditch effort to avoid all-out war the UN had quietly stationed NATO troops along the current boundary line.

But what made the United Nations uneasy was that if war broke out this time, it would be different than in the past. American intelligence reports claimed that chemical weapons, reported to be stocks of tabun, sarin and soman, which had been manufactured in the old Soviet Union, had been shipped to South America. These older nerve agents were persistent, remaining in the environment long after distribution, which created tactical problems for the troops that had to seize control of an area immediately. Therefore newer, nonpersistent chemicals had been developed by Moscow before the fall of the Soviet Union, and the older stocks had been pushed to the rear of the storage yards. These outdated chemical agents had been easy pickings for black marketers during the confusion Russia encountered during its own political changeover.

The bottom line was that both Peru and Ecuador had purchased the older chemicals from the Russian Mafia. And now both countries were primed to spread chemical holocaust on the other. If open warfare broke between the two nations, it was only a matter of time before one or the other played this ace card. And as soon as it did, the other would retaliate in kind.

The wholesale annihilation of thousands, perhaps millions, of innocent men, women and children in both countries would be the result.

The Executioner heard a slapping sound as a rubber stamp hit paper on top of the counter, and a man and woman at the front of the line moved away. He scooted his bags across the tile, inching forward, as he continued to wait in line. His mission to South America was both simple and complex. The simple part was the mission statement: find the chemical weapons and destroy them. It was the actual carrying out of that goal that became complex. He had no starting point.

The band went into a soft, sensuous number and Bolan continued to listen to the seductive female songstress as he waited to show his papers. But even as a mood of peace fell over the terminal, his eyes scanned the area. It was an old habit. Hard to break. And not one he wanted to break. It had kept him alive.

Small stalls along the walls, and cropping up like tiny islands above the dirty linoleum tile of the terminal floor, sold everything from candy and chewing gum to stuffed llamas, counterfeit pre-Colombian artifacts and T-shirts. People, both locals and visitors, hurried around these microbusinesses like running backs dodging tacklers.

A city of close to half a million people, Iquitos was one of the world's frontier gateways. More precisely, it was in the middle of the frontier. It could be reached only by air or river; no roads led through the world's largest jungle that surrounded it. And while the military buildup due to the political tensions was massive, the city was as wide open as an American Old West mining camp. Thousands of extra Peruvian army and air force personnel had been shipped into the area's military bases during the past few weeks. But they were there preparing to fight Ecuador, not to keep order among the citizens. Always wild, Iquitos would be even wilder than ever until this crisis was over.

Bolan's trained eyes continued to scan the crowd in the terminal as he waited. He saw many men, women and children, obviously natives, at the airport trying to make a buck any way they could in the sadly impoverished Peruvian economy. They had looked the same in Lima. Of the tourists, however, he noticed a major difference between visitors to Iquitos and the Peruvian capital. Iquitos's guests were cut from harder, leaner, more "fit" looking stock than their counterparts in Lima. Instead of expensive leather suitcases, they carried canvas or nylon backpacks and other luggage made to endure the rigors of the jungle. Their clothing was made up of baseball caps, blue jeans, khaki fatigue pants and jungle or hiking boots rather than the walking shorts athletic shoes, and souvenir I love Lima T-shirts Bolan had encountered when he'd cleared customs in the country's capital city.

All of which was to be expected, Bolan thought as he continued to wait. Few people came to Iquitos for an easy vacation. They came to experience the jungle.

The soldier heard the slap of another passport and behind him, a voice said, "Señor?" He took one last glance around the terminal, wondering why Harvey Scarberry—the man supposed to meet him—hadn't yet shown up. Maybe Scarberry had been caught up in traffic. Like major cities in so many Third World countries, traffic signs and regulations were regarded more as suggestions than law, and the result was frequently massive chaos.

Turning, Bolan reached into one of the multitude of pockets in his lightweight photojournalist's vest and produced his passport. The man on the other side of the counter had a thin mustache. He took the document, glanced at the picture, then looked back up into the Executioner's eyes. "Ah, Michael Belasko," he said. "You cleared Customs and Immigration in Lima?"

Bolan nodded.

"You are a writer, I see," the man behind the counter went on. "You are here to report on the situation with the Ecuadoran aggressors?"

Bolan smiled and nodded again. He wasn't sure whether it was the government of Ecuador or the government of Peru that was the aggressor in this conflict threatening to erupt at any second. And he wasn't sure he cared; at least about the governments. Like so many neighboring nations around the world, the two countries were age-old enemies and would no doubt be fighting each other for one reason or another for centuries to come.

What did interest the Executioner, however, was the welfare of millions of innocent Peruvian and Ecuadoran citizens who had no idea they were on the brink of decimation if the chemical agents were released.

"Please have nice visit, Señor Belasko," the man with the thin mustache said. "And please be careful. These are dangerous times."

"I'll do my best," Bolan replied. He turned back around and took a few steps away from the counter. A moment later, he saw a man roughly five feet eight inches tall hurry through the same door the Executioner had come in. Wiry arms extended from the sleeves of the black T-shirt the man wore under a lightweight nylon bush vest. The chest and shoulders beneath the vest and shirt, however, looked bulky—almost as if they belonged on a different body instead of the one sporting the sinewy arms. The man was in his midfifties with sandy-blond hair. In addition to the T-shirt and vest, he wore OD fatigue pants and sandals. Bolan could see the subdued black pocket clip of a folding knife in his right front pocket.

Harvey Scarberry—it could be no one else. Brognola had described his old acquaintance well. Scarberry had been a Drug Enforcement Administration special agent who had liked his final assignment at the Iquitos field office, and stayed on to live there after retirement. During his tenure along the Amazon, he had fallen in love with the mysteries of the jungle, and during his off- hours had become a jungle survival expert. He now ran a small business, Scarberry Adventure Training, that took clients on survival trips that lasted from two days to six months, depending upon the patron's pocketbook and desires. He knew the city, the jungle and the rivers like a research scientist knew test tubes and petrie dishes. According to Brognola, Scarberry was twice divorced and had fathered two daughters. But he had a young Peruvian girlfriend who was about the right age to be another daughter.

The Executioner raised his arm to catch the man's eye. To each his own, he surmised. Scarberry saw the soldier's up-stretched hand, made a quick turn toward the counter and started that way.

He never got there.

A steady stream of automatic rifle fire exploded from somewhere in the terminal, drowning out the music of the band.

WHILE HE SAW neither the weapon nor the man firing it, the Executioner recognized the distinctive gunfire—9 mm Uzi. And if the rounds buzzing past his head were any indication, the weapon was pointed at *him*.

There was no cover in sight, and the closest concealment was the counter directly behind him. Amid the terrified screams and frantic movements of the people inside the terminal, the Executioner pivoted on the balls of his feet, abandoned the duffel and shoulder bags on the floor where he'd set them and dived over the counter. His left shoulder drove into the soft belly of the shocked immigration official who had just stamped his papers.

More 9 mm rounds began to pepper the wall behind the counter. Bolan wrapped his arms around the waist of the stunned bureaucrat. In a flying tackle worthy of an NFL linebacker, he wrestled the man to the floor.

The autofire continued with no signs of letting up. The soldier thought briefly of the contents of the bags he had just left in front of the counter. In them, he had a wide variety of weapons and enough firepower to hold off a battalion for a few days. But that was a moot point now. He couldn't reach them. Drawing his .44 Magnum Desert Eagle from the nylon shoulder holster under his vest, he dragged the Peruvian official to one end of the counter. He was less than a half second ahead of a new burst of fire that drilled through the thin plywood between them and the rest of the terminal. The 9 mm bullets opened splintery holes in the backside of the counter before disappearing into the wall. Had he and the immigration official stayed where they'd fallen, the deadly lead would have done the same thing to them.

The soldier pushed the other man hard against the floor. "Stay down," he whispered. "And don't move."

The man with the thin mustache stared up at him, his eyes paralyzed in shock. He opened his mouth and his lips moved, but no words emerged.

Bolan released the man and waited for the gunfire to let up, then rolled across the floor behind the counter. He was the target—he knew that—but he needed to get as far away from the innocent Peruvian official as possible before the man took the rounds meant for him. He also needed to return fire, and to do so he'd have to expose himself momentarily behind the counter. Which would provide his attacker with a new target.

Bolan rolled to a halt at the end of the counter, away from the immigration man. He rose to a kneeling position, a thousand and one thoughts racing through his mind as he prepared to shoot back. What had become of Harvey Scarberry? Had the former DEA special agent been hit? Did the man with the Uzi even know Scarberry was his contact? What did Bolan actually face now? A gunman? Or *gunmen?*

He had heard only one weapon, but that didn't mean there weren't other attackers in the terminal, laying low to lure him from hiding before joining in the firefight.

Bolan took a deep breath, then stuck his eyes and gun hand up over the counter. He scanned the terminal for the source of fire, finally seeing the hardman partially hidden on the other side of the steel luggage conveyor. Strangely, almost comically, the bags on the belt continued to revolve as if it were business as usual in the Iquitos airport.

By the time Bolan had spotted his assailant, the man with the Uzi had also spotted him. The Executioner was forced to drop back beneath the counter, rolling again, as a flurry of new rounds exploded from the Israeli hand cannon. With no more emotion than a man viewing a war movie from the safety of a theater seat, Bolan watched more holes appear in the plywood just inches from his side. His mind continued to race. It was a fine line he had to walk if he didn't want to put the innocent mustached man in jeopardy or get shot himself. The counter offered limited concealment. He had no more than ten feet behind it in which to maneuver. And he couldn't get too close to the cringing bureaucrat at the other end. Each time he returned fire over the top, the enemy would get a new fix on his position. Then the gunman would aim directly beneath that position and hit the old man.

Bolan had managed to move quickly so far, but sooner or later, the man with the Uzi would snap to the fact that the Executioner was playing cat and mouse. Then he'd begin shooting to the sides of where Bolan last showed himself. Figuring that out wouldn't take long.

The bottom line was that the only thing more limited than the space in which Bolan had to maneuver was the time in which he had to end this affray.

The Executioner's jaw tightened. He waited for a lull in the firing, then rose again, the Desert Eagle pointed toward the steel conveyor belt. An OD backpack moved across the face of the gunman on the belt, then was replaced by a huge turquoise suitcase standing on its end. As he waited for the bag to move out of the way, Bolan's index finger took up the slack on the trigger. With his peripheral vision, he scanned the terminal.

Many of the other people inside the building had cleared out of the area as fast as their feet could carry them. Others had dropped to the floor behind chairs or other obstacles. One seemingly disoriented older man had simply frozen in place as if his aging limbs had turned to granite. The only movement he made was a slight trembling of terror as he used the walking stick in his hand to support legs numbed with fear.

But Bolan saw no sign whatsoever of Harvey Scarberry.

As the turquoise suitcase moved along the luggage conveyor, the Executioner pulled the Desert Eagle's trigger the rest of the way back to the trigger guard. A 240-grain hollowpoint .44 Magnum round exploded from the chamber, sounding like a nuclear bomb in the close confines of the terminal. The jacketed hollowpoint slug rocketed out the barrel of the pistol at close to 1400 feet per second, slicing through the steel rim of the luggage conveyor just to the side of the gunman's head.

The Executioner dropped back and rolled quickly to the other end of the counter. As he knew the man would do, the gunman sent his return fire bursting through the plywood directly beneath the spot from which Bolan had fired. As he watched the new holes appear in the pressed wood, the Executioner realized that yet another problem was about to enter the equation. By now, the number of rounds that had penetrated the counter had begun to open larger holes—large enough to see through.

Bolan waited, thinking, planning, as the rounds continued. He had seen the gunman behind the conveyor. The would-be assassin had dropped to a prone position, resting the Uzi over the edge of the steel rim. From the Executioner's angle, the man's face was clearly visible each time a space appeared in the revolving luggage. That face was an easy enough target for a man with Bolan's expert marksmanship.

The problem was that a face shot would kill the man, and that's not what the soldier wanted to do. At least not yet. He needed to learn who the attacker was, why the man was trying to kill him, and most of all how he knew who Bolan was.

That meant taking him alive.

Bolan lifted his head over the counter, then ducked back again before the gunman had noticed him. In addition to the man's face, he could see his calves and feet outstretched behind the luggage conveyor. But shooting the man in such extremities—even with the powerful Desert Eagle—wouldn't ensure incapacitation. Even wounded, the gunner might return more fire while Bolan moved in to question him. That would force a head or chest shot in self-defense, and the Executioner would be no better off than if he'd simply ended the shoot-out with a bullet to the face in the first place.

Round after round after round continued to drill through the plywood. The gaping holes in the counter grew. Bolan waited. It was impossible to count the shots fired, but he knew the man had to be nearing the end of the Uzi's 32-round magazine. When that came, there would be at least a brief respite while the gunman changed magazines.

The Executioner's jaw tightened again as a plan formed. It wasn't a perfect plan, he knew. In fact, it had holes in it almost as big as the holes now appearing in the counter between him and the gunman. But it was the only plan available under the circumstances.

The pause in the 9 mm autofire came a second later. Even as he rose, the Executioner heard the familiar scrape of metal on metal as the gunman ejected the spent magazine from his Uzi. Bolan's head shot up over the edge of the counter, the mammoth Desert Eagle extended in front of him. As he pulled the trigger, Bolan caught a quick flash from the corner of his eye—black and khaki, moving fast.

Scarberry. The former DEA man, he could see now, had suddenly emerged from refuge behind several overturned chairs and a trash can roughly twenty feet to the side of the gunman with the Uzi. He had drawn the lock-back folding knife Bolan had seen clipped to his pocket and was thumbing it open.

Bolan had aimed at the gunner's left calf as he squeezed he trigger. But even as the bullet left the barrel he knew he had missed. The gunman had shifted slightly at the last second as he shoved a fresh load into the Uzi.

The Executioner's round struck the tile to the side of the gunner's leg.

The barrel of the subgun turned back up toward Bolan, forcing him to hurry the next shot. It, too, struck wide of the man, leaving another gaping, jagged puncture in the gleaming steel rim around the edge of the luggage conveyor.

Dropping back behind the counter once more, Bolan heard the 9 mm explosions and watched the holes in the plywood grow even larger. It wouldn't be long until the gunman could see where he was. Besides that, it looked as if Scarberry was getting ready to undertake a fool's mission and go after the gunner by himself. With a folding knife.

Bolan had to do something.

The roars of the Uzi still filled the air as the Executioner shot up from behind the counter. As he did, he caught another flash-picture of Scarberry. The former DEA agent was sprinting toward the baggage conveyor, the knife gripped in his right fist.

Bolan squeezed the trigger and the Desert Eagle jumped in his hand. Before he even heard the Magnum roar, he saw the gun-man's calf explode in a flurry of red. A high-pitched shriek pierced the air above the lower tones of the gunfire. Rounds continued to fill the air from the Uzi but now they were far less concentrated in focus, flying over the Executioner's head to the wall; some even striking the ceiling. The attacker's mind was now divided between killing Bolan and his own pain and injury.

The Executioner dropped back and duckwalked to the end of the counter. Had he diminished the gunman's effectiveness enough to make it across the room without being killed? He didn't know, but he had to find out.

Darting suddenly around the corner of the counter, Bolan rose halfway and sprinted toward the conveyor belt at a forty-five-degree angle. After three steps, he cut back, letting a burst of fire pass harmlessly through the spot he'd just occupied. As he ran, he caught yet another glance of khaki and black.

Scarberry was nearing the man with the Uzi, coming in from the gunner's right, slightly behind the man. But before he got within killing range with the blade, he would enter the gunman's peripheral vision.

A new burst of 9 mm rounds forced Bolan to dive forward. Hitting the hard tile on his belly, he rolled to his side, then came up on his feet again. As he rose once more, he saw the man with the Uzi suddenly turn the barrel away from him and point the weapon at Scarberry.

Two quick bursts exploded from the subgun, one right after the other. Bolan watched impotently as Harvey Scarberry jerked back and forth like a crazed marionette in the control of some demented puppeteer. The former DEA agent took the rounds squarely in the chest.

Bolan extended his arm and snapped off another thunderous .44 Magnum slug at the gunman's lower leg. The round missed the man by inches but served to bring his attention back to the Executioner. A steady stream of fire forced Bolan to the ground once more.

Before he could rise again, the soldier heard a long shrill scream come from the man behind the luggage conveyor. It cut off suddenly and was replaced by a throaty, choking, gargling sound.

The Executioner frowned. It made no sense. He had seen his last shot miss. Then, as he popped back to his feet again, what had transpired suddenly became all too clear.

Next to the still-revolving luggage, Scarberry knelt on one knee above the man holding the Uzi. The former DEA man was already wiping the bloody blade of the combat folding knife on the collar of the gunner's shirt.

The man who had tried to shoot Bolan, and had succeeded in pouring two trios of 9 mm rounds into Scarberry, lay staring sightlessly at the ceiling of the airport terminal. Blood gushed from the cavernous slash in his throat.

Bolan's eyes scoured the terminal for any sign of a second attacker. Seeing none, he let the Desert Eagle drop to arm's length at his side and walked forward. Scarberry's back was toward him, but he had no doubt what he would see when the man finally turned his way. None of the rest of what had just happened made any sense if he didn't.

So it came as no shock to the Executioner when Scarberry turned to face him and exposed the six ragged holes in his black T-shirt. Or the white gleam of the bullet-resistant Kevlar vest peeking through the holes.

THERE WAS LITTLE, if any, reason to point out to Harvey Scarberry that he'd just blown any chance they had of finding out who the would-be assassin had been. At least not before they'd even met each other. Besides, it seemed that Scarberry realized his mistake the second after he'd made it. The man in the black T-shirt and two vests—the outer made of khaki nylon, the inner of bullet-resistant nylon—straightened and turned to the Executioner.

"Uh-oh," the former DEA man said. "I think I fucked up."

Bolan didn't answer. The Kevlar vest explained why the rounds from the gunman's Uzi hadn't killed Scarberry. It also accounted for the man's apelike appearance with a chest and torso too thick for his wiry arms. The Executioner looked down at their attacker on the ground as the man choked out the last of his lifeblood, then lay still, his sightless eyes fixed on the ceiling for all eternity. "Let's get out of here before the cops come," was all he said.

Scarberry nodded as he stood. "The cops are part of the military, and the military has Ecuador on the brain at the moment. A little thing like a shoot-out at the airport isn't going to get their panties in a twist."

"Unless they think the Ecuadorans did it," Bolan countered as he holstered the Desert Eagle.

Scarberry squinted then said, "Good point. In fact, damn good point. Let's go." He turned and started jogging for a side door, then looked back over his shoulder to make sure Bolan was following. "Belasko, right? Mike Belasko?"

Bolan stared at the carnage that had once been an immigration counter as he ran. "It'd be quite a coincidence if I wasn't, don't you think?" he said.

"Yeah. Guess it would."

As they ran to the door, Bolan took in more of the wrecked terminal. Bullet holes pocked the walls, floor and ceiling. One of the musicians' guitars was in splinters, the microphone stand had been nicked and the microphone now dangled from the cord, and blood stained the entire area surrounding where the gunner had been shot in the leg and had his throat cut.

It could be nothing less than a miracle that only one life had been lost. And that was one life that needed to go.

Scarberry led the way out of the building and across the concrete parking lot to a ten-year-old Nissan. "It ain't much," he said as he thumbed a remote control on his key ring to unlock the doors. "But it's all we have."

Bolan had picked up his bags on the way out and now threw them in the back seat before sliding into the car on the passenger's side. "As long as it gets us out of here without any complications, I'm happy," he said.

Scarberry got in behind the wheel and stuck the key into the ignition. A second later, the engine turned over. He backed out of the spot and steered the car to the highway leading into town. "It'll do that," he finally said, responding to the Executioner's last statement. When Bolan remained silent, he drove on. The soldier saw him checking the speedometer every few seconds, making sure he was under the speed limit but not by more than a mile or two. Good. It wouldn't do to get stopped for speeding at this point. But driving too slow could draw attention just as easily.

Bolan nodded to himself. Smart. The former DEA agent might have messed up their chances to question the gunman but he'd had no idea that was Bolan's intention. He'd been more intent on staying alive, and with nothing more than a folding knife to go up with against a submachine gun, he'd done a heck of a job.

They passed a sign pointing toward a large military base. Behind the chain-link fence, men and vehicles moved quickly about. The base was alive with activity as Peru prepared for war.

"You don't carry a gun?" the soldier asked, finally breaking the silence.

"Don't even have one anymore," Scarberry said. "Even when I was active with DEA we weren't supposed to be armed according to Peruvian law. Since I retired, and decided to make this place home, I've tried to play by the rules."

Bolan had learned over the years that all cops could be broken down into two general categories, depending on how they viewed their agency's policy manual. There were those who looked at the manual as another book of the Bible. Then there were those who thought it should be retitled *The Book of Suggestions*. According to Brognola, Scarberry had been of the latter group, a maverick who wasn't afraid to bend the rules when that was what it took to get the job done.

Bolan turned to face him. "From what I was told you used to make your own rules," he said.

Scarberry shrugged. "I said we weren't *supposed* to be armed," he said. "Didn't say I never was. Only a fool would hang out with the dopers in this part of the world without a piece." A grin crept across his face. "The truth is, since I retired I haven't had a need for anything but the 16-gauge single-shot shotgun the law allows. I take clients on trips into the jungle, where the worst dangers I face come from fer-de-lances, cascabels or other snakes. Hell, this is low jungle, there aren't even any cats to worry about. Out of the jungle, regardless of what people in the States may think, there's a lot less violence and street crime down here than there is back home." He guided the Nissan around a curve in the road and the city of Iquitos appeared, then chuckled. "At least there was until you got here."

Scarberry turned suddenly serious. "No, really, Belasko," he said. "Did you see any beggars at the airport?"

Bolan shook his head. "No."

"But you know how impoverished this country is," Scarberry continued. "That's no secret. Yet, no one's asking for a handout. Oh, they'll try to sell you every worthless piece of souvenir-tourist crap in the world. And if you offer them something, they'll take it. And they'll keep taking, without shame, until you're ready to stop giving because they need it. But nobody panhandles down here. They aren't used to getting anything for free, and they expect to work for everything they do get." He turned to meet the Executioner's gaze. "Our government might take a lesson from theirs in that respect."

Bolan couldn't argue. Experience had taught him that people who were pampered and allowed to survive without working soon grew to expect such treatment.

The soldier turned his eyes back to the road. At the airport, then all along the highway leading into Iquitos, he had seen the famous rickshaw cabs of Iquitos. Nicknamed after the people-powered Asian two-wheeled taxis, the Peruvian versions were motorcycles with trailers mounted at the rear. The trailer held a seat that could accommodate up to three tourists or what appeared to be countless locals. As he focused his attention on the rickshaw they were now passing, Bolan saw three women and seven children crowded in under the overhead awning. They were seated in an arrangement that he doubted could be duplicated again if their lives depended on it, and which would put the circus clowns who emerged from miniature cars to shame.

"Okay," Scarberry said, laughing. "Bottom line, yeah, if I'm going to hang out with you, I suspect I could use a gun. By the looks of the trouble that seems to find you, I could use *several*. Maybe a few grenades, a Hummer and a squadron of F-16s."

"I brought extra weapons. We'll get you fixed up when we get where we're going."

"Which brings us to my second question," Scarberry said. "Where are we going?"

Bolan paused, thinking. Under his guise as a journalist, he already had a room lined up in downtown Iquitos at the Hotel Florentina. But there was no need to go directly there and check in. If he was going to portray a journalist, he needed to be seen acting like one. Iquitos might be a large city, but he knew it operated like a small town. Word spread quickly—especially among the rickshaw drivers—and soon the entire population would know a new guy was in town. Word of the gunfight at the airport would also be the talk of the day, and while there were too many American journalists in town to immediately link him to it, even the lukewarm efforts of the police would eventually point his way. When that happened, the whole cover would fall apart. But he needed to put that time off as long as possible.

"Let's get something to eat," Bolan said. "Some place downtown. Preferably, out in the open with lots of people around." He reached over the seat and grabbed one of the shoulder bags. Pulling out an expensive 35 mm Pentax camera, he draped it around his neck on the strap. "You know any place like that?"

Scarberry laughed again, and Bolan saw a twinkle enter his eyes. "Oh yeah," he said. "I know a place like that. Ari's. Full name is Ari's Burgers."

"Hamburger place? I need some place where I can further my cover. Some place where we'll be seen."

"Don't let the name fool you, Belasko," Scarberry said. "Just trust me on this one. You show up at Ari's, word will spread fast."

ARI'S BURGERS HAD an international clientele. It made no difference which way he looked in the open-air corner café, Bolan saw people from all over the world. Japanese, Chinese, Germans and Russians were seated alongside native-born Peruvians and men and women from other Latin American countries. Bolan knew instinctively that many would be agents of their respective governments. Many others would be posing as legitimate businessmen whose real trade was in drugs, arms or illegal antiquities. The United States was well-represented, with DEA, BATF and Customs agents, State Department officials and Coast Guard sailors all trying—usually unsuccessfully—to pass themselves off as harmless bureaucrats.

Ari's stood on the corner of Prospero and Armas avenues, across from the Plaza de Armas in the center of Iquitos. Two of its four sides were open, one running along each of the two busy streets. Bolan and Scarberry took a seat at the last table available—next to the sidewalk and near the wall that joined the café with the souvenir shop next to it. Against the wall were a line of glass-doored refrigerators holding bottled water, ice cream, beer and various soft drinks. They hadn't been seated more than a few seconds when a beautiful young woman with deep berry-colored lips and the sharply defined features of an Indian princess walked over and kissed Scarberry on the cheek. Like all of the Ari's waitresses, she wore a very short woven skirt and halter top, which was decorated with Inca print and emphasized her perfect body. An off-white headband with neon green letters shouting Ari's Burgers was tied around her forehead, keeping her long black hair in place.

Scarberry wrapped an arm around her waist. The girl glanced immediately over her shoulder to an old man standing with his arms folded across his chest in front of the cash register. He had been scolding another of the waitresses when they'd entered the café, and now he stared at their table with a malicious expression on his face.

"Mike," Scarberry said, "this is Anita, Anita meet Mike. Honey, we'll both have a bottle of water, an Inca cola and an Ari's burger with fries. Now, you better get out of here before the old fart has a stroke." He glanced toward the cash register where the old man continued to glare. Anita kissed him on the cheek again and took off.

"My girlfriend," Scarberry said as soon as she'd gone. "And I don't need any more comments about our ages than I've already had." He chuckled, then said, "The old bastard by the cash register is some relative of the owner. His primary purpose in life is to make sure none of the girls have time to breathe."

Bolan nodded and continued to survey the café. American missionaries, he saw, were also in abundance, and they appeared to be the only people at Ari's who weren't trying to act like something other than what they actually were. Several were seated at the table next to Bolan and Scarberry, and most seemed enchanted by the exciting world they'd suddenly entered and fiercely dedicated to witnessing for Christ to the people of Peru. But one overweight woman who seemed to be in charge of a group of teenagers droned on and on in an incensed voice about the substandard sanitary conditions, a lack of motivation to "better themselves" and what she referred to as a "basic laziness" on

the part of the Peruvian people as a whole. Bolan had to wonder
about her true intentions.

A quartet of men who looked as if they could be mercenaries,
drug smugglers, gunrunners, or yet another group of American
agents of some sort were seated at a table catty-cornered from both
the missionaries and Bolan and Scarberry. Finally, a bulky, bald-
ing, middle-aged man had overheard all of the woman's bitching
he cared to hear. Turning in his chair, he faced her. "What did you
expect when you came down here?" he asked between the cigar
stub stuck between his teeth. "The fucking Holiday Inn?"

The woman rose indignantly and hurried her group of
teenagers out of Ari's and down the street.

"Missionaries are like everyone else, I guess," the former
DEA man said. "Some good, some bad. I've known a lot of them
down here. Most have their heart in the right place. A few, like
that one, can't seem to get past the fact that the toilets don't always flush and not everyone uses the latest shampoo. And almost
all of them—good and bad alike—are pretty naive." His eyes suddenly shot across the room to a table next to the sidewalk. "But
once in a while, you get one like that guy sitting over there. Dedicated as hell and is anything but naive."

Bolan followed Scarberry's gaze and saw a short, stocky man
seated alone. Another of the waitresses, dressed identically to
Anita, was in the process of bringing him his order. She set it on
the table, the two spoke briefly and she moved away. Bolan studied the man. He was dressed in what had begun life as a white
T-shirt. But years of sweat had dyed the shirt tan. The thick bi-
ceps and forearms of a manual laborer extended from the tight
sleeves, and at the end of the muscular neck that shot up from
the T-shirt's stretched-out collar was a weather-beaten face. He
wore black horn-rimmed glasses twenty years out of style and,
like the rest of the man's appearance, practically shouted that the
way he looked was low on his list of priorities.

"Lee Kinelli," Scarberry said, lowering his voice to a whisper. "One tough little bastard. And you may not believe it, but

he was tied into the Chicago Mob before becoming a missionary." He paused, then went on. "The rumor is—and this may be an exaggeration for all I know—that he took hits for them."

As if he had radar, Kinelli looked up from his food and then across the room. His eyes met Scarberry's, then he chuckled. "How are you, Harvey?" he shouted across the room over the noise of two dozen other conversations and the sounds from the street. "Missed you in church Sunday."

Scarberry returned the laugh. "Wasn't feeling well," he shouted back.

Kinelli laughed harder. "Been sick for quite a few weeks now, haven't you?" he asked. "I'll have to pray that you get well."

Scarberry shrugged, playing along with the game. "Been sick some, out in the jungle all the other weeks."

"Well, God loves you anyway, Harvey," Kinelli said. "I'll reserve a pew for you next Sunday."

"I'll be there."

"I won't hold my breath." The missionary laughed and returned to his food.

Few things surprised the Executioner anymore. But a Mob hit man turned missionary was a borderline case. "Is he for real?" he asked Scarberry.

Scarberry nodded. "Oh, yeah. We checked him out when he first arrived. Figured he was down here working some drug connection. But we never found anything but the good he was doing, and he's been here for years now." He glanced toward the missionary and watched the man eat as he continued. "The story is he almost got killed, and just like that hit man in *Pulp Fiction* he 'saw the light.' Got out of the Mob and then tried to get a job with one of the American foreign mission boards. They weren't having any part of him, so he came here on his own." The former DEA man smiled and shook his head. "What he did to finance his trip is a matter of great speculation at some of the finer cocktail parties." He turned to Bolan. "The Lord works in mysterious ways."

The Executioner nodded. While it was unusual to say the least, such a complete turnaround from demon to saint wasn't unheard-of by any means. He thought briefly of his own pilot who had brought him to Peru. Jack Grimaldi had once been a flyer for the Mafia. But he had been a good man inside, and Bolan had helped turn him around. Now, there was no one the soldier trusted more.

Scarberry broke into his thoughts. "Anyway, Kinelli preaches all over this area. He also helps folks build houses. He gets civic projects going, too. Parks, schools, the like. Anything to make these people's lives better. We've got a little joke around here about him when it comes to saving souls."

"What's that?" Bolan asked.

"The Reverend Kinelli just makes them an offer they can't refuse."

Anita returned carrying a round tray and set their order on the table in front of them.

Scarberry glanced over his shoulder, saw that the old man at the cash register was busy rebuking one of the other waitresses and pinched Anita on the butt. The young girl squealed, then slapped at his hand with the empty tray, giggled and walked away.

As soon as she'd gone, Scarberry turned serious. "Belasko, you ever been married?"

Bolan shook his head.

"I have been," Scarberry said. "Twice. Both times a disaster." He looked down at his plate for a second. "Part of it was the job. The bad hours, the stress, all that. And part of it was picking the wrong women. But part of it was just me. I wasn't ready." He glanced over his shoulder to where Anita was picking up another order from the kitchen. "Anyway, I think I might be now. Thinking about it, anyway."

"Good luck," Bolan said. "I wish you the best." The two men began to eat, and he got down to business. "I need to find out who the guy at the airport was," he said before taking a bite of his hamburger. "My primary goal is to locate and neutralize the chemical weapons Brognola told you about. But that's connected to the guy who tried to kill me. I don't know exactly how, but it has to be."

Scarberry bit into his own hamburger and nodded. "Yep," he said. "Has to be." As soon as he'd swallowed, he said, "You've got a leak somewhere."

The Executioner knew that already—it was the only thing that explained how the man with the Uzi had fingered him. But he didn't know where the leak was, or how to plug it before it got worse.

"Who knew you were coming down here?" Scarberry asked as he squeezed ketchup out of a container onto his french fries. "By the way, this isn't the kind of ketchup you're used to," he added. "It's made out of some kind of peppers instead of tomatoes." He handed the plastic bottle to Bolan.

"Just Brognola, you and me," the soldier said as he took the ketchup and set it down. "At least we're the only ones who knew the real reason I was coming."

Scarberry looked up as he used his fork to stick a french fry in his mouth. A moment later, he said, "I've known Hal Brognola a long time. Good man. But he's with the Justice Department." He moved his fork through the ketchup on top of the fries and as he looked back down at his plate. "You aren't."

"What makes you say that?" Bolan asked.

"Just a feeling."

Bolan sat quietly, waiting.

When he got no response, Scarberry looked up again. "Okay. Some things I need to know, have to know, and some things I don't and I'm better off not knowing. And I don't need to know exactly who you are, just that Brognola vouches for you. That's enough. Hell, I'm even willing to keep calling you Mike Belasko and pretend I believe that's really your name if that's what you want."

"It is," Bolan said simply.

"Fair enough. So where do you want to start?"

Bolan glanced around the café, watching the street hustlers and the old man by the cash register. Each time his attention was diverted in any way, they entered Ari's and began trying to hock their wares to the closest tourist. But each business venture ended almost as quickly as it had begun. As soon as the old man saw them, he shuffled angrily their way, his arms flapping up and down at his sides like some enraged vulture, and the would-be sellers were forced back to the sidewalk. The cracked pavement appeared to be neutral ground.

Bolan's eyes fell back on the Reverend Mr. Lee Kinelli. The man had finished what looked like fish and was now eating a cup of the local ice cream. Turning his attention back to Scarberry, the Executioner said, "I need you to set up some interviews for me. As an American writer."

Scarberry set down his fork and took a drink of Inca cola. "No problem," he said. "Who do you want to see?"

"For a start, the colonel in charge of the air force base," Bolan said.

"That would be Colonel Imenez."

"Whoever." Bolan took a sip of Inca cola, found it too sweet and switched to the bottled water. "And there's another air force base, right? "

"There is," Scarberry agreed, bobbing his head up and down as he continued to chew. "ESSEL. *Esquela de Supervivencia de la Selva.* Downed Pilot Jungle Survival School. Very small compared to the main base, but they're quartering some of the troops there as they get ready to move toward Ecuador."

Bolan looked up briefly as the old man at the cash register screamed out a string of angry Spanish. His arms flapping again, he scuffed the soles of his shoes over the tile toward a table of younger men the soldier had pegged as probably U.S. Coast Guard. One of the street vendors—a reed-thin man with a stringy mustache and rotting brown teeth—had entered the café and was trying to hustle several cheaply framed butterfly specimens.

When he saw the older man coming, he hurriedly dropped the frames back into the box suspended around his neck and hurried out of the café.

Bolan took a bite of his burger. He wasn't sure exactly what it was, but he'd bet his life it wasn't beef. He glanced out toward the sidewalk where the street hustlers were pushing everything from alligator and jaguar teeth to bright red T-shirts that read I Love Iquitos in bold white letters.

Bolan was familiar with ESSEL. The Peruvian Air Force Downed Pilot Jungle Survival School trained not only their own in-country troops but those of friendly nations, as well. Britain, France, Germany and many other countries had sent their top soldiers, and quite a few U.S. Navy SEALs, Army Special Forces, and other American personnel were also graduates.

"Who's running ESSEL these days?" Bolan asked Scarberry.

"Commandant Suarez." The look Scarberry now gave his own hamburger made it appear he'd come to the same conclusion Bolan had. "Horsemeat, would be my guess," he said, then took another bite. "Ramon Suarez. Good dude. You'll like him."

"You know him?"

"Oh, hell yeah," Scarberry said. "He was still a captain when I was still with DEA. Assigned to the joint DEA-U.S. Coast Guard-Peruvian narcotics task force."

The Executioner was familiar with the task force. The U.S. Coast Guard provided a continuous patrol, up and down the Amazon and its tributaries, with unarmed gunboats. DEA agents joined the Coast Guard personnel and provided the expertise necessary to root out the boats transporting cocaine and other illegal drugs. The Peruvian military rode along to make the whole thing legal.

"Yeah," Scarberry went on. "Suarez is okay. We've downed many a beer together over the years. And since ESSEL is smaller than the main base, he'll be easier to get to than Colonel Imenez. So we'll contact him first. What do you say I give him a call later this afternoon?"

Bolan nodded as he finished eating and tried another sip of cola. He wondered how much about secret chemical weapons either Suarez or Imenez would know, and how much they'd be willing to pass on the foreigners like him and Scarberry if they did. The answer was, he didn't know, but it was a launching pad for this mission. He had nothing better to go on at this point.

The cola wasn't any more to his taste the second time than it had been the first, and the Executioner set it down again. He was reaching for the water when a familiar eerie feeling suddenly crept up his spine and his battle radar suddenly went on full alert. His hand froze halfway to the water.

The Executioner held little, if any, belief in extrasensory perception. What he did believe in, however, was experience. Battle was what Bolan had been trained in. War, both formal and informal, was his experience. He had gotten no more than a feeling that something was wrong many times over the years, and each time that feeling had saved his life or the lives of others.

He had that feeling now, and he wasn't about to ignore it.

The soldier looked up to see the man who had attempted to sell the butterflies earlier walking toward him. A thin hand was invisible inside the box suspended from his neck on a dirty rope. But that wasn't unusual, and not what caused Bolan to halt his hand before it reached the water bottle. What had brought on the alarm inside the Executioner's head wasn't the strange expression on the street hustler's face, or even the bizarre look in his eyes that hadn't been there before. Nor was it the stiff, almost Frankenstein-like plodding pace that now propelled the man toward Bolan and Scarberry's table.

What had tripped the Executioner's battle radar was the very essence of the man.

This man was about to kill someone.

Him.

As the street vendor continued toward him, Bolan forgot about the water and reached under his vest for the Desert Eagle.

2

As if in slow motion, the Executioner watched the street hustler bring the SIG-Sauer P-226 out of the box. His first thought was that not only did this man not own the gun, it had come into his hand only moments before. Even at street prices, SIG-Sauers were one of the most expensive of all handguns, and this man was of Iquitos's poverty-stricken class—he simply couldn't afford it. And if he had stolen it, he would have traded it for something of more immediate need to his survival. Like food. In addition to that, Bolan's brain registered the fact that the man's hand was wrapped too far around the pistol. His wrist wasn't straight, and wouldn't absorb the recoil when the weapon was fired. And he had far too much finger on the trigger. When he pulled the double-action mechanism all the way through, his shot would tend to go left of his target.

It was as if the entire world around him was suddenly operating in slow motion while Bolan moved at the same pace. He processed the information his eyes picked up and transferred to his brain, and knew someone had just given the gun to the man. As the barrel continued to rise, the Executioner would have bet his life that the man hadn't had the gun when the old proprietor chased him out of Ari's less than a half hour earlier.

But there was more—perhaps a hundred additional details

racing through Bolan's mind as he continued to watch the man move. What the soldier saw before him was an Iquitos street hustler who was far too busy trying to scratch out a day-to-day living to bear him, Scarberry, or anyone else any malice. Bolan was an American, and to this man Americans meant only one thing. Money. And money meant survival. At least for another day. And the man with the SIG would never kill the "goose that laid the golden egg."

Unless someone had offered him so much money that a man in his position had been unable to refuse.

Even as he finally began to move, the Executioner realized that his assailant wasn't an evil man. The feeling he had gotten—the feeling that had penetrated his very being and caused him to look up as the man entered the café again—wasn't one of evil or hatred or malice of any sort. The aura that had emanated from the street vendor's soul was a combination of four other emotions. Desperation and fear were the first two. And the first two brought on the second pair: regret and guilt.

This recognition produced an emotion in Bolan. Sorrow. He felt sorry for the man who was about to try to kill him. And he had no desire to kill this street vendor, even in self-defense.

But he wasn't going to let this man kill him.

Still feeling as if the rest of the world were at half speed, Bolan began to come up out of his chair. As the SIG rose higher, the barrel angling closer toward him, he held no false hope that the man would change his mind. The glint of a cheap, corroded wedding ring could be seen on the hand not holding the gun, and it told Bolan that somewhere, eating whatever scraps they could find and sleeping on floors of hard-packed dirt beneath worn and patched mosquito nets, this man had a family. A family to whom would go whatever money he received for killing the Executioner.

Yes, this man was afraid to act. He felt guilty about doing it, and he knew he would regret doing it for the rest of his life. But he was going to do it. The desperation component within his emotional quadrangle would ensure that he saw the murder through.

Bolan's hand had moved automatically toward the Desert Eagle. But now he let it fall away as he thrust the rest of the way to his feet. The street vendor stopped three feet away from the table, directly across from him. The man's hand trembled as he attempted to point the unfamiliar gun at his target.

Bolan leaped with all the power in his thighs. Flying across the table headfirst, he stretched out both of his arms to his sides. Harvey Scarberry, who had continued eating and not noticed the approaching man, suddenly looked up and said, "What the fu—" as the Executioner's legs dragged across the tabletop, sending plates, bottles and silverware flying through the air around him. His legs were still in the air as one hand found the gun and the other grabbed the street hustler's wrist. His shins came down on the tabletop, striking painfully against the metal. His fingers found the butt end of the weapon and told him—by feel—that the double-action pistol had not been cocked into single-action mode. He clamped a thumb over the hammer, trapping it flat against the slide.

The man holding the gun screamed in surprise. He hadn't known what to expect—he was not an experienced killer. He tried to pull his hand free from the Executioner's grip but the strength—the will to continue—had drained from his body.

Bolan crashed into the man, and the two tumbled to the floor between tables. Gasps and other surprised sounds issued from the mouths of Ari's other patrons. With a quick jerk, the Executioner ripped the SIG-Sauer from the street vendor's grasp. When the man reached for it again, Bolan snapped it downward, rapping a wrist and bringing forth another scream—this time of pain rather than surprise.

The Iquitos street hustler fell to a sitting position, his head bowed, eyes to the floor.

Behind the counter that held the cash register, Bolan could see one of the beautiful young waitresses on the phone. But her terrified eyes were glued to the Executioner. Leaning over, he grabbed his would-be killer by the arm and jerked the man to his feet. "Who told you to do this?" he demanded in Spanish.

"I didn't know him," he said. He was fearful for his life, but his shame outweighed his fear. A tear dripped down the side of this face as he said, "I will give you the money if you don't kill me." He reached slowly into his pocket, and extended his hand.

It held a ten sole bill. Between two and three U.S. dollars.

Bolan snatched the bill out of the man's hand, stuffed it into the box on the floor and lifted it into the air. With his other hand, he hauled the man to his feet. Behind the counter, he could see the waitress speaking excitedly into the phone. "Get out of here," he ordered the street vendor. "The cops are on their way."

Turning to Scarberry, he said, "We'd better go, too."

Scarberry nodded and followed Bolan out onto the sidewalk. As they turned down the street, the Executioner glanced back into Ari's and saw the man who had tried to kill him hurrying out of the café. He had taken the ten sole bill out of the box and held it against his chest, clenched in his fist, as if it might be the most precious diamond on earth. Before he turned back, Bolan's eyes fell on Lee Kinelli. The former mobster turned missionary had a mixture of amusement and benevolence on his face beneath the black horn-rimmed glasses. His eyes met Bolan, and he nodded his approval.

But that was not all that the Executioner saw. Beneath the table, gripped in the Reverend Mr. Lee Kinelli's right hand, the two-inch barrel of a small blue revolver was visible.

No one but Bolan seemed to see the missionary casually slip the gun back under his T-shirt.

THE HOTEL FLORENTINA was not five-star accommodations. The fact was, if such celestial measurement had been used to rate the inn, it wouldn't have received even a brief twinkle from an ancient burned-out star.

Bolan led Scarberry up the steps to the lobby, dropping his bags in front of the counter. Directly ahead, on the other side of the registration desk, he saw an open door. Through the entrance, a line of rooms stood to the left, with an unkempt courtyard to the right.

Across from the registration desk was a small, shabby lobby.

Two couches, one with only three legs still shakily supporting it, the other slanting forward with both of the front supports missing, occupied most of the room. Several threadbare armchairs formed a semicircle around a black-and-white television set on which a Spanish game show was in progress. Excited chatter buzzed forth from the scratchy TV speaker among bells, buzzers, whistles and Latino hard rock music.

The only person seated in front of the TV was a beautiful young woman in her early twenties. Long, shining black hair cascaded down her neck and back, partially concealing the high round breasts visible above her neckline. Sultry brown eyes looked up as Bolan stopped at the desk. The woman smiled seductively.

Bolan returned the smile, but shook his head.

The woman affected a pout with her sensual lips. She held up the fingers of both hands, closed them, then opened them again. Twenty soles. A little over five dollars. The young prostitute was ravishing, and could have earned an easy five hundred dollars an hour in any large U.S. city. A wave of sadness swept over Bolan as he turned away from her and back to the desk.

A man with a three-day growth of beard had come in from the courtyard. "Yes?" he said, taking up his station behind the counter.

"Belasko." Bolan said. "Reservation for two." He held up two fingers, glancing over his shoulder. Scarberry had stopped just behind him and was grinning at the young woman.

The room for two cost even less than the prostitute had asked. The desk clerk led them through the door into the courtyard. He handed Bolan a key and pointed toward a door just past a five-gallon glass water container perched atop a tall stool.

Bolan led Scarberry into the room and set his bags on one of the two beds. A lone sheet—which might have been washed during the past year or might not have been—covered the mattress. There was no pillow. Nor were there any attempts to decorate the cracked plaster walls. A small wooden table pressed against the wall between the two beds. A lone straight-backed wooden chair was the only other furnishing.

"Eh, what the hell," Scarberry said, dropping to a seat on the other bed. "I've slept in worse places. Haven't you?"

"One or two," Bolan said, then turned and sat facing the former DEA agent. Nodding toward the door, he said, "Make your call. To the commandant at ESSEL."

Scarberry nodded, rose to his feet and walked out of the room. He disappeared toward the lobby.

Bolan stared at the cracked wall in front of him, his eyebrows lowered in concentration. The street vendor who had tried to kill him at Ari's had been the second attempt on his life since he'd reached Iquitos—a city where he was supposed to be known as a harmless journalist. He didn't know how but his cover had been compromised. Maybe not completely blown but someone knew he wasn't what he was portraying himself to be. He closed his eyes and rubbed his temples with both hands. As Scarberry had pointed out, there was a leak somewhere. Right now, it might only be whoever was behind the two attempts on his life—and he had no doubt that they had come from the same source. But word would eventually spread, until even the average man on the street knew he was more than he seemed.

Which meant he had to work fast.

Bolan stood, opened one of his bags and pulled out a metal coffee cup. He walked out into the courtyard and held it under the spout of the glass drinking water container. He glanced around the courtyard as the cup began to fill.

He had chosen the Florentina for its location and anonymity. It was in the heart of the city, close to the action, where he could grab quick rickshaw rides to both bases, and was within fast walking distance of several Internet cafés that he intended to use for communication to the States.

When the cup had filled, Bolan held it to his lips and took a sip, then returned to the room and the edge of the bed. While he had judged it a good idea to leave Ari's right after the incident with the street vendor, he doubted that the police were going to make much of what had happened. He was a foreigner, and a journalist at that. In that role, he would be viewed by the cops as a bottom feeder who was there to profit from the misfortunes of their war. In short, most cops wouldn't really care if he got killed or not.

The thought brought a smile to his face. Such apathy could be used to his advantage. The smile faded almost as quickly as it had come. Such apathy might well be his only advantage.

Footsteps sounded on the broken concrete outside the room, and Bolan's hand moved unconsciously toward the Desert Eagle. But a moment later, Scarberry appeared and the hand fell back away.

"Good news," the man said, resuming his seat on the bed. "The commandant can see you in an hour."

"How long will it take to get to the base?"

"Five, ten minutes max. That's by rickshaw."

The soldier nodded. Reaching behind his back to his belt, he pulled out the SIG-Sauer he had taken from the man at Ari's. "I've got extra rounds if you want this piece," he said, extending the weapon across the room to Scarberry. "But that's the only magazine."

Scarberry took the SIG but his face was one of disgust. "I'm from the old school," he said, dropping it on the bed next to him. "I *hate* autos. Especially double-action, and especially 9 mm."

"So Brognola told me," the Executioner replied. He reached into his duffel bag and produced two black leather pistol cases. "Which is why I brought these." Unzipping the first case, he pulled out a Smith & Wesson N-frame Mountain Gun in .45 ACP.

Scarberry smiled. "Ah," he said. "That's more like it."

Bolan handed him the big revolver and two 50-round boxes of .45 slugs. Reaching into the bag once more, he came up with an unopened cardboard and plastic container of half-moon clips. They would be necessary in order to eject the spent brass that was actually manufactured for a semiauto rather than a revolver. But they also served as the fastest wheelgun speedloader ever devised, not even having to be removed from the cylinder when a fresh load was inserted.

Scarberry began loading the clips for the Mountain Gun as

the Executioner unzipped the other case. Another S&W revolver appeared. This wheelgun, however, was smaller—a 5-shot J-frame .357 Magnum hammerless in stainless steel. Known as the Centennial, it was both an excellent backup and pocket gun for those favoring revolvers. He handed it, a box of .357 rounds, and a half-dozen Safariland speedloaders to the man across from him.

Scarberry had dropped the first clip in the Mountain Gun's cylinder and now he stood, pulled up his T-shirt and stuck it in his belt. The Executioner let his eyes fall to the Spyderco-Keating Chinook folder clipped to the former DEA man's pocket again. Scarberry now had a knife and two handguns, and enough ammo to fight a war. There were long guns in the duffel bag as well, should they need them.

Which they would.

Bolan waited while Scarberry loaded the Centennial, then dropped the revolver into the front pocket of his vest. He balanced it out with the speedloaders on the opposite pocket, looked up and smiled. "I feel fifteen years younger."

"Then you're ready?" Bolan asked.

"Ready," Scarberry said. "Let's hit the town and see who tries to kill you next."

THE TWO-WHEELED motorcycle taxis—properly called motorcars but more commonly dubbed rickshaws—buzzed up and down the street in front of the Florentina. They looked very much like ants hurrying to and fro around a colony, all moving, all intent on accomplishing whatever task they had set out to perform. In the case of the rickshaws, that task was to coax the highest fee possible out of the tourists, get them where they wanted to go, then move on to the next fare as quickly as possible. Little thought or no observance at all was given to traffic laws. The soldier was somewhat surprised not to see a wreck on every block of the city.

Several of the vehicles pulled to the curb the moment he and

Scarberry appeared in front of the Florentina. Bolan ducked under the canopy of the closest rickshaw, with Scarberry sliding in behind him.

"ESSEL," Bolan said.

The driver twisted around on the motorcycle seat. "Four soles," he said.

Scarberry was an old pro at this. "Two," he countered.

"Three," the driver said and turned back around, knowing this was the sum they'd been working toward all along.

The strange vehicle merged with other similar taxis zipping up and down the street. A few minutes later, the driver slowed.

Bolan was surprised to find the jungle survival school located right in the center of the city. He got out as the driver pulled up to the main gate and Scarberry handed the man three coins. Two guards—both armed with Soviet surplus AK-47s and wearing OD pants—stood at the door in the fence. Their T-shirts were of a slightly lighter shade of green and bore large block letters. Bolan has no time to read what they said as the guards ushered them inside, making no attempt to check papers or even ask their business.

As soon as they had entered the compound, Bolan glanced at Scarberry. "Security always this lax?"

Scarberry shrugged. "Commandant probably told them to expect us," he said. "But yeah, it's usually more lax than this. Sometimes they have guards out, sometimes they don't."

Bolan frowned as they walked on. With the threat of a war with Ecuador hanging over their heads, he would have expected more. The fact that they were both obviously Americans meant nothing. Latino terrorist groups, as well as Latino governments, often employed mercenaries from other countries. And for all these two guards knew, he and Scarberry could have been just that.

Scarberry, who had obviously been to the base before, now took the lead as they walked along a cracked concrete pathway. The predominate building ahead appeared to be the barracks.

Two stories tall, the outside walls had been painted in a jungle camouflage pattern. It overflowed with men—some visible through both the open doors, others hanging around outside on the porches and stairs. Other soldiers had set up tents on the grassy areas. None of them looked particularly ready for war. But all were armed with AK-47s as the gate guards had been.

Bolan nodded to himself as they walked on. There were far too many troops for the base to be currently functioning as just a jungle survival school. ESSEL was being used as a housing site for troops ready to march toward Ecuador should the need arise. Jungle training, for the time being, had probably been suspended.

In front of the barracks stood a swimming pool filled with chocolate brown water and floating cigarette butts. Several of the men, however, had doffed their uniforms and were swimming. Off to the side, a raised walkway led over a small pond to a large gazebo that appeared to be an outdoor mess hall. Cutting between the barracks and the bridge, the two Americans headed toward another building set off to the side.

Bolan glanced out across the base as they walked. Beyond what appeared to be a concrete soccer court, he saw several Peruvian air force personnel cutting the tall grass with machetes. Beyond them, on the other side of another fence, a small Peruvian army base abutted the air force site. Several helicopters— again old Soviet surplus—stood neglected on a landing pad.

Scarberry opened the door to the office building and ushered the Executioner inside. Bolan saw that the walls, floor and everything else seemed to be in great need of a soap and water. This lack of cleanliness was reflective of what he'd seen so far of the base in general, and had this been an American military site, someone would be on permanent KP if not facing a full-blown court marshal.

Scarberry, again, seemed to read his mind. "Don't let the state this place is in fool you," he said. "These guys are tough sons of bitches when it hits the fan."

Commandant Suarez's office lay at the end of a long hall. Scarberry continued to lead the way. Bolan followed his new partner past several open doors before they turned into the final office.

A pretty receptionist wearing civilian clothing sat behind a desk filing her nails. She dropped the file as the door opened as if embarrassed to be caught in such a trivial task. Looking up, she said, "Mr. Scarberry and Mr. Belasko?"

Both men nodded.

The secretary reached for the phone on her desk and spoke into the instrument. Returning the receiver to the cradle, she said, "Commandant Suarez will see you now." She stood and clicked her high heels across the tile to another door, opened it and moved to the side, letting them pass.

Bolan took the lead this time, entering the office. While neither cleanliness nor order appeared to be or paramount importance on the jungle school base as a whole, Commandant Ramon Suarez's office, and the man himself, were a study in both spotlessness and systematization. The wood-paneled office walls were covered with photographs, certificates of achievement and other documents—all skillfully matted inside matching frames. The furniture, consisting of a desk, two couches and three padded leather chairs, were of the same set. A long row of two-drawer filing cabinets stood to the side of the desk, and while they didn't match the rest of the wood it was obvious that great thought had gone into choosing colors that would match with the general decor. The floor was covered with a spotless green carpet, and a slight odor of pine-scented disinfectant hung in the air.

Suarez, himself, looked immaculate as he rose and extended a hand across the desk. He was dressed identically to the gate guards and other soldiers they had seen at ESSEL, but his green pants and the T-shirt were carefully starched and pressed. Bolan now had time to read the block letters on the T-shirt: Prepare for the Worst, Hope for the Best. As he grasped the man's hand, Bolan noticed a navy blue baseball cap hanging from a hook on the wall behind the desk. It sported the logo of a palm tree shading the sun above the abbreviation ESSEL. The Executioner had already seen several of the soldiers wearing the same cap around base. But their headgear had been soiled, sweat-stained and battered. Suarez's cap looked as if it had just come out of the box.

"I am very pleased to meet you," Suarez said in flawless and nearly unaccented English. "Won't you please sit down?" He indicated the chairs and couches on the other side of the desk. As Bolan and Scarberry found seats, the commandant came around the desk and sat with them. It was an important move from a psychological point of view; the fact that the ESSEL commander had come out to meet them, rather than remain behind his desk in a position of authority, meant he was treating them as equals rather than subordinates.

Before the conversation could begin, the woman who had ushered them into the office came through the door carrying a silver tray. She set tiny china demitasse cups and saucers in front of Bolan, Scarberry and Suarez, then placed a small stainless-steel pitcher of milk between them. Suarez motioned for her to leave the tray. She set it down and walked back out of the room.

"Please," Suarez said, indicating the table in front of the other two men with a nod.

Bolan looked down into his cup and saw that it was filled three-fourths of the way full of milk. Lifting the pitcher, he poured a small amount of the near-mud consistency coffee on top. As he stirred the mixture with a silver spoon Suarez said, "I hope our coffee is to your liking. Some Americans find it too strong."

Then, without waiting for a response, he turned to the man at Bolan's side. "So, Harvey, of what service might I be to you and your associate?"

Scarberry let Bolan answer. "I'm here to cover the upcoming war with Ecuador," he said.

Suarez raised an eyebrow. "Yes, of course," he said. "And may I ask you, Señor..."

"Belasko."

"Señor Belasko," the commandant continued. "May I ask you what your politics are concerning the situation?"

"My politics on this situation are the same as my politics on all situations," Bolan said as he raised his cup toward his mouth. "I have none." He took a quick sip of the coffee and milk and set his cup back on top of the saucer. "I'm a journalist. I only report the news. And I do so as impartially as I possibly can."

Suarez nodded and smiled. Whether the smile and nod were sincere, and if he had actually bought the story, were anyone's guess.

Suarez leaned forward. "I will answer your questions to the best of my ability," he said. "Unless, of course, the answer is classified information. But first, I would ask that you answer a question of mine."

The Executioner waited.

The smile never left Suarez's face as he said, "You have been here only a few hours. Why would two attempts have already been made to kill you? A simple American journalist?"

Bolan paused a moment before answering. Even with all of the other violence erupting around the city he had known word of the incidents would travel. He had just not known how fast. After a moment, he replied, "As you might guess, that is a subject I have given great consideration."

Suarez's eyes sparkled with mischief for a moment and he chuckled. "I can imagine I would do the same in your position."

Bolan returned the smile. "All I can come up with is that I've been confused with someone else. Someone that somebody else wants dead. Or maybe someone got some wrong information about me."

Suarez continued to nod but his face became deadpan. "Someone might have been...misinformed, told that perhaps you are not actually a journalist," he said. "That, perhaps, the journalist story is only a cover, and that you are, in reality, an American agent of some sort. Perhaps an agent of the CIA?"

"Yes," Bolan said. "That could be a possibility." They were playing a game, now. Suarez at least suspected that this wasn't misinformation at all but the truth. At the moment, the Executioner saw no choice but to play along.

"But of course, you are not," Suarez said, the nod turning into a head shake as his lips pursed slightly.

"No," he said. "I can honestly tell you I am not a CIA agent."

"Of course not," Suarez said, the smile returning to his face. It was obvious that the man wasn't convinced. He shrugged, though, breaking the somber mood that had fallen over the room. "So, shall we proceed with your questions?"

Bolan pulled a small notepad and pen from the pocket of his safari jacket. "What would you say would be the likelihood of an all-out war between Peru and Ecuador?"

Suarez stared down at the tiny white cup on the table in front of him and spouted out the party line. "That will depend on Ecuador," he said. "I can assure you that Peru will not instigate any hostilities. But if Ecuador attempts to steal land that is rightfully ours..." He took time to draw in a deep breath and shrug his shoulders. "We can do nothing but defend what is ours."

The conversation went on for several more minutes, with Bolan asking the questions he knew a journalist would ask, and Suarez returning the answers he knew his government wanted him to give. Finally, Bolan looked up and said, "Commandant, there are rumors that both sides—Peru and Ecuador—have obtained quantities of chemical warfare agents. Weapons of mass destruction. If this is true, it takes this potential war into a new arena involving innocent civilians. What can you tell me about this?"

A quick flash of surprise flickered in Suarez's eyes. It didn't last for long. "I have heard the same rumors," he said. "But I have seen nothing to indicate that there is any truth to them." The man's eyes contradicted his words.

"Would you—would Peru—use such weapons against the Ecuadorans?" Bolan asked. "Knowing it would not be just the enemy soldiers you killed? Knowing that hundreds, thousands, of innocents would suffer? Die a horrible death?"

"Of course not," Suarez said quickly. "Of course, as mere commandant of this base, I wouldn't be the one making such a decision. But I can assure you that no one in the chain of command wants to kill innocent people regardless of their national origin."

"That wasn't what I asked you, Commandant," the Executioner said. "I didn't ask if you *wanted to kill them.* I asked if you *would kill them* in order to win a war with Ecuador."

"No," Suarez said. "But again, I must tell you that all I have heard on this subject is what you have heard. Rumors. My personal opinion is that Peru doesn't even have such chemical agents." Again the look in Suarez's eyes spoke otherwise. And in those eyes, Bolan also saw more than deception. He saw fear. He saw a man who wanted, with all his heart, to tell the journalist seated across from him that yes, Peru did have chemical weapons and yes, of course they would use them if it came that.

But Suarez was a good soldier. A patriot to his country. He wasn't going to betray it to some American journalist who probably wasn't even really a journalist.

To make things look good, Bolan asked several more questions and wrote down several more responses. Finally, he said, "Commandant, I'd like to thank you for your time." He stood.

Scarberry and Suarez rose to their feet as well. All three men shook hands.

"You will be visiting with Colonel Imenez at the 42nd Air Group?" the commandant asked.

"We plan to, yes," Bolan said. "So far, we haven't been able to arrange a meeting."

The light in Suarez's brown eyes flickered again for a moment. "As you can imagine," he said, "the colonel is a very busy man right now. But perhaps I can help." He reached down and lifted the telephone receiver. "Harvey," he said, "perhaps you would like to stay and help me make the call. Belasko, if you would be so kind to wait in the outer office?"

Bolan nodded. It was apparent that Suarez wanted to talk to Scarberry alone, which was hardly surprising, since the two men were old friends.

Bolan exited the inner officer and walked outside, closing the door behind him. The secretary quit doing her nails again, smiled seductively his way as he took a seat along the wall and began to make small talk. He answered her questions politely, even adding a few remarks himself. But he played dumb to her obvious flirtations. She was attractive. Actually, more than attractive. And Mack Bolan was only human. But he wasn't likely to have any time for even a short R&R of that nature on this mission.

A few minutes later, the door opened again. Scarberry stepped out and said, "Ready?"

Bolan rose to his feet and they left the office. On the way out of the door, the soldier said, "He get us a meeting with Imenez?"

Scarberry shook his head as they walked along the cracked sidewalk. "No, and he doesn't think he can. The man's up to his ears in war preparation right now. But we may not have time to waste there anyway."

They were nearing the gate and Scarberry became quiet as one of the guards opened it for them. The two men stepped onto the street to flag down a rickshaw.

"Then what was your private conference all about?" Bolan asked.

Scarberry reached into his pocket and pulled out a small scrap of paper as they waited. Bolan unfolded it. He saw only an E-mail address written there. "So what's this?" he asked.

"Someone we need to contact," Scarberry said. "Suarez doesn't believe for a second that you're a reporter. And he all but came right out and told me that they do have chemical weapons." The former DEA man glanced back over his shoulder, but the two men at the base gate were too far away to hear. "Ramon is a concerned about it all as we are. But he can do nothing officially."

Two of the motorcycle taxis pulled up against the curb in front of them. They got in behind the first driver, which brought on a stream of Spanish curses from the second. "He doesn't like the idea of being court-martialed and losing his job," Scarberry whispered out of the corner of his mouth.

Bolan nodded as the rickshaw took off. "But he gave you a lead. It pays to have old friends."

"I guess," Scarberry said, nodding. "At least I told him the same thing. Know what he said?"

The Executioner turned to face the former DEA man.

"That he was doing it out of both friendship and concern. But that if word leaked out that he was the one who gave me this E-mail address—" Scarberry held the scrap of paper up in his hand "—friendship wasn't going to keep him from putting a bullet in my head or cutting my throat. Or both."

THE SOUND OF FRANTIC clucking was suddenly halted as a dull thud pierced the stillness of the late afternoon jungle. Kenji Rivas looked down the small descent to the creek. A chicken's head had fallen next to a log embedded in the muddy bank. A geyser of crimson shot forth from the neck of the bird still gripped in the hands of the man who had killed it. The blood mixed with the brown water around the log, turning it even darker. White cloud-like feathers floated up into the air as the man holding the chicken turned it upside down. The body continued to dance in his hand as the last of the blood drained out.

The man who had beheaded the chicken was Solari, one of Rivas's lieutenants. He now held the carcass up for inspection and grinned a smile of satisfaction. For a man who had supposedly spent so much time in the jungle he had surprisingly white teeth. And his skin wasn't as wrinkled like many who spent their lives in the bush.

Rivas turned his attention to the area where they had begun setting up camp. The steady sound of machetes eating away at soft wood thudded as both his New and Free Peru men and the members of Ecuador's CONAIE Lightning Bolt faction had begun setting up camp. Most of the men from both countries habitually slept on the ground. Some carried lightweight net hammocks that were now being slung between trees. A few were even hard at work chopping forked branches that would be driven into the soft earth and used as the posts for jungle beds. Once the four corners were established, longer limbs would be cut to form a

frame and then pieces of canvas tarp, worn out military para-
chuting, or even rain ponchos would be tied to the wood with
vines.

Rivas watched the men work. Regardless of what style of bed
they chose, they all carried mosquito netting. This area of the
Amazon Basin was low jungle, and while it might lack the
jaguars and some of the other dangers of higher terrain, it was
rampant with mosquitoes and other insects that carried disease,
poison and perhaps the most dangerous curse of all to men in the
jungle for weeks on end—irritation. A cumulative buildup came
from constant itching and the burning sting of mosquitoes, fire
ants and other less-than-lethal bugs. Eventually, this culmination
could drive a man to distraction and poor judgment. Rivas had
once watched a man who'd been bitten by too many mosquitoes
finally give in to the desire to scratch. In a half-crazed euphoric
daze, he had spent an entire night turning his arms, shoulders,
legs and every other spot on his body he could reach into what
looked like raw hamburger meat. The entire time he had dug his
fingernails into his own flesh he had uttered moans of relief not
unlike a man in orgasm.

But infection came easily in the damp climate of the Amazon. And it had killed him a week later, long after his ecstatic
moans had turned to howls of agony.

Solari climbed up the muddy ascent from the stream as he
pulled feathers from the chicken carcass. He gave Rivas another
smile as he passed and continued on to where some of the
Ecuadorans had begun getting the fire started. Between the two
camps, they had two large steel pots. One would be used to boil
the remaining feathers off the chicken. The other would contain
the stew eventually brewed from the chicken, rice and a variety
of herbs gathered around the area.

Next to the fire, Rivas saw the main nicknamed Relámpago
talking to one of his men. Slowly, both of the Ecuadorans glanced
his way.

Rivas nodded to himself. Alejandro Carillo—Relámpago—

and the other men of the Lightning Bolts didn't fully trust the New and Free Peru men yet. Fine. That was as it should be, for trust shouldn't come easily in their line of work. But eventually, credibility would be built. It had already become clear to the Peruvian that if he could convince Relámpago that their goals ran parallel, the Lightning Bolts would be an invaluable asset to him. At least for a while. The more he considered it, the more a new plan—far grander than any that had formerly occupied his brain—had begun to form. He would discuss that plan with Relámpago later, over the chicken stew. Actually, he would only discuss *part* of the plan.

Rivas looked up at the darkening sky. The stew, and the discussion, wouldn't be long in coming now. Darkness fell early over the jungle—usually by six o'clock or so. And it stayed dark until six the next morning. Unless a mission of vital importance needed to be carried out, the smartest thing a man could do during those twelve hours was to barricade himself inside his mosquito netting and wait it out. It was common practice to lay there, catching as many snatches of sleep as the insects—which invariably invaded even the most carefully constructed netting—would allow. To wander far from camp during the black hours of the night was to invite disaster; there were simply too many things out there that bit, stung, tore or otherwise injured. It was hard enough to avoid such things, from poisonous thorns to vipers, even in daylight. Unnecessary risks at night, except in emergencies, simply weren't warranted.

A half hour later, the only illumination where Rivas stood came from the few stars peeking through the treetops and from the fire. Slowly, he made his way to the line of men who had formed. As they filed by, Solari ladled the chicken stew into their steel and pottery eating bowls. While the Ecuadorans and Peruvians were still mostly segregated, a few words were now and then being exchanged between the groups. Rivas smiled to himself in the darkness. Yes, it would take some time to before they were willing to fully rely on each other. But eventually, they would learn to trust each other. And in the naked wilds of the jungle, it didn't take nearly as long to know a man as it did within the obscure world of civilization.

Rivas noticed that Relámpago waited until all of the men—both his own and the Peruvians—had been through the line before walking toward the pot himself. Again, the leader of New and Free Peru smiled. Different commanders had different ways of letting their troops know, or at least making them believe, they were cared for. This was obviously one of Relámpago's ways. Rivas filed it away as a possible ploy of his own sometime. It never hurt to have trust-building tricks in reserve.

The NFP leader walked up and took a place behind the Ecuadoran Indian. When Relámpago had been served, he stepped forward, got his own ration of stew, then followed the Lightning Bolt leader to the edge of the fireside. Both men squatted on their haunches. Silently, they began eating.

"It is good," Relámpago finally said in Quechua, breaking the silence.

Rivas answered in the same language. "My man Solari," he said around a mouthful of chicken and rice. "He is a good lieutenant. Perhaps even a better cook." He nodded toward the pot. "Long ago, he was once the chef for the Brazilian ambassador in Bogotá."

The Lightning Bolt leader snorted. "He has a far more primitive kitchen in which to work now. And far fewer ingredients to include in his stews."

Rivas chuckled. "Just as many," he said, sweeping the hand that held his steel spoon in front of him to indicate their surrounding. "But different ones. As you know, the jungle has everything a man needs to live, and live well. He just has to know where to find it."

The Ecuadoran nodded, then reached into his bowl and pulled out a large, round white object. "Ah," he said. "No wonder the stew is tasty. Where did you find them?"

"Solari located them yesterday," Rivas said. "A rotten tree was filled with them and we took in a large number. They will not keep long, as you know, so I ordered him to use as many as possible in the stew. You like *suri?*" Rivas pulled one of the grub worms out of his own bowl and popped it into his mouth.

The man nodded. "Yes, very much," he said. "Although my people do not call them that. And we prefer them raw but this is good."

Rivas laughed. "I will eat them raw when I must." he said. "But even after I have pinched their heads I worry that they will bite me back when they hit my tongue." The two men continued to eat and talk in the flickering firelight as the rest of the two groups gradually finished and retired for the evening. Crickets chirped in the darkness, and here and there a bird could be heard. Small, unidentifiable animals moved away from the camp as insects of a thousand varieties moved in. All in all, a spirit of primitive tranquility seemed to permeate the camp. It was man with nature. Man in the wild. Man ten thousand years ago.

Man, some said, as man was meant to be, Rivas thought. But not the way *he* intended to be. He glanced once at Relámpago and noted the deep lines in the man's face. The leader of the Lightning Bolts had spent his whole life living like this. And would spent most of the rest of it this way, as well. He knew nothing else, no better way.

Kenji Rivas did. Although he had grown up in the jungle, he had moved on to a far superior lifestyle in Colombia later. He had known the luxury and easy life that money could bring, and he had liked it. He had sworn he would never return to the jungle, and only one thing would have made him break that vow as he had for the last year.

Money. And, of course, the power that came with it.

Finally, Rivas worked the conversation around to where he wanted it to be. He laid out his plan—at least part of it—to the Ecuadoran. He watched the other man's eyes change from listlessness to interest, then to intrigue and finally an obvious, if not animated, excitement.

"It can work," Relámpago said when Rivas had finished.

"It will work."

For a moment, Relámpago's face took on its earlier apathy in the firelight, and he said, "It is unfortunate so many people must die."

Rivas knew just how to answer that. "It is not unfortunate, it is tragic," he said. "But there is no other way. Some must die so the rest can truly live."

Slowly, Relámpago nodded.

The two men said good-night and retired to their beds. Rivas looked up through the mosquito net above his head at the tree-tops and the stars beyond, and smiled. He was always amazed at how easy people were to persuade.

Relámpago would be helpful. He would work hard for his Quechua people, believing he was helping free them from the slavery of the Ecuadoran government. Together, he and Rivas would turn the course of history in South America. Yes, many people who didn't know it yet were about to die. But they would serve a cause just as Rivas had told Relámpago. They would die so others could live. And live well.

The NFP man suppressed a laugh as he realized that "others" meant *him.* He listened to the snoring of the men around the camp, wondering which noises came from his NFP followers and which ones came from the noble savages from Ecuador. The very term "noble savages" made him want to laugh harder, and he stuffed the back of his hand into his mouth and bit down on flesh and bone.

It didn't matter who the snores came from. No one in this camp except himself would be alive to snore in a few more weeks.

3

The personal computer boom in the United States and other countries had prompted small businesses, collectively known as Internet cafés, to spring up around the globe. Usually set in store-fronts in busy commercial areas of the larger cities, at first glance these establishments looked somewhat like video arcades. They served two vital purposes. First, they allowed access to the In-ternet and E-mail to the citizens of impoverished economies—people who would work for less yearly income than even the most basic home computer would cost. Second, they provided com-munication back home for Americans and other travelers who had grown accustomed to this quick, easy, and inexpensive method of communication. For less than fifty cents anyone who wished could enter one of the Peruvian cafés, log on and do business.

The only downside to the operation were the machines them-selves. Much like the famed "Mexican Market" for used cars, a trade in secondhand modems, screens and keyboards had leaped into existence between North and South America. This meant that the vast majority of computers available to the public were an-tiquated, agonizingly slow to connect and then to operate, and that at least one glitch, which had to be worked around, existed in every setup. There was one rule of thumb when entering an Internet café—the savvy user did his best to look for the least

battered equipment he could find. Chances were that if it looked
new it was stolen rather than secondhand. And the chances of it
working were far higher as well.

In Iquitos, there were three Internet cafés within easy walking distance of the Hotel Florentina. Harvey Scarberry led the
way down the street toward the nearest one. He stopped outside
the dirty glass storefront, shielded his eyes with a hand like a
frontier scout scouring the plains and peered through the glass.
Bolan did the same and saw that the seats along both walls were
all full. Without a word, they walked on.

The next Internet café was less than two blocks away, and they
spotted several of the booths open. Scarberry led the soldier inside past a splintering wooden desk where a teenaged Peruvian
proprietor sat reading a magazine. They found adjacent seats near
the end of the room, and Scarberry began tapping the keys.
"Want to just contact this guy from my address?" he asked as the
slug-slow machine began to turn over like a cold automobile.

Bolan frowned, thinking. Finally, he said, "No. Let's set up a
dummy address. We don't know who we're dealing with, and
there's no reason they should know, either. At least not yet."

Scarberry nodded and continued tapping the keys, waiting,
then tapping again. Five minutes later, they were registered as
jungleman307. The former DEA man pulled the scrap of paper
Suarez had given him out of his pocket, tapped an icon that read
send new mail and typed in the address. The code name was
cigarsycigarillos.

Scarberry turned to face the bigger man. "Okay," he said.
"What do you want me to say?"

"Suarez give you any idea how to break the ice?"

The former DEA man shook his head. "He gave me the address, said we should contact this guy, then he threatened my life
if I let the cat out of the bag as to where we got the intel," he said.
"Then he wanted me out of the office, fast." He cleared his throat.
"That's it."

Finally, Bolan said, "Scoot over."

Scarberry stood and the two men exchanged seats.

Bolan looked at the screen, then moved the mouse to the message box. *Information needed,* he typed onto the screen. *Willing to pay well. Discreet. If interested, reply.* He hit the send icon and the message flashed away into cyberspace.

Bolan turned to the man standing behind him. "Why don't you go settle with the guy at the desk?" he said.

Scarberry frowned for a moment, then what Bolan was really saying dawned on him. He chuckled softly, and the Executioner could read in the former DEA man's eyes the fact that he knew Bolan wanted to send another message. Privately.

As soon as Scarberry had stepped away, Bolan typed in one of Stony Man Farm's secret and untraceable E-mail addresses. This one would lead directly to Hal Brognola. Without undue introduction, he simply informed the Farm's director that two attempts had already been made on his life and that the only answer could be a leak in the system somewhere along the line. Brognola would handle it from his end.

Bolan stood and pushed his chair away from the computer terminal.

From across the room, Scarberry saw him. The former DEA agent walked back to Bolan. "What do we do now?" Scarberry asked.

The soldier led the way across the room toward the door. "Wait," he said. "We'll check it in an hour or so and see if there's been any reply." Although Scarberry had already paid for the computer time, he dropped another dollar on the desk in front of the young man reading the magazine. The kid looked up, grinned and snatched up the money. It disappeared into his pocket.

"So," Scarberry said as he followed Bolan back onto the street. "What do we do while we wait? Play a game of chess?"

The soldier came to a halt, looking both ways. Three blocks back toward Ari's, someone had set up on the back of a pickup with a bullhorn and was shouting in Spanish. A crowd had started to gather. The speaker was too far away for Bolan to make out his words, but the cheers of the crowd told him they liked what they heard. As the rickshaws ripped by in both directions, he turned the opposite way and saw block after block of storefronts and sidewalk stands selling everything from quilting swatches to machetes and clothing.

"Yeah, in a manner of speaking, that's exactly what we do," the Executioner said. He turned to face the end of the street. "Is the Belen district that way?"

"Yeah." Scarberry's face took on a mixed expression of curiosity and concern. "But why would you want—"

"Let's go," Bolan said. Holding up a hand, he watched half-dozen rickshaws pull into the curb. The two men got into the back of the strange motorcycle cab and Bolan said, "Belen."

The driver looked over his shoulder with the same expression Scarberry had just given him, then shrugged and twisted the throttle. A moment later they were tearing down the street, weaving in and out, honking horns once again.

BOLAN AND SCARBERRY got out of the rickshaw, paid the driver and gave him an extra tip. They found themselves standing at the edge of the market, next to a stand where a woman who looked half-gypsy sold roots, herbs, potions and fetishes of all kinds. Easily identifiable animal body parts floated in sealed glass jars and bottles, many of which were labeled with colorful pictures that depicted Christ, angels, Satan, saints and odd combinations of all four images. The prevailing religion seemed to be a combination of Christianity, voodoo and the Hispanic culture Santeria.

Harvey Scarberry's eyes had fallen on the same booth. "Seems like they're trying to cover all the bases," he said offhandedly. With the roar of the motorcycles, the wind and the street noises of Iquitos filling their ears, it had been too noisy for the two men to talk during the ride to Belen, the most poverty-stricken district in the city. Now, however, Scarberry said, "Okay, want to tell me why we're here? I don't think you got a sudden urge for fresh fish."

Bolan looked down the steep, cracked asphalt embankment that led to the edge of the Amazon. Both sides of the narrow street were crowded with fish stalls and rickety wooden booths selling foods and other items. The structures extended out onto the water, where many of them floated on rafts. All appeared to be constructed of scrap wood and tin, and looked as if a stiff wind would tear them apart like wet Kleenex tissues through an oscillating fan. Most of the people in the Belen district were natives, either workers or shoppers who had come to bargain for meager amounts of fly-covered food. And they were packed together almost shoulder to shoulder—almost as numerous as the flies.

Floating on the water at the end of the other raft-shacks was a larger building of some sort. As rickety as the rest of the structures, it looked as if it might collapse at any moment from the weight of the hundreds of birds perched on its roof. The birds waited for whatever scraps of fish might be discarded when night fell and the humans went home.

Here and there, mixed in with the natives, a few brave tourists were checking out the wares. Most had done their best to dress down for the occasion, and there were very few Banana Republic, Travelsmith, or other clothing articles that mark the affluent traveler. But the tourists still stood out. They were far too clean to have spent much time at the fish market.

"We have some time to kill," Bolan finally said, "and I had an idea. A long shot, granted, but better than sitting around doing nothing while we wait."

"Well..." Scarberry said, a sudden yawn forcing him to pause before he went on. "Care to let me in on it? I might be able to help."

"You're not only going to help," Bolan said, "you're going to be the major player. Who runs all this?" He swept a hand in front of him.

"Runs it? What do you mean?" Scarberry said.

Bolan turned to face him. "I've never seen an area like this where somebody wasn't getting rich. There's money everywhere,

Scarberry. It's just that in some places, only one or two men have all of it. Who is it here?"

Scarberry nodded his understanding. "Luis Alvarez," he said. "He's head of the fisherman's union. Not a union like you'd have back home. Just more of a loose-knit group that gets together and sets prices."

"You know where to find him?"

"Not right off the bat," Scarberry said. "Not everything he does is exactly what you'd call legit. Runs a few guns, artifacts, that sort of thing. And the rumor is he's been sick lately."

"I've never seen a place like this where the top dog's influence didn't lap over into the rest of the city, either," the Executioner said. "That's the part of Luis Alvarez I'm interested in. How about dope?"

Scarberry shook his head. "No way," he said. "And I can vouch for that personally. We were constantly spot-checking at DEA." He paused a moment, then went on. "That's the funny thing about Alvarez. He'll break some laws but not others. You can believe me or not but he's got morals. His own set of morals maybe, but there are lines he won't cross. And drugs is one of them. In fact, he's reported to have had several of the dealers in Iquitos killed."

"So he doesn't mind killing drug dealers but he won't sell dope."

"Yeah, I know it sounds odd," Scarberry answered.

"Not to me," Bolan said. He felt the same way.

Scarberry glanced around to make sure no one else was listening, then lowered his voice. "He used to feed us intel when I was still with DEA," he said. "He's got one hell of a network going."

"That's why I wanted to come here," Bolan said. "There's always a Luis Alvarez in a place like this. Although they rarely have such rigid moral codes. You said you didn't know where he was. But can you find him?"

"Probably. At least I can try. We'll have to find someone who knows him. In addition to trying to stay one step ahead of the cops on the guns, antiquities and some shady union business, he has to do the same with the drug dealers. And like I said, I hear he's been sick. He—" The former DEA man turned jungle guide suddenly halted in midsentence and frowned.

Bolan followed Scarberry's line of sight into the crowd where a young man in his midtwenties, wearing black denim shorts, a white ribbed tank top and Nike cross-trainers was making his way up the street toward where they stood. At first glance, he didn't appear any different from the other people mingling through the market. And he appeared to be alone. But a second look told the Executioner that all was not as it appeared. For one thing, the man's shorts and shirt were spotless. His Nikes—a highly prized item in Peru—were new.

And as he broadened his gaze, Bolan saw that two men were walking in front of the man in the black shorts, their eyes skimming across the faces of the people in the market. Behind the man walked two more, doing the same. All four of the bodyguards wore loose shirts outside their trousers. But with each new step they took as they ascended the steep incline, suspicious bulges pressed against the fabric just above the waistline.

"What are you Belasko, magic?" Scarberry asked with a grin. "You just want to meet somebody and will them to appear, or what?"

"That's him?" the soldier asked, his eyes still on the young man in the black shorts. He was far younger than Bolan had pictured him, and he didn't look like he'd been sick a day in his life.

Scarberry shook his head. "No, but it's the next best thing. That's Arturo Alvarez. Luis's son." The former DEA man stepped forward as the young man and his protection team neared the top of the hill. *"¿Como estás, Dobla A?"* he half shouted to them.

Bolan watched them closely. *Dobla A.* Double A. It had to be a nickname for Arturo Alvarez.

All four of the bodyguards' heads had snapped toward the sound of Scarberry's voice. Their hands had shot automatically toward their belts. One of them, a big man who might have moonlighted as a Peruvian Sumo wrestler, carried a small laptop case in his left hand. His arm, riding against his side, had lifted the tail of his shirt to reveal both a roll of hair-covered flab and the butt of a Makarov pistol.

Alvarez held up his hand and the men froze. A wide grin covered his face. *"Madre de dios,"* he said, changing his path and starting toward Bolan and Scarberry. "If it isn't my old friend Tarzan."

Scarberry laughed politely. Out of the side of his mouth he whispered, "He calls me that 'cause of my guide service. The kid hates the jungle. Can't understand why anybody—especially an American like me—would ever want to go into the jungle."

Alvarez stopped in front of Scarberry and looked him over head to foot, still smiling. "You are looking very healthy," he said as he extended his hand. "Young Peruvian girls will do that for a man."

"Up yours," Scarberry said, laughing again as he squeezed the man's fingers. "She's free, white and twenty-one."

"No," Alvarez said. "She is free and only twenty years of age. But we shall consider that close enough." There was more laughter, then Scarberry inquired about Alvarez's father.

A look of true sadness entered the young man's eyes. He should his head. "Not good. It has spread rapidly. It is now in his liver."

There was no mention of the word cancer. It was understood. "I'm sorry," Scarberry said.

Bolan nodded his head in agreement. He continued to study Alvarez. He had heard the young man speak enough now to conclude that much of his English had come from books and tutors. He displayed precious little of the slang most Americans sprinkled into their conversation.

"Double, I want to introduce you to a friend of mine," Scarberry finally said, turning to hook a thumb at Bolan. "This is Mike Belasko. An American journalist."

Now it was Bolan whom Alvarez studied from head to foot. Finally, he smiled warmly at the Executioner. "Ah, Mr. Belasko," he said. "A pleasure. Any friend of Jungle Jim's a friend of mine." He shot out his hand. "And you are a journalist?"

Bolan nodded as he took the man's hand.

"Then I suspect you are not a very good journalist," Alvarez said, still smiling. Before either Bolan or Scarberry could ask why, he answered the question. "Because your arms and even your face show me scars. Some old, some not so old. Tell me, do your readers become that angry at what you write?"

Scarberry cleared his throat and skipped over the question. "We need to talk to you, Double," he whispered. His eyes rose to take in the four bodyguards who had formed a protective circle around the young man. "We'll give you the straight story. But it needs to be in private."

Alvarez glanced up. "Pepe, take the men for a beer," he said.

"But Señor Arturo," the overweight bodyguard protested, "your father has ordered us not to—"

"Now!" Alvarez said in a more stern voice. "I will be fine." He glanced at Scarberry and grinned ironically. "I have our retired DEA friend and—" he swept an arm in Bolan's direction and grinned even more "—what appears to be America's toughest journalist to protect me."

Reluctantly, the four bodyguards shuffled off to the side, out of hearing distance.

"So," Alvarez said, draping an arm around Scarberry's shoulder and guiding the man toward a small café just off the market. "How may I be of service to you and your *journalist* friend." He was still smiling. He didn't seem to want to know who Bolan actually was as much as to make sure that it was obvious that he knew what Bolan wasn't.

TRUJILLO WAS Peru's second largest city, and certainly the most important site of the country's northern region. Trujillo was known for many things, among them a charmingly formal-but-simple lifestyle and fierce patriotism. Founded in 1535 by Francisco Pizarro, cousin, contemporary and rival of Herman Cortez,

the South American Spanish conquistador had named the city
after his place of birth. It grew quickly as a convenient stopover
during tenuous treks along the coast between Lima and Quito,
Ecuador. Many of the old colonial homes built during that era
survived to remind the traveler of Trujillo's historical past.

Which is exactly why Kenji Rivas had chosen Trujillo as the
site to launch the first in a series of terrorist attacks that he
planned to occur with the speed of bullets leaving a high rpm machine gun.

Alone, Rivas took in a deep breath of the early-morning air
as he walked leisurely down the sidewalk. Ahead, on his side of
the street, he could see the colonial-style building and the sign
announcing the Hotel Libertador Trujillo. Beyond the hotel, a
section of the park within the Plaza de Armas was visible, and
old men dressed in loose cotton shirts and straw hats sat pretending to read the morning papers as they actually dozed.

Rivas drew abreast of the hotel and passed rows of tiny windows set in the side of the building. Barely visible through the
panes, he could see men, women and children inside the dining
room eating breakfast. A group of giggling, gossiping young
mothers, all carrying shopping baskets in one arm and small
children in the other, passed him on the sidewalk heading away
from the plaza.

These women had finished their shopping. They and their off-
spring would live to shop another day. But there were bound to
be other mothers and children within the Plaza de Armas, and
they were doing their last shopping. Along with the old men he
had seen seated on the benches, and the uniformed schoolgirls
who he saw now as he turned the corner, they were all about to
die.

Rivas shrugged indifferently. What did it matter? Relámpago
rationalized such deaths as the few sacrificing for the many. This
need to justify his actions forced the Ecuadoran to fall back on
meaningless clichés, such as the fact that "there are always casualties in war." Rivas had even listened to him earlier as they

man compared the sacrifices these few would make to the sacrifices his ancient Quechua-speaking ancestors had offered up their gods. What rot.

Rivas walked on, glad he didn't feel any need to play such a childish game. The simple fact was that he saw no reason to rationalize what he was about to do. Yes, people would die. There would be sacrifices. But he looked at it almost directly opposite to the way Relámpago did. In his case, many would be sacrificing for few. He laughed silently. And the few were very few, indeed. One, in fact. Him.

The NFP leader crossed the street to the plaza and stepped onto a grassy area. He strolled on, cutting through and around the old men on the benches. He passed the schoolgirls who were seated on the grass, giggling and whispering secrets into one another's ears. One of them looked up and smiled at him, her dark brown eyes dancing.

Rivas returned the smile and walked on.

In the center of the plaza stood a bizarre statue, a running figure with wings who gripped a torch. The statue was called Liberty. But what made this Liberty so strange was that the running legs were far too short for the rest of the figure. Rivas knew the reason for this—the disproportionate legs had been a compromise to the authorities within the cathedral in front it. They feared that given full size, the monument would be taller than the cathedral itself.

How Peruvian, Rivas thought as he neared the statue. Such thinking, and the statue itself, represented everything that was, and always had been, wrong with his country. Compromise. Capitulation to superstitious religious powers. But the short legs were symbolic to the NFP man in another way. Simón de Bolivar had set up his revolutionary government in Trujillo, and this city had been the first in Peru to declare its independence from Spain. Ever since then the country had tried to run. But for one reason or another, it always seemed that its legs were too short.

A curious mixture of anger and determination now filled

Rivas as he walked on, studying the deficient statue. He would change all that. When he was through, Peru would run on the long sturdy legs of the finest Thoroughbred stallion.

And he would be at the reins.

Thirty feet from the statue, Rivas saw the empty bench and headed toward it. Casually, he dropped onto the hard steel and pulled the folded newspaper from the inside breast pocket of his well-worn and frayed light cotton sport coat. He hated the worn-out coat he was forced to wear in order to blend in. As he settled into the bench and crossed his legs, his eyes caught a flicker of the cheap imitation leather sandals on his feet just beyond the soiled cuffs of his permanently stained khaki work pants. On his head, he wore a straw hat that looked as if some ravenous animal had taken a bite from the brim. He hated all of the clothes that he wore—almost as much as he hated the time had been forced to spend in the jungle as he gathered together his band of mindless followers.

Rivas glanced around him. But the clothes were doing what they were supposed to do. No one had given him a second glance. Although younger than many of the men in the park, he easily passed for an unemployed laborer in a country with an unemployment rate of ninety percent.

Sighing to himself, Rivas looked back down at his newspaper. This wouldn't last forever. Soon, he would be wearing the same expensive suits that had been his daily garb in Colombia. No. They would be even more expensive.

The New and Free Peru leader pretended to read his paper for a few minutes, but his thoughts were on other things. He knew an American agent was in Iquitos—his government contact had told him the man was coming even before the big American arrived. He didn't know what the man's assignment was, but he had paid the contact to have him killed. So far, two attempts had failed, and Rivas wondered how his incompetent contact could have ever worked himself so high in the government. It only proved that the government itself was inadequate.

Rivas looked up, surreptitiously scouting the area. Nothing unusual. Two minor police officials stood on the corner. No other uniforms in sight. He supposed that some of the men seated around the plaza, or even some of the other young mothers who came and went with shopping bags, could be police officers in undercover roles. But that was unlikely. It had been less than two hours since he had first shared his carefully planned strike with the rest of his men, and it would be next to impossible that word of what was about to take place could have leaked out and a counterstrike set up within that time framework.

Letting the paper fall to his lap, Rivas closed his eyes three-fourths of the way. He continued to watch beneath his squinting lids for five more minutes before finally drawing a small cell phone from the side pocket of his jacket. Thumbing the on button, he tapped in a number.

"Yes," the voice at the other end of the connection said.

"Send in the first team," Rivas stated. He waited until he heard the other voice confirm that he had heard the order, then killed the connection, stuck the phone back into his jacket and returned to his paper.

Less than thirty seconds later, the first man appeared. Dressed similarly to Rivas, he shuffled across the ground and disappeared into the cathedral. He came back out just as a second man appeared, entering the central courtyard area from the opposite direction. As the second man walked leisurely toward the winged statue, the first man shuffled back out of the plaza and started down the street.

The second man walked slowly past the statue. Anyone not watching him closely—and no one but Rivas had reason to do so—would have missed the fact that the hand in his pocket suddenly snaked out and dropped something at the base of the statue.

As the second man disappeared down the street after the first, a third, then a fourth, then a fifth, sixth and seventh man entered the plaza. Rivas kept the paper in from of him as he watched them all walk nonchalantly past the entrances to various government buildings. He saw some of the quick hand movements they made that others failed to catch.

When the last man had left the plaza, Rivas pulled the phone from his coat again. "Second team," was all he said before hanging up again. Reaching into another pocket of his coat, Rivas retrieved the set of steel military dog tags that Relámpago had given him. They still hung from their chain. He kept them behind the newspaper as he stared at them. Half of the steel tag had been charred by fire and was unreadable. That was good. If he made it too easy on investigating officers, even the imbecilic Peruvian police would smell a setup. And the "burned" theme went well with what was about to happen anyway.

Rivas broke the chain but left it threaded through the tags. After a last glance around to make sure no one was paying him any attention, he dropped the entire charred and broken mess on the ground between his feet and stood.

Rivas crossed the street to the Hotel Libertador Trujillo again. He was just starting up the steps toward the dining room when the first bomb went off. Which gave him, like everyone else within hearing distance, an excuse to stop, turn and try to see what had happened.

More explosions sounded like rapid small arms fire as the bombs—small charges of C-4 plastique—went off. Each one would kill only those people within a twenty- to-thirty-foot area, and Rivas estimated that would amount to no more than fifty dead bodies, maximum. He could easily have blown the entire plaza to shrapnel—but that wasn't his plan.

Loud screams of terror sounded from inside the park as men, women and children began to run in panic. One woman, her hair and clothes on fire as if she were a giant matchstick, sprinted along the grass, then dropped and rolled across the ground. Her action did nothing to extinguish the flames.

Three minutes later, Rivas heard the first of the sirens. A few seconds after that, a police car screeched its tires to a halt almost directly in front of him. Two uniformed officers leaped out, weapons drawn.

Rivas let his hand fall into the side pocket of his coat where the .32-caliber pistol was hidden. Just in case. The cops had no reason to suspect him of being anything more than another curious onlooker. But it didn't pay to take chances.

Without giving him a second glance, the police officers ran past the woman's smoking remains toward the center of the plaza. A second car stopped, siren screaming and red lights flashing, and two more officers emerged.

Rivas waited until eight patrol cars and the van that transported Trujillo's SWAT team had all arrived at the scene before tapping numbers into the phone one final time.

"Team three," he said.

The New and Free Peru leader held the phone in his hand this time as more explosions suddenly erupted around the plaza. This time, fire was far more prevalent, and he saw at least two dozen of the uniforms burst into flame. Some of the police officers tried the drop-and-roll technique as the woman had done but had no more luck with it than she had. The homemade napalm—consisting primarily of everyday over-the-counter dishwashing detergent—stuck to the men's clothes and skin like the most super-adhesive glue.

As the unfortunate men burned, four large half-ton trucks arrived. As complete and utter chaos broke out within the plaza, the drivers calmly braked the vehicles to halts along the four streets encircling the area. No further movement was seen at the trucks until several of the burning, screaming, frantic officers stumbled toward the streets.

At which point two dozen New and Free Peru men, all armed with submachine guns, poured out of the backs of the trucks.

As the fiery, tortured, incoherent figures made their way toward the streets they were joined by other officers who had escaped the explosions. Regardless of whether they were aflame, they now broke ranks and ran. But they didn't run far.

The NFP men opened up with the submachine guns, mowing

them down like a harvesting machine sweeping its way through fields tall with ripened wheat. Rivas smiled. It looked very much like a carnival shooting gallery in Hell.

Rivas took notice that his men were following his orders—shooting for the legs rather than the torso of the men who were on fire. A bullet through the heart or head would stop the torment of the flames. And that wasn't what he wanted. The officers who weren't on fire were shot anywhere. With them it didn't matter. The shrieks, screams, gasps and chokes were so loud that they all but drowned out the roars of the subguns.

The first waft of burning human flesh reached Rivas's nostrils, and he couldn't help but grin. He loved it when one of his plans went smoothly. The only glitch had been the one napalm bomb that had gone off prematurely during the first wave explosions—the bomb that had set the woman on fire. The initial C-4 charges had been designed not to kill massively but rather to ensure a massive turnout by police. The *real* targets.

The NFP man waited until all of the police officers had fallen and the torturous sounds of agony were dying down before he turned away from the Plaza de Armas. He had taken several steps before he remembered the Ecuadoran dog tags. He turned quickly.

Rivas smiled. Across the street in the plaza beneath the bench where he had sat, glimmering in the light from a burning body, he saw the metal ID and broken chain.

"MY USUAL, INEZ," Alvarez shouted to a beautiful young woman behind the counter as they took seats at one of the café's three tables. The waitress brought a large bottle of carbonated water and three glasses. She set it all in the middle of the table and left.

"Allow me to do the honors," Alvarez said. He unscrewed the cap and a loud hiss emanated forth as the gas escaped. Filling each man's glass, he twisted the cap back on and stared at Scarberry. "So," he said, "what can I do for you?"

"We need to talk to your father," Scarberry said.

Bolan saw a slight flinch in Alvarez's shoulders. "I am sorry, my friend," the young man said. "He is receiving no one but the immediate family." He waited a moment, then went on. "But you may tell me what you need. There is little my father could help you with that I cannot do myself. And with all due respect to him, it will soon be me who is charge of our business anyway."

Scarberry looked at Bolan.

The Executioner thought a moment, then nodded. Turning to Alvarez, he said, "Somebody's been trying to kill me."

"From what I have heard," the young man said, "at least two men."

Bolan nodded again. "But the same source is behind both attempts. I want to know who it is."

This time it was Alvarez's turn to nod. "And you would like us—me, my father...our...shall we call them employees—to find out who that person is for you?"

"If you can," Bolan said.

A smile of wisdom that seemed to contradict his tender years slowly crept across Alvarez's face. "Oh, we can," he said. "At least we can find out who the man was who tried to kill you at the airport. And we already know who the street vendor at Ari's is. He will tell us who hired him."

"I questioned him briefly myself," Bolan said. "I don't think he knows who the man was."

"We will have more time," Alvarez said. "And perhaps more persuasive methods."

Bolan shook his head. "Talk to him. But not too hard, if you get my drift. He didn't want to kill me any more than I wanted him to. My guess is the man's family was starving."

"Ah!" Alvarez laughed. "A humanitarian! A man who understands the plight of the Peruvian poverty-stricken. My hat is off to you, Señor!"

Bolan knew the man seated across from him was poking mild fun at him. But Alvarez's eyes danced with amusement; he meant no harm. He had simply seen too many foreigners—most of them Americans like Bolan and Scarberry—profess sorrow at the plight of the impoverished. But he had seen very few willing to lift a finger to actually do anything about it.

"You are correct," he finally said in a more sober tone of voice. "I know this man. He made a pact with the devil in order to feed his family. If he knows more than he told you, he will tell us willingly for a few dollars."

"You'll be reimbursed," the Executioner said. "And I'll pay you for your services as well."

Alvarez laughed again. "Friend," he said, "I already have more money than I know what to do with. And you couldn't afford what I would charge anyone." He waved a hand in front of his face, dismissing the idea, then indicated Scarberry with a toss of his head. "This is on the house. A favor for my old friend George of the Jungle."

Bolan thanked him. "Where can we reach you?" he asked.

"That will be difficult," Alvarez said. "But I can find you." He frowned, thinking hard. "This will either take minutes or days," he said. "I cannot know which yet. Where will you be in—" he glanced to the watch on his wrist "—two hours?"

Bolan thought about the E-mail message he had sent earlier. It was time to check to see if there had been a reply. "I have some business at one of the Internet places," he said.

"What, you need to check E-mail?" Alvarez asked. Without waiting for an answer, he looked out from the open café and snapped his fingers. "Carlos!" he shouted.

The Peruvian sumo wrestler waddled up to the table carrying his laptop.

"Where are you staying?" Alvarez asked Bolan.

"Hotel Florentina."

The young Alvarez made a face and shook his shoulders. "Ugh!" he said. "Abominable. No air-conditioning. But tell Marina I said hello."

"Marina?" Bolan said.

"You have seen her. Beautiful girl. She works the lobby."

Bolan thought of the lovely young prostitute he'd seen earlier. "I'll tell her for you," he said.

As he spoke, Alvarez had motioned for his gigantic bodyguard to set the laptop on the table. He indicated it with his hand. "Please," he said. "Be my guest."

The battery-operated computer was soon humming to life. Bolan wondered about using it—no matter what he did to the messages afterward, there would be a telltale trail that could be followed to them by any computer "nerd" in Alvarez's employment. The question was moot. There had been no reply from "cigarsycigarillos" to "jungleman."

Bolan shut the top of the computer and pushed it across the table toward Alvarez. "Thanks," he said.

"No luck?"

"No," Bolan confirmed.

All three men stood.

"My luck will be better," Alvarez said. "If the poor man who assaulted you at Ari's does not know any more, there are other people who will. It is simply a matter of finding the right ones and spreading around a few dollars." He smiled. "We can be very persuasive when we chose to be."

"Like I said, don't hurt him," Bolan reminded Alvarez.

The man nodded. "I understand, and I don't hurt men such as him anyway. I will do what you Americans call kill two birds with one stone. I will give him money for the information. I will contact you at the Florentina as soon as I have something."

"If we aren't there, just leave word that you called," Bolan said.

The three men shook hands.

Then, with another snap of his fingers Alvarez was suddenly surrounded once more by his bodyguards. The five men walked out of the café.

4

The Executioner still wasn't satisfied with his game plan. It seemed he and Scarberry were getting nowhere, and every hour that passed brought a rise in tension between Peru and Ecuador. He had some thinking to do. Some strategic planning. And he often thought best on his feet, in motion. So, forgoing the rickshaws, he decided to walk the mile or so back to the Plaza de Armas section of Iquitos where the Hotel Florentina, Ari's and the Internet café he had used earlier were located.

Out of nowhere the machete came at his head.

For what could have been a hundredth or merely a thousandth of a second, during which time seemed to stand still, the machete was all he saw. It was all he knew.

The Executioner ducked instinctively, hearing a *whoosh* as the thick blade swept over his head, clipping a lock of his hair which, like his mind itself, seemed to hang suspended in time for a moment before gravity began pulling it downward. The *whoosh* was followed by a *thunk* as the weapon continued on to sink into the frame around the doorway to his right. Like any well-trained and seasoned warrior, the Executioner had kept his eyes up as he ducked, and he watched the long heavy blade embed itself in the wood. The handle of the weapon, too, was made of wood— rotten and cracked with age, and held in place by a wrapping of dull copper wire. The flat sides of the blade had been darkened by use, rust, and time. But the edge—the edge that was now lodged in the door frame at the exact level where his throat had been only moments before—had been sharpened to the keenness of a barber's razor and sparkled in the sunlight.

Only then did Bolan consciously register the man who was prying the blade free from the doorway.

Even as Bolan prepared to counter, the machete came free with a crunch and splintering sound. He had no time to reach for either the Desert Eagle or the Beretta as his attacker freed the weapon from the wood. The man was right-handed, and he now stood with that arm across his body, ready to swing the vicious blade backhanded toward his prey. Still squatting, Bolan stepped forward as the machete began to move. He straightened his bent knees again, shooting his head and torso up and forward, inside the arc of the swing.

The attacker's forearm hit the Executioner's shoulder. The machete—and the power of the blow—was behind his back. With the adrenaline pumping through this veins, Bolan barely even felt the impact. He pressed forward, keeping his chest against the attacker's upper arm, and reached up with both hands to grab an elbow and forearm to trap the offending limb against his body. He was taller than the attacker and, with both hands busy, his next instinctive move was to jerk his neck down in a head strike. He aimed the skull bone at his hairline for the attacker's right eyebrow, hoping to split the skin and send a flurry of blood down into the man's eyes. But even as his head descended, the attacker looked up.

The soldier's forehead struck the man squarely on the nose, and the result was no less effective. Bone crunched and cartilage cracked as a spray of crimson shot from both of the attackers nostrils. Behind him Bolan heard the steel machete that had still been gripped in the attacker's fist clatter to the sidewalk.

The head strike had knocked the attacker slightly down and back. Bolan drove a short uppercut into his chin to straighten him again. A short left into the man's gut jackknifed him double once more and then a powerful overhand right to the back of the neck knocked him to his hands and knees on the concrete, semiconscious.

The Executioner straightened and looked up and down the sidewalk, then across the street. What had just transpired hadn't gone unobserved. Several people had obviously witnessed what had just happened, but none of them seemed outraged or even particularly surprised. One middle-aged woman, her arms full of bags containing fresh produce, had frozen in place and stared curiously at Bolan, her expression reflecting that she wasn't convinced she hadn't just hallucinated the whole incident. But even as he returned her gaze, she shrugged and began walking down the sidewalk.

Peru was about to go to war. Violence was expected. Whatever had happened between the man with the machete and the big gringo wasn't the worry of the people of Iquitos. They had plenty of other things to occupy their minds without borrowing the problems of others.

Scarberry, who had been a half pace behind the Executioner as they walked along the sidewalk, now stepped forward holding the fallen machete in his hand. "Well," he said, looking at his watch, "it was about time. Nobody's tried to kill you in what...three, four hours?" He looked at the man on the ground. "I'd have offered to help but you seemed to be doing so well, and it was so much fun just watching."

"We've got to get this guy out of here," Bolan said. "I want to find out what he knows." He reached down and grabbed the attacker under the armpits. He now had time to study the man more closely, and what he saw told him volumes. The man who had wielded the machete looked to be around thirty years of age. He wasn't dressed in rags but neither did he look as if he were on his way to a photo shoot for *Esquire* or *Gentlemen's Quarterly*. A three-days' growth of beard pocked his chin and cheeks over old acne scars. But there was something about the man that didn't fit the rest of the image he portrayed, and it gnawed the depths of the Executioner's subconscious as he tried to define exactly what it was.

Before he could solve the puzzle, Scarberry moved in and quickly patted the man down for more weapons. He looked to Bolan and shook his head. Other than the machete, the man was clean.

A moment later, Bolan and Scarberry were escorting the still-dizzy man down the street, steering him toward the Hotel Florentina. A few people glanced curiously their way, but none was interested enough to do more. Scarberry had jammed a bandanna into the man's nostrils and the bleeding from his nose had all but stopped. He made no protest as the two Americans half guided, half lifted him up the steps to the Hotel Florentina's lobby.

The good-looking hooker—Marina, Alvarez had called her—had either found a customer or left the lobby for other reasons. But the desk clerk was on duty, his eyes glued to the black-and-white TV and what appeared to by a South American soap opera. He gave them a glance as they arrived at the top of the steps. Harvey Scarberry's hands were both holding one of the machete wielder's arms so he indicated the man with a nod of his head. *"Mucho cerveza,"* he told the desk clerk by way of explanation. Too much beer.

The desk clerk nodded and returned his attention to the soap opera. He couldn't have cared less whether the man was drunk or the whole Ecuadoran army was at the Iquitos city limits.

Bolan and Scarberry steered the man through the lobby and into the courtyard. The Executioner held him next to the water dispenser while Scarberry fished a key from his pocket and inserted it into the door. A moment later, the two men threw the man on Scarberry's bed. He groaned as he landed on the sheet facedown, his legs still off the bed, both toes of his shiny white Nike cross-trainers touching the floor.

"Roll over," the Executioner ordered.

The man lay flat where he had fallen.

Bolan snapped a kick in the back of the man's calf. The kick brought a yelp of pain.

"I said roll over," the soldier repeated.

Slowly, the man used his arms to push his chest off the bed, then twist himself to his side and finally onto his back. Scooting up to rest his back against the wall, he took several deep breaths, then reached up with one hand to explore the damage to his face. His nose had swollen to twice its normal size, and both eyes were already blackening. His glazed brown orbs, sunken deep inside the swelling, stared at the two men before him. He was still in too much shock to actually register where he was or what was going on.

"Sit up," Bolan said.

The man didn't need a second kick to obey. He pulled himself farther up with more of his back resting against the wall. He was still breathing hard, and the bleeding had started at his nose again. Scarberry walked quickly into the bathroom and returned a moment later with a roll of toilet paper. He tossed it to the man on the bed and said, "We've got questions for you, amigo, so get that snout plugged up."

The man on the bed held a wad of toilet paper to his face and waited.

"What's your name?" the Executioner asked.

"Juan," the man replied from behind the toilet paper. "Juan Torres."

"Who sent you?"

Torres pressed the toilet paper harder against his nose. To Bolan, it looked more like an effort to stall for time than an attempt to further control his bleeding nose.

It had to have looked the same to Scarberry. He turned to the soldier. "You have no idea how much fun it is not to have to put up with all that Miranda crap anymore. Mind if I handle this?"

"Be my guest," Bolan said.

Scarberry drew the S&W .45 ACP Mountain Gun from under his shirt and stepped to the edge of the bed. Jamming the barrel of the big wheelgun into the wad of bloody toilet paper, he said, "Listen, my friend and I have no time to fuck around with you.

Start talking, and start talking fast. Otherwise I'm going to give you a third nostril and, I promise, it's going to bleed a hell of a lot worse than the two you've got right now."

Slowly, Torres let his hand, and the blood-soaked toilet paper, drop from his face to his chest. His eyes almost crossed as he stared at the gun barrel, which stayed in place. "I don't know who the man was," he whispered hoarsely.

"If you can't tell us who he was, then you'd better start telling us a hell of a lot about him," Scarberry said. He leaned forward slightly and jammed the S&W barrel between the man's swollen nose and his upper lip.

The Executioner studied Torres closely, and again his brain registered the fact that something didn't quite jibe with the man's overall appearance. But this time, what it was became clear. The growth of beard on his face wasn't unusual; few men in Peru shaved every day as they did in the States. Torres's shirt and pants weren't new but they weren't old, either. Bolan's eyes traveled on down to the man's shoes, and there he found the answer.

Torres wore what looked like new Nike cross-trainers. They were a model that ran over a hundred dollars a pair in the U.S. and would cost even more in Peru. Import tax and shipping and handling put them into the ridiculous range, and none but the country's very wealthy—like Alvarez—ever wore such footwear. Even they usually had them brought down in person by visiting friends or relatives to avoid the tax.

Torres didn't appear to have come from the sewers of Iquitos. But he wasn't one of Peru's "landed gentry," either.

The distinctive sound of the revolver being cocked echoed though the sparsely furnished room. Two almost inaudible clicks followed by a slightly louder one as the hammer locked back into single-action mode. When he spoke again, Scarberry's voice was even lower than the whisper in which Torres had spoken. "We're waiting, Juan," the former DEA man said. "But we're not going to wait much longer."

Torres's eyes might still have been crossed. It was impossible to tell because the lids were clamped tightly over them. "He...he...will kill me..." he breathed. "He swore that he would if I talked...."

Scarberry glanced at Bolan. "Don't you hate it when they say that?" he said. "It sounds like he's in some really bad, low-budget movie. And then I've gotta say, 'I'll kill you if you don't' and I sound just as bad as him."

He shook his head in disgust and then turned back to Torres. With a short sigh, he said, "Okay, I'll play the game. We'll kill you if you *don't* talk."

Bolan caught Scarberry's eye again. He indicated that the former DEA agent should step to the side. As soon as he was out of the way, Bolan moved in to take his place directly in front of Torres. The man's eyes opened as the S&W's barrel moved away from his face.

The Executioner reached out and pulled the room's one chair over in front of the bed, then sat down. He was about to play the good guy in this variation of the time-proved good-cop, bad-cop routine, so he left the Desert Eagle and the Beretta in their holsters. But he didn't want to overplay the part or Torres would see through it. So he let the tails of his vest fall to the sides to make both weapons visible.

Torres's eyes jerked from one gun to the other, then finally returned to Bolan's face.

Bolan smiled. He stared at the man's nose. "Bleeding stopped?" he asked.

Torres nodded. "Yes. I think so."

"Good," the Executioner said. "Okay, Juan, let's look at this situation from your point of view. See what options you have open." He waited a second to let it sink in, then continued. "We want to know what you know. That is, who hired you to try to kill me. You with me so far?"

Juan Torres nodded.

"But you're afraid that if you tell us who it was, word will get back to him and he'll kill you. Right?"

The man with the blood-caked, swollen face nodded.

"My friend here has just informed you that we'll kill you if you *don't* tell us. And we're here right now, so normally the decision should be pretty easy. Better go along with the guys who have the opportunity to kill you now, rather than later, right? Still with me?"

This time there was no nod. Torres simply stared into the Executioner's eyes, waiting.

"But it isn't quite that easy for you, is it?" Bolan went on. "No, somebody has thrown sort of a wild card into the game and it's confusing you. And I think I know what it is." He paused long enough to let what he had said sink in, then continued. "You've heard about the guy who tried to shoot me at Ari's. Maybe you even know him. Iquitos isn't that big a city. But in any case, you've heard that I could have killed him but I didn't. So, you're asking yourself right now if I won't probably let you live, too. You're thinking maybe this guy isn't really a killer. Maybe he doesn't have it in him. Tell me, Juan, am I pretty much on the mark so far?"

Again, there was no response, either verbal or physical, from Torres. But the man's eyes seemed to change right in front of the Executioner. Torres could tell that Bolan was leading toward something. What that something was, he didn't know.

But it scared the hell out of him, and it showed in the eyes behind the swollen face.

"Let me tell you why I didn't kill the guy at Ari's," the Executioner continued. "And I think that'll solve your dilemma. That guy was nothing. A poor street hustler trying to feed a family by selling alligator teeth and mounted butterflies and other jungle bugs. He'd never have hurt a bug himself except somebody came along and took advantage of his situation. Put a temptation in front of him he couldn't resist. So the guy saw a way to help his family, Juan. Maybe he could buy his son a decent shirt or his little girl a new dress. Or maybe the new dress would be for his wife. Maybe they could all have something more than corn for dinner for a night or two." He paused to take a breath. "That's why I couldn't bring myself to kill him even though he tried to kill me."

The speech had brought a spark of life and hope back to Torres's eyes, and the man suddenly perked up. "Yes!" he almost shouted. "It is the same. I, too, am a poor man with a family. I would never have agreed to do such a horrible thing if my children weren't starving."

Bolan looked sadly down at the floor and slowly shook his head. "No, Juan, I don't think that's the case. I don't think that's the case at all."

"Señor!" Torres almost cried. "It is true! I wanted only to feed my family. They are starving. I can tell you are a good man. You must believe me."

Bolan looked up but continued to shake his head. It was almost time to move. Almost time for the second scene of this psychological one-act play designed to frighten and confuse Torres to the point where he willingly opened up and talked. "Thank you, Juan," he said. "And I do like to think I'm a good man. But I just can't believe you. Do you want to know why?"

"Why?" Torres asked anxiously. "Why cannot you believe me?"

Bolan moved faster than a jaguar as he reached down, ripped one of the man's white Nike cross-trainers from his feet, then came out of the chair and landed with his knees on Torres's thighs. Torres screamed as the Executioner's full weight pulled his shoulders down from the wall and he found himself on his back on the bed. Bolan edged forward until his knees straddled the man's chest in the classic wrestling mount position. He slammed the rubber sole of the shoe across Torres's face and the blood shot out of his nose again. Then, reaching down, he grabbed a handful of the man's hair with one hand and jammed the shoe into his face with the other.

To the sides of the shoe, the Executioner could see the man's eyes. They were wide in amazement, with terror quickly setting in behind the shock. Bolan's sudden change in demeanor had worked, and worked well. Just as it always had in the past.

"This is how I know, Juan," the Executioner growled in a low menacing voice. "Men with families to feed do not buy themselves shoes like this. At least if they care about their families they don't. So either you don't have a family, or you don't care about them, and either way, it won't bother me to kill you because any family with a father like you is better off without him."

Throwing the shoe against the wall with mock anger, Bolan reached under his armpit and drew the mammoth .44 magnum Desert Eagle. He placed it exactly where Scarberry's S&W had been a few minutes earlier and looked down into Torres's terrified eyes. "Start talking," he said.

Torres told him everything he knew, and Bolan believed every word he said. The problem was, there wasn't much. Torres admitted that he was known as a something of a tough guy in the Belen district. A man—Peruvian by his accent—had approached him and offered him fifty dollars to kill the big American. The man had pointed out Bolan while he and Scarberry sat talking with Alvarez.

"You were supposed to meet him later," Bolan said. "Where?"

"No," Torres said. His nose was filled with blood and he could barely get the words out. "I was not supposed to meet him. Ever again."

"You're lying," Bolan said. "You had to meet him in order to get your money."

Torres shook his head violently and drops of blood flew each way. "No, señor," he pleaded. "I had already been paid."

"You're still lying," the Executioner said. "How could he know you wouldn't just take the money and run?"

"You do not understand. He showed me a gun. And he watched the whole thing from a store window. Across the street. He said if I tried to run away with the money he would kill me."

The Executioner eased up the pressure on the hand cannon. Torres's story was unusual but not that far-fetched. And under the conditions—knowing he was one pull of the trigger away from death—it was almost certainly true. That meant the man behind this had not only been there while he talked to Alvarez in the café, he had also been less than twenty feet away when Torres attacked with the machete.

Bolan sat up and frowned. One thing didn't make sense. If the guy was that close to him, why didn't he just shoot the Executioner himself? Why hire Torres to do it?

There could be only one reason. This man, whoever he was, was worried about being recognized. Maybe not to the people in the Belen—at least not to Torres—but perhaps to people in other areas of Iquitos. The Executioner reminded himself that they had been several blocks from the fish market when the attack had come. The mystery man figured he could face the heat of simply being in the same area in which a murder took place, but he didn't want to be seen in the act or get caught with the smoking gun in his hand. Did that mean he lived in Iquitos?

He also seemed to have connections all the way back to the States, because he could somehow find out that Bolan wasn't really a journalist even before the big guy's plane had landed. Was he Coast Guard? DEA? State Department?

Bolan got off the bed but continued to stare at Torres. "You said his accent sounded Peruvian. From this area or another?" Like all large countries, people from one area had slightly different speech patterns than those living in others.

"No," Torres said, shaking his head. "Not Amazonian. He sounded more like...perhaps from the Andes."

The Executioner's eyebrows lowered in thought. That didn't mean the man didn't currently live in Iquitos. Just that he probably hadn't been born here. So what did he have? A man born in the Andes who had moved to Iquitos. And was at least semirecognizable.

Bolan reached across the bed, grabbed Torres by the shirt, and hauled him to his feet. He holstered the Desert Eagle and opened the door with his other hand, then shoved the machete man out into the courtyard.

"Where are we going?" Torres asked in a quiet, timid voice.

He stared up at the Executioner, his swollen face now the size, and somewhat the shape, of a small pumpkin.

"For a walk," Bolan said. He waited until Scarberry had joined them in the courtyard, then closed the door.

ALEJANDRO CARILLO no longer thought of himself by that name. He had been called Relámpago so long that it had taken over in his mind as his own appellation. Often, when thinking, he realized he also now referred to himself in the third person in his own mind. Relámpago is thirsty, he would think. Or Relámpago finds that girl quite attractive. Had he been a more educated man, particularly in the field of psychology, Relámpago might have realized that this was a way of distancing himself from what he knew—at some level of consciousness— he had become.

Relámpago had begun his career as a freedom fighter with idealistic hopes of bringing equality to the Quechua in Ecuador. He had found out quickly that this equality couldn't be achieved without killing, and that many of the lives he would be forced to take would be from individuals far removed from the mistreatment of his people. At first, the deaths of such blameless men, women and children had made him sick. More than one night he had fallen to his knees in prayers begging forgiveness. More than one night those prayers had been preceded by, and followed by, vomiting. But then, as he orchestrated the demise of more and more human beings who had nothing to do with the problem, it had become merely a distasteful necessity. Shortly after that, he had lost all remorse—all feeling whatsoever.

But while Alejandro "Relámpago" Carillo would have scored in the superior range on any intelligence test, he was not an educated man.

Sweat had broken out beneath the sweater-vest he wore over a long-sleeved shirt with a button-down collar. He glanced at the carefully pressed brown slacks and the squeaking leather shoes and wondered how some of his Quechua brethren—those who had given into the rule of the modern-day Spaniards who controlled Ecuador—could stand dressing this way every day.

Relámpago passed a large picture window in one of the ancient buildings among which the sidewalk wound. A sigh escaped his lips. For him, at least, this costume of the invaders would be only temporary. And such clothing, as well as the briefcase he now held in his left hand, was necessary to the illusion he had to project if what he was about to do was to succeed. He walked along the concrete path as a student came toward him. The young man's arms were loaded with law books, which he almost dropped as he looked up at Relámpago. A moment of confusion clouded his eyes as he failed to recognize the older man's face. But he recognized the costume, and without further hesitation said, "Good morning, professor."

Relámpago merely nodded. He walked on.

Loja, Ecuador, stood seven thousand feet above sea level and was his target of choice because of its proximity to the Peruvian border. Both the Zamora and Malacatos rivers, which emptied into the Amazon, ran through this subtropical town. In addition to the rivers, one of the great Inca highways that had once joined Cuzco and Quito lay in the hills that surrounded the town. So, in addition to the location near the border, the site held both ancient and modern significance for what Relámpago was about to do.

As he walked on through the university campus, he let his mind wander. Ecuador and Peru had fought a war in 1941 over the thousand-mile swamp in the Amazon basin. Peru had won, and Ecuador had never forgiven them. War had broken out again in 1981 and 1991, and a few shots had even been fired in 1994. But the argument now was over a much smaller stretch of land known as the *Cordillera del Condor*—a fifty-mile stretch of high jungle that lay between two rivers. According to the *Protocol de Rio de Janeiro,* which had officially ended the war in 1942, one of the rivers served as the border between the two countries. The dispute was that no one seemed to know which river it was. The *Protocol* was unclear in its wording. There were rumors of heavy gold deposits between the two rivers. Gold that each country wanted.

Gold, Relámpago knew, that belonged to neither country. It belonged to the Quechua.

The man masquerading as a law professor took in a deep breath and was again reminded of the odor that he found offensive. In addition to this law university, Loja boasted of being the center of Ecuador's quinine industry. The quinine was produced from the bark of the cinchona tree, which was abundantly cultivated in the area. The quinine trade had not, perhaps, been as responsible for the disruption of his Quechua way of life as the oil industry, but he hated it nearly as much. And striking back at modern industry in general had a certain satisfaction for the man who everyone, including himself, called Relámpago.

The sidewalk curved slightly, then straightened as a branch led off the main pathway toward a one-story building more modern that those he had just walked past. Through the windows of the wall facing him, he could see roughly a hundred young men and women seated at long banquet tables. They were eating. Though he couldn't see it, he knew the cafeteria line stood farther back beyond the tables. He had sent men the day before to recon both the layout of the cafeteria and learn what time of day it was the most crowded with law students.

Relámpago glanced at his wristwatch. Then, looking back up, he saw four men dressed similarly to him approaching the cafeteria from other campus pathways. All four men also carried briefcases. Another glance at his wrist brought on a smug smile of satisfaction.

The Lightning Bolt leader used his free hand to push open the glass door that led into the cafeteria. He stopped just inside, seconds ahead of the others. He watched the faces of the law students as he waited. Few looked up. Even fewer registered any surprise at seeing an unfamiliar face. They were all too busy in conversation with one another, or with their attention glued to the many textbooks which lay open amid their plates and glasses.

One by one, the other four men entered the cafeteria, stopping just inside their respective doors as Relámpago had done. When the last man had arrived, the Ecuadoran gave a brief nod of his head.

The briefcases fell to the floor to reveal a variety of firearms.

Relámpago was the first to fire, cutting loose with a long full-auto burst of 9 mm rounds from his Calico M-950 submachine gun. It was impossible to count precisely, but he estimated that during his first burst of fire he burned roughly twenty rounds. That meant that eighty remained in the huge, 100-round top-mounted drum magazine atop the weapon. He watched the law students at the table nearest him dance in death. From other parts of the cafeteria, he heard the explosions from the weapons of his men. And everywhere, he heard screams.

The Quechau leader fired another long burst and more students fell. He glanced across the room where a young woman with bleached blond hair rose from her seat and tried to run. The counterfeit yellow hair didn't go well with her dark skin, and was yet another indication of her traitorous behavior toward her own Quechua people. It irritated him, and he took even more than the usual pleasure in swinging his Calico her way.

A long stream of 9 mm slugs skimmed over the table toward the young woman. The first several rounds of the volley struck her in the side, ripping her blouse and causing her to jerk in staccato jolts. He raised his aim slightly and the remainder of the burst trailed up her neck and through her head

The screams, screeches and shrieks of horror gave way to moans and groans of agony as the students continued to fall. Most found a resting place on the floor, but others fell across the tables, sending plates, silverware, glasses, and books and papers sliding. Both the tile and the tabletops were soon slippery with crimson. Relámpago glanced at his feet and saw that the soles of his shoes were now wet. A veritable river of blood seemed to be washing across the ground.

The Quechua sloshed a few steps to his side to reposition himself. From his new vantage point, he could look through a window into the kitchen where three women dressed in white and wearing hairnets stood frozen in shock and terror.

You feed those who will someday continue the subjugation of my people, he thought.

Relámpago cut loose with another burst from the Calico. Tiny holes appeared in the women's clean white uniforms, spotting them as if the cafeteria workers had spilled red pepper over their clothing. But the spots grew quickly, and soon it looked more as if they had fallen into a giant institutional vat of ketchup.

A young man wearing thick black glasses panicked and ran straight toward Relámpago. The movement was sudden and unexpected, and before the Quechua leader could swing the Calico his way the law student was inside his arms. A flurry of fists drove the leader through the door through which he had entered. The landing blows were weak and ineffective, but he was impressed with the young man's courage nonetheless.

Regaining his balance, Relámpago brought the Calico around in an arc and slammed the heavy machine pistol against the student's jaw. A loud crack echoed off the surrounding building, not unlike the sound of a wooden baseball bat hitting the ball. The young man fell to his hands and knees in front of the Lightning Bolt leader, his face toward the sidewalk.

Relámpago pressed the barrel of the Calico against the back of the boy's neck and pulled the trigger. Flapping waves of blood rose to splash the Quechua in the face and soak his sweater-vest. The student fell forward onto his face, almost headless.

He looked down. He would have no more opportune time to do what he had to do than this.

Reaching into his pocket, he pulled out the ripped shred of material. It had been torn from the shoulder of the uniform blouse of a Peruvian army sergeant, and still contained part of one stripe designating the man's rank. Squatting, he opened the student's hand, pressed the material into the palm, then closed the dead fingers around it. It would look as if the young man had ripped it from his attacker before dying. This young man would be touted as a hero—one who had fought back against the attackers. And perhaps he deserved to be remembered that way, he thought. And if anyone chanced to survive the massacre and had seen the student back Relámpago out the door, it would be no problem. Even an amateur forensic lab like that of the Ecuadoran government would identify the scrap of uniform with the hated Peruvians. The fact that Relámpago hadn't worn a uniform would get lost in the retelling of the story.

When he reentered the cafeteria, it was over. An eerie silence had replaced the roar of the gunfire, which itself had replaced the buzzing chatter of the law students that had preceded the attack. He surveyed the room. The tables, floors, walls and even parts of the ceiling were awash in blood. His fellow Lightning Bolts had already left. He took a final look at the dozens of dead bodies that littered the cafeteria.

The Quechua picked up his briefcase from the floor and dropped the Calico inside. Turning, he exited the building once more and walked swiftly along the sidewalk, retracing his steps. A few students and professors had heard the gunfire and were making their way curiously, if timidly, toward the cafeteria. One of them saw his blood-covered face and chest and stopped cold on the sidewalk. "What happened?" he asked.

Relámpago shook his head as if in confusion. "An attack of some kind," he said, feigning shock. "I don't know...perhaps...the Peruvians." He hurried on past the student, his blood-soaked face breaking out in a grin. The young man considered him one of the victims rather than an attacker, and he would be reported to the authorities as some unrecognized professor.

The car was waiting exactly where it was supposed to be when he arrived at the parking lot. Two of the other four men were already inside. Relámpago got into the back and dropped the briefcase on the floor between his feet. No words were spoken. There was more work ahead, and the time to celebrate victories was still far in the future.

THE STREETS WERE practically deserted as they made their way from the Hotel Florentina back toward the Internet café. It was late afternoon, the tail end of siesta. The few men and women who moved on the streets did so languidly and seemed irritated that they weren't observing this age-old Latino custom of rest as were many of their fellow Peruvians. Ari's was on the way, and Scarberry wanted to say hello to Anita so they stopped briefly. Bolan waited with Torres on the sidewalk. But the former DEA man came out soon after he went in. Anita hadn't been feeling well and gone home. They walked on.

Bolan led the way into the Internet café with Torres behind him. Scarberry brought up the rear in order to keep an eye on the man. The former DEA agent had the would-be machete assassin covered with the small .357 Magnum pistol in the pocket of his vest. Bolan had explained to Torres that one false move would mean his death. But he had hedged his bet that Torres would cooperate, promising him that if he went along with them he'd live.

Torres had been compliant ever since and apparently believed him. Which made the Executioner happy. The last thing he needed right now was the further complications that would come from Scarberry gunning down a man in broad daylight as they crossed the Plaza de Armis.

The café attendant recognized the soldier from his earlier visits and the tip. All the computers were busy, but he walked to the one Bolan had used before, spoke in a bullying tone to the frail man seated there and hooked a thumb toward the door.

Bolan didn't like it, but he suspected that what he was doing outweighed whatever computer project the small man was involved in. The simple fact was that this man who was now being ushered out of his seat might not be alive to continue his pursuits if the Executioner didn't work quickly.

Taking the vacated seat, Bolan logged onto the Internet, found his mail site and pulled up his account.

A message was waiting.

Bolan opened the message and began to read as Scarberry stepped in behind him. "Turn and look the other way," the former DEA man ordered Torres in a low voice. "Don't even think about looking at the screen."

The Executioner heard Torres's feet shuffle as he began to read: *Dear Jungleman: I know who you are, and I have what you want.*

Bolan felt his eyebrows lower in concentration. Okay, fine. But exactly how did he know who the Executioner was and what he wanted? Was this man a player in the Iquitos underworld who knew the American journalist had already been involved in several skirmishes? Bolan's adventures under that guise were undoubtedly part of the current gossip among rickshaw drivers and other townspeople. Then another possibility, which should have seemed obvious from the start, suddenly dawned on him. Colonel Ramon Suarez had been the one who gave Bolan and Scarberry the mysterious E-mail address. Bolan had assumed that the E-mail address led to someone Suarez knew—someone who was either in the government or the Iquitos underworld. Someone who knew more about the chemical weapons than Suarez did, and who was in a better position to help them. Someone who wouldn't have to risk being tried as a traitor or losing his position in the Peruvian air force.

But there was another possibility. Cigarsycigarillos might well be Suarez himself.

That was the simplest, and most likely, answer to how Bolan's identity and information needs were known. On the other hand, he couldn't completely rule out the possibility that he was wrong. Perhaps Suarez was burning the candle at both ends and had told this contact himself in exchange for a cut of the money the Executioner would probably pay for the intel he needed. Nowhere was it written that selfless and selfish motives couldn't sometimes go hand in hand.

There was also always the chance that Suarez was setting up Bolan and Scarberry rather than helping them.

Before reading on, Bolan swiveled slightly in his chair. Now, he could see Torres standing with his back to him, staring through the front windows to the street. Scarberry had half turned to keep an eye on both Torres and the screen.

"You know Colonel Suarez well," the Executioner stated without expecting any answer from Scarberry.

The former DEA man answered anyway, with a nod of his head. "I've told you that already."

"But exactly how much do you trust him?"

Scarberry shrugged. "I worked with him a lot of times, Belasko," he said. "He never turned me around or circled me. At least not that I know of."

Bolan frowned again in thought. Scarberry was being as honest as possible—more honest than many men, even men who had been in the DEA and other agencies who worked with informants—knew how to be.

Scarberry knew that almost all men had a price, and that knowledge caused him to add, "Look, I think I'd be one of the last on his list to double-cross. But the man is human and he lives in a country with a dead economy and a history of bribery and graft. For enough money..." His voice trailed off for a moment and he squinted his eyes, trying to find the right words. Finally he just settled for "...he might."

Turning back to the screen, the soldier finished the message. *I will meet you tonight at 8:00. Walk straight to the river from Ari's. I believe you know where that is. Stand along the white railing where the water has receded. I will find you. Come alone.*

The message had not been signed. Not that the Executioner had expected it to be.

"I don't like this," Scarberry said.

"I'm not crazy about it myself," Bolan agreed.

"You'll be completely out of control of the situation," the DEA man went on. "*He'll* find *you?* That's bullshit. I know that area where he wants to meet. There's a walkway along the river. Teenagers and others hang out there at night. He could come by and put a bullet in the back of your head before you knew who he was."

Bolan shrugged. "It seems like a chance we'll have to take," he said. "We've got nothing else. Unless you have a better idea, in which case I'm willing to listen."

Scarberry clenched his teeth. "No," he said. "Except that I think I should follow you. I won't be able to get close enough to be of much use or he'll spot me. But I can get close enough to get to your body before it gets cold." He paused, and the laugh he gave out held no mirth. "At least I'll feel better."

Bolan nodded his consent.

Scarberry glanced at Torres who still stood frozen in place, staring out the window. "So, what we do with our new little buddy here? I can't go trailing after you like James Bond and keep him in tow at the same time."

The soldier fixed his gaze on Torres and set his jaw in thought. The machete-killer wannabe had told them very little of use. He was a midlevel predator within the Iquitos underworld, subsisting primarily on what he could mug from unwary tourists and a small armed robbery now and then. He had been approached by a man with long brown hair and a short well-trimmed beard—both which Bolan suspected were false—and offered fifty dollars to kill the American journalist calling himself Belasko. His retainer, who also appeared to be American, had provided him with a set of photos.

Bolan pulled four crumpled grainy pictures from his pocket now and looked at them. They had been taken at the airport soon after he'd first arrived and before the shooting began. They showed him getting off the plane that Jack Grimaldi had flown, then entering the terminal. In the final picture, he was standing in the immigration line and just beginning to turn, mere seconds before the full-scale gun battle began.

Which meant that the man who had hired Torres had been there the whole time. And that he knew there was a chance that the hit at the airport might fail. Otherwise, why would he have bothered with the pictures? That, in turn, meant he knew far more about Bolan's true identity than the Executioner would have liked. But most of all, it meant that his knowledge had originally come from somewhere in the United States of America.

Scarberry had gone silent as Bolan thought. The problem was, the Executioner didn't want to kill Torres—he hadn't only promised the man his life if he cooperated, the machete man might prove useful in the future. New intelligence that they picked up along the way might spark other details in Torres's brain that, combined with the new information, provided answers to questions yet to be asked.

On the other hand, he couldn't baby-sit the man from now on nor could he let him walk. And he couldn't leave him with Grimaldi. If he needed him, he would need him immediately. Grimaldi wasn't close enough. And there was always the chance that Torres would report back to his mysterious retainer if allowed to go free.

Bolan's jaw clenched tighter. He wished he could somehow put Torres on dry ice for a while, lock the man away in a little box until he needed him again.

Slowly, the Executioner's jaw began to slacken and a smile crept over his face.

Maybe he could do just that.

"YOU DO NOT UNDERSTAND," Juan Torres pleaded. "This is not the United States. They will kill me!"

"No, they won't kill you," Bolan said, shaking his head. "You might take a few lumps, but they won't kill you. And you deserve a few lumps anyway."

The two men sat at a table at Ari's. Scarberry was on the phone in the hall next to the rest room. He had been concerned about Anita ever since finding out she had gone home sick.

"For what?" Torres almost cried. "I have done everything you asked. I have told you everything I know. For what do I deserve a beating?'

Bolan looked him in the eye. "How about trying to cut off my head with a machete?" he asked. "Or a thousand and one other crimes you've committed that you didn't get caught for?"

Torres's lips clamped shut as if he had no further argument, and the question went unanswered. Shaking his head in disbelief, he looked down at the table.

Scarberry came back. "No big deal," he said. "Just sick to her stomach. She's okay now and worried about the money she lost by not working."

Bolan nodded. "You ready, then?"

Scarberry said yes, and Bolan turned and led the way out of Ari's and across the street to the Plaza de Armas.

On the other side of the plaza, between Ari's and the Hotel Florentina, stood a building they had passed several times, both on foot and in rickshaws. Bolan suspected the building contained a residence, and that it housed either a high-ranking military officer or some other government official. The reason for his suspicion was simple: two uniformed guards were always outside on the corner.

Though the faces changed, the uniforms never did. They weren't the uniforms of Loreto state or even the federal police but rather military police who stood watch. There were always two men, and they always carried both Soviet AK-47s and 9 mm Makarov pistols. They eyed everyone who walked by but spoke to no one. And no one seemed inclined to speak to them.

Following Torres, Bolan and Scarberry let the man gain twenty feet on them. "Keep in mind," Scarberry said just before the machete wielder left whisper range, "you try to run, I'll shoot you before you get five feet."

Torres's tone was surly as he spit over his shoulder, "Does it matter how I die? From your bullet or theirs?"

Several benches stood on a grassy area near the corner of the Plaza. Bolan and Scarberry dropped into seats facing each other. From this vantage point they could appear to be in conversation but keep the corner in sight. Children played nearby, and young couples walked arm in arm as the two Americans watched Torres. The man who had tried earlier in the day to kill the Executioner slowed his pace as he neared the street. Just before crossing toward the two guards, he stopped and turned.

Torres looked at Bolan and Scarberry, then across the street to the cops, then back to Bolan and Scarberry again. He was obviously weighing his odds of escape versus what might happen to him if he did as the Executioner had ordered him.

Just to help him decide, Scarberry lifted his vest with the hand wrapped around the gun in his pocket.

Torres shook his head in disgust. Evidently, he feared the Americans more than the cops, because he finally turned and walked purposefully across the street.

Between the corner building and the broken concrete curb, the two military police officers stared straight ahead. Torres came to a halt directly in front of the nearest cop and said something that Bolan and Scarberry couldn't hear. But they distinctly heard what came next as, a second later, the machete man's open hand slapped across the face of the military policeman in front of him with a resounding pop.

For a second, the two cops stood stunned, reluctant to believe what had just happened. Then the one who had been slapped brought the butt of his AK-47 across and rammed it into Torres's jaw. Torres went down, maybe out, maybe just smart enough to fake unconsciousness. In any case, he got off easy, taking only a half-dozen kicks from the two men before they halted. The man who had been slapped pulled a walkie-talkie from his belt and spoke into it.

Bolan and Scarberry waited until the military police jeep showed up to tow Torres away. The two cops each treated themselves to a final gut punch before throwing the machete man at the officers who had shown up to get him. The new men took a turn as well, but it was equally brief.

"Not bad for a career mugger and armed robber," Scarberry said.

Bolan nodded. "Less than he deserves." He turned and the two men started toward Ari's and then the river beyond. "Let's hope that Suarez can get him out of jail if we need him." *And let's hope the commandant turns out to really be on our side,* he thought but didn't say.

"We'll do just that," Scarberry agreed. "Until then, let's just stay alive the rest of the night." He glanced at his wrist. "Aren't you a little overdue for another murder attempt?"

5

Dusk had come and gone, and the darkness of night had fallen over the Amazon basin. A few ancient lights cast their dim eerie glow over the river but even more had burned out long ago and never been replaced. Still, the moon was full and the Executioner could see the gently rolling waters quite well.

The water level was low, and Bolan gazed out at the mossy green land that had so recently been uncovered as the river receded. He knew that not too many miles from where he stood, alligators would be frolicking on the banks as they looked for food. On the Amazon, nature was never more than a step away from turning the cities into jungle once more.

The Executioner leaned against the white concrete rail, his eyes flicking back and forth to the corners of the eyeglasses he wore. They had been cheap plastic sunglasses before he'd knocked out the dark lenses and glued tiny mirrors to the inside of the frames. They were a crude—yet effective—surveillance tool, allowing him to watch behind him as he appeared to be looking out over the water. With a mirror in both corners of the frame, he now had almost 360-degree visibility.

The sounds of music blasted out from a café directly behind him. In the mirrors, Bolan watched as the teenaged boys and girls of Iquitos loitered in the wide walkway that led to the river. It was courting time. In the tiny mirrors, he saw girls strutting past with exaggerated walks. Boys flexed their muscles. Both sexes pretended they didn't know the other was watching.

For a moment, the Executioner thought back over his life, wondering what it might have been like had he chosen a different path. Perhaps he would have courted girls in the traditional way had a war not come along for him during those years. Perhaps he would have found a girl and settled down to have children if things had been different. But as it was, his war had never ended. It had only expanded as new enemies joined or replaced the old. And it looked now as if it would never end.

Bolan forced the thoughts from his mind. It would do no good to think of what might have been. It didn't matter. He had a job to do.

The soldier glanced to the right-corner mirror and saw the street leading away from the river and back toward Ari's Burgers. Somewhere, along that street or nearby, Scarberry waited. For what, Bolan wasn't certain, for as the former DEA man had said, there was nothing he could do to help if assassination was what was on their contact's mind.

The Executioner was on his own.

Ten minutes passed, then twenty. The laughter and shouting behind him grew louder as cheap wine was passed among the boys and some of the girls. A fight over one of the girls broke out and ended as quickly as it had begun. It was all posturing and no one was hurt.

A figure that seemed somehow out of place appeared in the corner of the Executioner's vision. He switched his concentration to the left mirror on his glasses and watched as a man strolled down the walkway in his general direction. What set him apart from others was not only his age but his manner of dress. Clean blue jeans, black and green jungle boots, a light khaki T-shirt and a baseball cap. Suddenly, he spotted the Executioner and almost stopped. Then, walking more slowly, he stared directly at Bolan as he made his way toward a spot along the railing perhaps thirty feet to the soldier's left.

Slowly, careful to keep the movement from giving him away, Bolan leaned over the railing. Shielded by his body, his right hand inched across his chest to find the grips of the Beretta 93-R under his arm.

The man coming toward him had long brown hair and a short well-trimmed beard.

Bolan drew the Beretta but kept it under his jacket.

The long-haired man quit watching him as he entered into what would have been Bolan's normal field of vision had he not worn the mirror-glasses. He looked out over the river, taking in a deep dramatic breath and expanding his chest with exaggerated casualness. Bolan watched in his peripheral vision. Something told him this man was no problem.

That something was bad acting ability. His lack of professionalism at appearing unconcerned with what was going on around him.

The long-haired man waited half a minute or so, then began to ease his way along the railing. Bolan was growing tired of the amateur performance. He glanced at his watch as he stuffed the Beretta back into his shoulder holster, then turned and walked directly up to the man.

"Cigarsycigarillos," he said.

The man with the hair and beard had been glancing the other way when Bolan made his move. Now, he froze where he stood. Slowly, he turned to face the Executioner. "Excuse me," he said with a British accent. "Were you speaking to me?"

"Cut the crap," Bolan said. "I was—" He stopped in midsentence as he saw Scarberry suddenly round the corner and walk quickly toward them. The former DEA agent was hurrying but his face showed no stress—just aversion. He was shaking his head.

"Hello, Richards," he said sarcastically as he neared. "I might have known you'd be mixed up in this somewhere."

The man called Richards turned slightly. "Harvey!" he said. "Good to see you. The more the merrier."

Bolan looked from Scarberry to Richards to Scarberry again. "Okay, someone want to explain old-home week to me?"

Scarberry's face was still filled with loathing. "Long story short," he said. "William Richards—Willie to his friends and that's why I call him either Richards or William—"

"See now, Harvey—"

"—has another jungle guide business here in Iquitos. He's tried every dirty trick in the book to get me run out of business, busted, thrown in jail, deported, or in any other way out of competition with him. And he's always got his finger in something—jungle or not."

Bolan looked back at Richards. "That the story?" he asked.

"Crudely put," Richards said, smiling. "But essentially correct, yes."

"And you're Cigarsycigarillos?" Bolan asked.

Richards nodded, effecting a slight bow. "At your service, Mr. Belasko."

Scarberry took another step closer and addressed Bolan. "Let's go," he said. "We're wasting our time with this crumpet-eater."

Richards pretended to be offended. "Tsk tsk," he said. "Such racism is not becoming of you."

"That's not racism, you idiot, it's nationalism," Scarberry said. "You and I are of the same race, I'm sorry to say." He turned to Bolan. "Come on. Let's go. It's a dry run. This fool can't even find his ass with both hands."

Bolan had started to follow the former DEA man when Richards reached out and touched his arm. "Goodbye, then," he said.

The Executioner walked past him. He had taken three more steps when he heard the Briton say, "I suppose I'll just have to lead someone else to where the chemical weapons are hidden."

Bolan and Scarberry turned back to the man.

"You know where they are?" the Executioner asked.

"Well," Richards said, "at least some of them. And I can lead you to the location." He raised a hand and glanced down at his fingernails, then brushed them against his T-shirt as if it had a lapel. "For a price, of course, Mr. Belasko," he said.

THE PRICE had been agreed upon, and it included transportation along the Amazon to the spot on shore where they would enter the jungle. Dawn was breaking as Richards angled the tiny fishing boat toward shore.

Most of the night had been spent preparing for the trip, loading the boat, then traveling along the dark river. Richards might not have been Scarberry's favorite person, but he had proved to be an intelligent and resourceful man, well-educated in the ways of the Amazon. During the night's darkest hours, they had made it through a whirlpool, which was the product of drastic underwater currents. And twice, they had avoided being spotted by U.S. Coast Guard gunboats, which would have caused a slight delay as the DEA agents and Peruvian military officers searched the boat and questioned them. The real delay would have come if they discovered all the weapons on board.

Delays for which they didn't have time. At least not if what Richards had told the Executioner was anything close to the truth. According to the Briton, some of the chemical warfare agents purchased by the Peruvian government had been stored north of Iquitos, off the Napo River, which fed into the Amazon. The Napo, which ran its course across the border and into Quito in northern Ecuador, provided the perfect conduit to transport the deadly agents to the enemy's capital city once war broke out. By spreading chemical death throughout Quito, Peruvian forces could neutralize top government and military leaders with a single well-planned strike. But, as the Executioner knew all too well, the same chemicals that killed enemy soldiers were incapable of discriminating between politician, soldier and civilian. Thousands of innocents would also die if chem-war erupted in the Ecuadoran capital.

Bolan had no intention of letting that happen. At least it wouldn't happen while he was still breathing.

The small fishing craft hugged the shore for a few hundred yards. Bolan scanned the water ahead for another patrol ship but saw none. He was mildly surprised when Richards guided them around a tiny outcropping of swampy land, then made a sharp left turn toward what appeared to be solid shore. The Executioner pulled a topographical map from his pocket and used a tiny flashlight—suspended from his tactical vest on a short lanyard— to look down at it. He frowned. The Amazon didn't connect to the Napo for several more miles.

Before he could voice his question, however, Richards said, "Duck, boys," and all three men crouched on the deck of the fishing boat. They drifted straight into what still appeared to be land with limbs scraping across their backs and the tops of their heads. Leaves broke from the limbs to carpet the deck around them in green. A moment later they emerged into open water again.

There was no need to ask the question now. Bolan had the answer. The hidden passage through the overgrowth was a shortcut. When the waters of the Amazon and the other rivers that fed into it around Iquitos rose, they flooded certain lower areas—the same ones, year after year. Canals were formed between the twists and turns of the rivers and stayed in place until the water retracted again. Although the Amazon was quite low, this shortcut looked as if it might be deep enough for a small craft such as theirs. If it was, it would lead them to the Napo and would save many miles. And time.

Whether it was a genuine difference of opinion or just his obvious dislike for William Richards, Harvey Scarberry didn't agree with the turn they had just taken. "The water level is down, Richards," the former DEA man said. "We're wasting valuable time trying this. We're going to get halfway to the Napo and find ourselves on dry land. We'll have to backtrack and start over." He looked at Bolan for support.

The soldier remained silent. The truth was, he didn't know.

"Nonsense, old boy," Richards said as he guided the boat by the tiller. Now that they had slowed and entered this isolated strip of water surrounded by nearby vegetation on both sides, the small outboard motor, which had been all but lost on the Amazon, sounded as loud as machine-gun fire in their ears. "I was out here a few days ago. The water is receding, of course, but hardly gone."

Scarberry looked at the deck, shook his head in disgust and mumbled a few semiintelligible obscenities under his breath. The words brought a huge smile to Richards's face as he steered them on.

The sun was up now, and the sounds along the banks began to change as the nocturnal animals retired for the day and their daylight counterparts took their place. Gone, for the most part, was the click of crickets and the hum of the other insects of the night. In their place came the early-morning calls of birds, and the sluggish just-waking movements of the small animals that inhabited the surrounding tangles of green growth.

Bolan reached into the left breast pocket of his vest and pulled out the small plastic bottle of insect repellant. Never knowing when, and for how long, he would be in the jungle, he couldn't take Larium or other antimalaria medications. Such drugs were basically poisons in their own rights, and their long-term effect on the liver and other organs became more of a threat than the diseases they prevented. On the other hand, the Executioner's schedule didn't include "downtime" while he shivered and sweated out the fevers of malaria. He kept his shots for yellow fever and all other diseases up-to-date, but would have to rely on the repellant to ward off the mosquitoes who bore malaria. Already, he had seen several perch on his skin at their odd forty-five-degree landing angle. Not all of them carried the disease, and he suspected he had brushed them off before they could inject their infectious toxin. But once they entered the jungle, he would be preoccupied with other things, and there would be too many of them to battle under any conditions. He was taking no chances, and he covered all of the exposed areas of his skin with the repellant.

The fishing boat continued to putter though the water as Bolan returned the repellant to his vest. The body of the garment was actually a nylon knit shell with strips of webbing sewn across it from which clip pouches and other attachments could be hung. Unlike tactical vests with permanent pockets, it allowed the wearer to locate the equipment he wanted and permitted those locations to be changed quickly and efficiently in the field should a mission take an unexpected change and suddenly call for different gear.

Another fifteen minutes brought the three men to the point where the shortcut merged with the Napo. Although nothing was said, Richards shot a condescending grin toward Scarberry. The former DEA agent ignored the Briton, but the look on his face made Bolan wonder if he would have been happier had he proved to be right, and they had run out of water and had to turn back.

The Napo River was a darker brown, and the current moved slower than that within the Amazon. "How much farther?" Bolan shouted over the motor and the wind.

Richards frowned at the shoreline, then glanced to his wrist. "Five, ten minutes," he said. "Gear up if you like." He turned his eyes to the equipment packed with the boat, then back to the water. A few minutes later, true to his word, the Briton steered the boat toward an area of land that had been flattened by the rising river before it had receded once more.

Jumping out of the boat, the three men pulled the light craft onto the marshy bank.

As always, Bolan had brought along his Desert Eagle and Beretta 93-R, with extra magazines for both. In addition to the handguns, he toted a Heckler & Koch MP-5. From the arsenal the Executioner had brought into the country on the plane flown by Jack Grimaldi, Scarberry had chosen a 12-gauge Winchester pump-action shotgun to go with his pair of wheelguns. The man was definitely from the old school of police weaponry, when the revolver and scattergun had been favored over the semiauto pistol and rifles or subgun. While the Executioner was not of that school of thought, he saw the wisdom in it for someone like Scarberry. It was better to be good with a slightly outdated weapon than mediocre with something state-of-the-art.

In the end, it was never a weapon that killed the enemy. It was the man who wielded that weapon.

Bolan glanced at Richards, who had just tied down the boat and drawn a machete from the Kydex sheath on his belt. He was chopping foliage around the site and covering the boat with it to camouflage the vessel from curious eyes. He had already retrieved his single-shot 16-gauge—the only legal firearm for private citizens in Peru—from where it had been carried in the boat. On his hip was the machete. They were his only weapons, and Bolan hadn't offered him more. Harvey Scarberry didn't like or trust Richards—he had made that fact abundantly clear. Whether his dislike and distrust came from purely personal reasons, or the fact that Richards was really no good, the Executioner didn't know. But until he did, Bolan didn't plan to give the man any more firepower than he already had.

If Richards did prove treacherous, the Executioner didn't care to be killed with a gun he'd supplied to the man.

Sliding his arms into a green backpack, Bolan waited while Scarberry and Richards hoisted their own packs. With a nods all around but no words, Richards led the men away from the water.

Bolan fell in behind the man on a narrow trail that led upward, away from the shore. A light rain began to fall, turning the already damp ground into sludge as their jungle boots slid through the mess. The Executioner had brought along a custom-made RTAK, a heavy version of the machete. The RTAK could be used for heavier camp tasks as well as clearing a trail, not to mention the fact that in the hand of a skilled warrior, it could lop off an arm, leg or head with one stroke. But it was clearing the trail for which he now used the big jungle knife, chopping twigs and vines out of his face as they made their way deeper into the Amazon jungle.

Soon, the only light by which they moved was what drifted down through the high treetops. Mosquitoes and other insects moved in, dive-bombing their faces and buzzing their ears. The light rain increased steadily. Each step was an adventure of its own, with vines ready to trip or thorns eager to tear.

A rustling in the wet leaves covering the pathway ahead caused Bolan to halt in midstride. From beneath the dryer foliage under the soaked leaves on top slithered a bushmaster snake. The bushmaster could grow to twelve feet, and often took up residence on such jungle trails. It was one of the most feared serpents in the Amazon, not only for its deadly venom but for the fact that, unlike most snakes who did their best to avoid people, it often decided to actually *chase* human prey.

The Executioner shifted his grip on the RTAK handle slightly, bringing the heavy blade back over his shoulder. The best strategy when dealing with this deadly species was to throw it something to avert its attention. But the snake ignored Bolan and the other two men and slithered off the trail into the undergrowth to the side of the path. The soldier gave it time to get cleanly away before taking off down the trail after Richards again.

Richards led them down into a large area of flooded lowland. But the water was quickly rising as the rain threatened to become a downpour. They stopped long enough to slip into their ponchos, then began making their way across the water using trees and other taller growths as stepping stones. Richards slipped at one point, fell from his foothold and splashed into the water. His head dropped out of sight for a moment. When it broke the surface again, he was spitting out mouthfuls of water and muttering between each sputter.

Bolan heard a soft chuckle come from behind him, then Scarberry's voice said, "Something wrong there, Willie old boy? Wish I had a shot of that to put in your advertising brochures."

Richards ignored him as he climbed out of the water onto the bank and waited for the other two men to finish crossing the flooded lowland. Together, they started the steep incline once more. By now, the rain had turned the trail into a mud pit with the consistency of just-poured concrete, and they all slipped as they struggled up the bank. It was two steps forward, then a sliding step down and back. They used any and all available limbs and vines that grew from the muddy bank to pull themselves along. But more often than not, the makeshift handholds broke and snapped with their weight and they slid back to the base of the embankment.

Finally, Bolan reached the summit of the steep slope. Taking a firm footing, he reached down and first helped Scarberry, then Richards, the rest of the way. Pulling a canvas-covered canteen from his vest, he unscrewed the plastic lid and handed it to Scarberry. Rain hammered through the treetops to mix with the sweat on the face of the former DEA man as he drank, before handing it back to Bolan. The Executioner started to pass the canteen to Richards, but the Briton was already drinking from a plastic water bottle he'd brought along. So, tipping the canteen up, Bolan drank.

"How much farther?" Scarberry demanded of Richards.

"Hour. Hour and a half in this rain, maybe."

The downpour increased with an intensity that could only be found in the tropics. The Executioner pulled the hood of his poncho over his head, his mind settling into thought as they took a brief rest period.

According to Richards, chemical weapons had been buried near a small stream deep in the jungle. As Scarberry had said, Richards seemed to have his hand in everything around the Iquitos area. He'd been tipped to the fact that soldiers from the army base next to ESSEL, who had been told they were about to hide airtight canisters of emergency rations in the jungle in the event that they were needed by Peruvian special forces troops fleeing back from the Ecuadoran border, were actually about to transport the deadly chemicals. He'd been slightly disappointed when the men left the base carrying nothing that even remotely resembled a chemical weapons container. But he had trailed them anyway, keeping far enough back that they never suspected they were being followed. Still hidden from sight, he had watched them clear a landing zone with their machetes, then signal to a helicopter. The chopper landed, and the men unloaded seventeen steel containers roughly the size of industrial dairy cans. Richards had then hotfooted it back to Iquitos, where he intended to sell what he knew to the highest bidder.

That first bidder had been Bolan, and Bolan had convinced Richards not to hear any more offers. In addition to a reasonable amount of cash, the soldier had also used another bargaining tool—the Briton's life.

The torrent of rain continued to pound them as they started off through the jungle once more. Bolan performed a quick check of his MP-5 to make sure the rain had not affected its function. Maybe the soldiers at the army base adjacent to ESSEL thought they had buried emergency rations, but their commanders had to know the truth. Wasn't it likely that Ramon Suarez, as the commandant of the air force survival school right next door, might catch wind of it, too? That might further explain why Suarez had given them Richards's E-mail address. The chemical death had come from close to home, which made it more personal.

The long, wet, slippery and dangerous trek though the jungle continued. Bolan walked behind Richards. Leaves and clumps of mud had stuck to their water-soaked bodies as they had struggled up the bank, and now a few tumbled off with each step they took. The going got rough as the dense foliage became even more dense, and they were forced to hack and slice their way through areas that had grown over the little used trail. Bolan divided his attention between where his feet fell and glances at the limbs overhead where boas and anacondas often waited in the low-hanging limbs.

Suddenly, Bolan felt as if a red-hot ice pick had been driven into the back of his left thigh in three quick consecutive stabs. He slapped hard at the back of his pants, then stopped on the trail, bending to loosen the ties where he'd tucked the pants into his boots. Shaking his leg, he saw what he'd known he'd see as a trio of crushed fire ants tumbled out into the mud. The stinging grew stronger, spreading as he retied his pant leg. He felt as if his entire leg from buttock to knee had been doused in gasoline and a match held to it. The pain, he knew, would get even worse before it got better. But it lasted for no more than a half hour or so, and was far from serious.

Trudging on through the rain, humidity, heat and mud, the three men resumed their pursuit of the buried chemical agents. Periodically, they came to jungle bridges spanning creeks and ravines. The plunge below these structures in the Amazon were rarely more than thirty to fifty feet. But that was still the equivalent of falling off a three- to five-story building, and more than enough to ensure serious injury or even death. Many of the bridges were nothing more than thick logs that had been felled and spanned the deep culverts below. Some had makeshift and undependable hand railings for assistance but others did not. Either way, the jungle bridges were now wet with rain, turning the already precarious footways into the equivalent of narrow, sky-high skating rinks. At some of the treacherous bridges, the pace of the three men was reduced. And each time they slowed, Bolan was reminded that the race toward war between Peru and Ecuador had not. Each minute brought the two countries closer to the hostilities that would eventually, inevitably, lead to the release of deadly chemicals over thousands of innocents.

Finally hitting an area of less density, the three men broke into double-time to make up for the slow progress. Forty-five minutes later, Richards stopped, turned and held a finger to his lips for silence. When Bolan and Scarberry had approached within whispering distance, he said, "We're close. Maybe five minutes away."

Bolan nodded. "Keep it slow and quiet," he warned the other two. "They may still have guards out." Scarberry and Richards both nodded. Taking off their ponchos, they started forward again at a walk. They had gone only twenty yards farther when Richards stopped again before a Tessaria tree to the left of the trail. With his machete, he made a small cut in the bark. Then, without a word, he stepped off the jungle trail and into the dense foliage itself. Bolan and Scarberry followed.

The three men were forced to cut their way through the thick leaves and branches, and lift their knees high over the tangled vines at their feet. Total silence was impossible if they expected to make any progress at all. But they worked slowly, keeping the noise to a minimum. Getting lost would be as easy now as falling off one of the log bridges, so they cut more tree trunks, following the age-old jungle rule of marking the trail on the right so they could return looking for the skinned bark on the left.

As the worked their way on, a faint odor of fouled water found its way to Bolan's nostrils. Gradually, the stench grew stronger. They had to be nearing the stream next to which the canisters had been buried.

Richards suddenly dropped to one knee and held up his free hand behind him for silence. He parted the limbs in front of him with his machete and leaned forward, the back of his head moving right, then left, then right again he surveyed what lay ahead. Bolan inched forward next to him and looked through the same opening. Through the tunnel in the branches, he could see a large, recently cut clearing. The middle of the newly opened space in the trees was piled at least five feet high with the refuge that had been cut to clear the landing zone. On the other side of the clearing he could see the stream.

The ashes of three small fires—a signal to the helicopter that had transported the canisters—could be seen equal distances apart. A flash of bright yellow caught the corner of Bolan's eye, out of place in the greens and browns of the jungle. He turned toward it, the corner of what appeared to be a yellow rain poncho sticking out from under the huge pile of downed tree trunks, limbs, branches and vines. He nodded his head. In addition the fires, the soldiers had used their bright yellow ponchos to mark the landing spot for the helicopter. This one had been forgotten and left behind. In his mind, Bolan visualized the international air-land signal they would have used: a large triangle with a smaller square set to the side of the upper right hand corner. Secure for landing.

Richards had led the way to the spot but now, without a word needing to be spoken, both he and Scarberry knew that the Executioner would take the lead. A final glance through the leaves showed Bolan no signs of human occupancy, so he rose to his feet. The MP-5 led the way as he stepped out of hiding and climbed onto the highly piled debris in the clearing.

Bolan heard the other men follow as he bounced across the springy surface of the downed foliage. He had no idea where the canisters were buried, but that wasn't his primary concern. First, he needed to further convince himself that there had been no sentries left to guard the site. Just because he couldn't see them didn't mean they weren't there. And if they were, they would have had to have been deaf not to hear him and the other two men approaching the site.

In the trees overhead, the birds had been singing. Now, as the Executioner walked over the leaves, branches and vines, they stopped. As soon as they did, so did Bolan.

But the jungle didn't grow silent. At least not for long.

The peaceful singing of the birds was suddenly replaced with the explosions of automatic rifle fire. Leaves, twigs and pieces of green jungle vines jumped into the air to his side. Bullets flew down around his feet, chopping the already cut foliage. As he turned toward the source of the fire, the Executioner's jungle boots sprang up and down on the limbs and leaves as if he were standing on a trampoline.

Behind him, he heard a scream. Then a moan. Then the man-made sounds of pain were lost in the midst of more rifle fire.

KENJI RIVAS SETTLED in against the back seat of the car as his driver navigated the busy streets of Cuzco, Peru. Overall, he was satisfied with the way things had gone so far. True, another attempt had been made on the big American and failed, but it didn't matter. The man didn't appear to be interested in the New and Free Peru movement. Even if he was, what could one man do? Very little. So he wasn't worth worrying about.

Rivas was happy with the success of the bombings in Trujillo. And after the phone call from Relámpago a few minutes earlier, it sounded as if his Ecuadoran counterpart's mission north of the border had gone equally well. Both Lima and Quito newspapers were reporting the attacks, and even though word of the Ecuadoran dog tags and Peruvian sergeant's stripes hadn't yet been made public, both countries were being blamed for the atrocities in their neighbor's land. As soon as the governments themselves were convinced—and Rivas was counting on the planted false evidence to make it sooner rather than later—war would begin.

From there it would be simple. A matter of very predictable steps. One of the countries—it made no difference which—would fire the first shot. The other would retaliate. Before long, one side would be losing and their chemical weapons would be used in desperation. This would bring on a retaliatory massacre of chemical death from the other nation, and the result would be a massive loss of life and total chaos. During the turmoil, both his and Relámpago's men would carry out a carefully orchestrated series of assassinations in Lima and Quito. Rivas estimated that roughly one-third of both militaries would either be dead or have deserted by that time. And with the key officials gone as well, it should be easy enough for him and the Quechua leader to take control of their respective countries.

Rivas thought back to the two days and nights the NFP and Lightning Bolt men had camped together in the jungle. It had been the time during that he had laid out his plans to the Lightning Bolt leader. Relámpago had quickly agreed to join him, as he saw it as a final chance to free his Quechua people. The two men had even stood in the light of the campfire before their troops and taken a blood oath to support each other. Then, as if in afterthought, Rivas had turned to his men and ordered them to join Relámpago should he be killed. With tears in his eyes, the Ecuadoran had reciprocated. If death befell him, the Lightning Bolts would become one with the NFP.

"Relámpago commands it," the Ecuadoran fool had said in that irritating way he had of referring to himself in the third person. Rivas thought it made him sound like some half-literate Apache chief in a bad American western movie. He wondered sometimes how the Quechua could ever have become leader of even a small band of men. He supposed the answer was charisma. And while charisma and intelligence weren't mutually exclusive, they didn't necessarily go hand in hand, either.

Rivas glanced through the car window as they made their way down the street. Soon, he would no longer have to listen to the Lightning Bolt leader's ranting proclamations of a new Inca empire. Relámpago would be dead. Rivas planned to let the man live only long enough to carry out the assassinations of the Ecuadoran president and other top government figures and then have him killed. Considering their new blood oath, it should be easy enough to plant one of his own men—probably Solari—with the Lightning Bolts and get it done quickly and easily.

Rivas turned his eyes away from the window and closed them. He was on his way to another strike, one that should be far less complicated in its execution than the one in Trujillo had been. This was to be a simple "in and out" job. There was little chance of anything going wrong on this one. His target was Rafe Gutierrez, one of the Peruvian president's top aides. Gutierrez was famous for sneaking away from his bodyguards. It had even become a sort of joke within the Peruvian government. The official reason for Gutierrez's disappearances was claustrophobia. According to the president, the man needed his privacy.

Rivas knew this was, at least partially, true. Gutierrez did indeed need his privacy. But that need had nothing to do with claustrophobia.

The New and Free Peru leader opened his eyes once more as the driver drove on. A light sprinkle began to fall on the windshield, and the driver turned on the wiper blades. Rivas looked out at the city. Although of immense historical value, he had seen Cuzco far too many times for it to retain any charm for him. Besides, he thought, as a weary sleep drifted over him, he could never become more than half interested in Peruvian history. His father had been a native of this country, certainly. But his mother, and all of his other ancestors on that side of the family, were full-blooded Japanese.

He let his mind wander in his half-sleep. Was it the Japanese blood that drove him? Surely, like only a few other warrior races around the world, the Japanese had never passed up an opportunity to conquer.

Was it his Japanese blood that caused him to leave the life of luxury he already had in Colombia and come back to the country to which he had sworn he would never return? Was it because what he could now achieve here was even greater riches than he'd had in Bogotá? Or was it the simple need for a challenge? The need to conquer? Rivas shrugged, not caring, but knowing it was so, whatever the reason.

The Peruvians had once been conquerors, hundreds of years ago when all the tribes that inhabited these lands had been under the rule of the Incas. But since the Incas's defeat by the Spanish, what had once been a great and noble warrior bloodline had been diluted as the Indians gradually bred with inferior races.

A horn honked next to him, and Rivas jolted forward into full consciousness. He realized he had almost given in fully to the lure of slumber, and as always happened when he first awoke, a jolt of anxiety shot through his chest. What had occurred while he slept? What had he missed?

"Nothing to worry about," a familiar voice said. "Just traffic as usual in beautiful downtown Cuzco."

Rivas glanced across the car to Paco Real. Although there were things about Real that bothered him, next to Solari he was Rivas's most trusted lieutenant. The man was his driver this day, because Solari was away on a mission of vital importance. Rivas had sent the former Brazilian chef to check out what might prove to be an unexpected stroke of luck for the NFP.

Real was smiling, and Rivas forced back a smile that then became a yawn. "We are getting close," the lieutenant said. "I know you are tired and need your rest. But perhaps you should awaken."

Rivas nodded groggily and sat up straighter in the back seat. He glanced out the window again and saw that they were passing by Cuzcos's Plaza de Armas. Like every major city in the country, Cuzco had a plaza so named. But Cuzco's Plaza de Armas had once been nearly twice as large as it was now. The area that remained had been called the Square of War by the ancient Incas. It had been the site of great civic buildings and councils, and was surrounded by buildings that had once been palaces. Somber parades had filed down the streets, and great assemblies had been held. Among the rituals had been one Rivas had always found curious. Each time the Inca nation conquered a new tribe, soil from that territory had been brought there to be symbolically mixed with the dirt of the *Aucaypata*. The ceremony had represented the incorporation of the new people into the great empire.

What bullshit, Rivas thought. When someone conquered, act like a conqueror not a social worker.

Leaving Cuzco, the car traveled into the mountainous countryside. They passed a radio station, its tall tower rising high to defeat the tall rocky peaks that surrounded it, then the amphitheater of Qenqo. It boasted Inca stone carvings inside a large hollowed-out stone that held an altar. Here, he knew, blood sacrifices of divination had once been performed by his father's ancestors.

The NFP man smiled. Blood sacrifices. They made far more sense than the silly symbolic mixing of dirt. In fact, he was about to perform a significant blood sacrifice of his own.

The driver slowed as they neared Puka Pukara, which meant "Red Fort." Reputed to have been an Inca fortress, many current historians believed it more likely that the site had been a guest house where travelers and beasts of burden had lodged for the night as they went about their journeys. It was primarily known for its breathtaking view, and a small modern guest house had even been built a few yards away.

This new inn was Rivas's goal.

Leaning forward slightly, the NFP man tapped the driver on the shoulder. "Pull into the ruins," he ordered. "As if we are tourists." He glanced at his khaki cargo shorts as he spoke, laughing silently to himself. They had disguised themselves as just that, with clothing stolen from Americans over the past few months. In addition to the cargo shorts, both Rivas and Real wore batik print shirts with the tails hanging over their belts, to hide weapons. Both wore baseball caps.

The car stopped. No other visitors were present, and Rivas breathed a silent sigh of relief. While he was always willing to kill in front of witnesses when it was necessary, he preferred not to do so. It always meant killing them, too, so they couldn't identify him later. It wasn't that he minded the killing so much, but it meant more work.

Rivas and Real got out of the car and opened the trunk. Both men pulled out large backpacks. They slung them over their shoulders as if they were about to take off on an extended adventure through the mountains and valleys before them. Instead, with a quick glance toward the modern guest house to the side of the ruins, Rivas started toward it.

Only two vehicles were parked at the inn. One, a twenty-year-old Ford pickup, stood outside the office. The other was a modern sedan, and it was parked just in front of a room with the Roman numeral IV nailed to the door. It bore nondescript numbered license plates. But in the bottom left-hand corner of the rear windshield Rivas could see a tiny sticker bearing the Peruvian government seal.

Rivas and Real walked side-by-side directly to the door. There was a window next to it, but the curtains were closed. There was little chance that anyone was peering through to watch their approach. Even if they were, they wouldn't recognize the two NFP men. And even if they did, there was nothing they could do about it.

The inn, Rivas knew, had no telephones.

At the door, the two men stopped long enough to reach into their backpacks and pull out MAC-11 submachine pistols. The guns were old and had fired many rounds having once been in the hands of the Shining Path, and then the FARCs in Colombia before finding their way to New and Free Peru in a trade that involved both guns and cocaine. But they had been well cared for over the years, and still functioned flawlessly.

Without ceremony, Rivas raised a foot and kicked the door just below the knob. The wood splinted, the door flying inward. He stepped inside the room with Real right behind him.

There was a furious rustling of sheets and then two heads rose from beneath the covers on the bed. One of the heads was topped with the thinning gray hair of Rafe Gutierrez. The other bore the surprised face and smooth skin of a slender young man in his late teens or early twenties. Both men looked bewildered. Neither had time for it to be replaced by fear.

Gutierrez opened his mouth to speak, but he never got a chance for the words to get past his lips.

Rivas held back the trigger and the MAC-11 began to fire. Real had taken a step to his side and drawn even with him. He, too, began shooting.

The MAC-11 had been one of fastest-firing submachine guns in existence since its origin, and now the individual rounds had so little space between them that they sounded almost like one big explosion. In a matter of seconds, both 30-round magazines were empty. Sixty 9 mm hollowpoint rounds had perforated Gutierrez, his friend, the bedding, the headboard and the wall behind it. Neither Rivas nor Real bothered to reload as their weapons clicked on empty chambers. There was no need. What remained in the bed was barely recognizable as having once been human. There was no doubt that all life had been driven from the two men.

The white sheets had soaked a deep burning red, and more blood had seeped from the sides of the bed to pool on the tile floor. Rivas walked forward, planting one of his boots in the nearest puddle. Then, carefully lifting it straight up, he stepped back, turned and followed Real out the door. He turned again just outside the room, looking back to survey the bloody tracks he had left. He nodded. They weren't perfect tracks, but perfect tracks would have been too obvious. But they were good enough that the lab technicians who lifted them would recognize the distinctive tread found only on the boots issued to Ecuadoran infantrymen.

Dropping their subguns back into their backpacks, Rivas and Real replaced the packs in the trunk of the car and got back into the vehicle. The driver started back to Cuzco, and soon they had returned to the city. Once again, Rivas stared through the glass as they passed a cathedral dating back to the 1600s and to its right the first Christian church built in Cuzco. He had lost all pretenses of the religion with which he had been raised, and neither structure held any significance for him.

Turning to Real, he asked, "Have you heard anything from Solari? Before, I mean. While I was sleeping?" He pointed to the small cell phone in the breast pocket of Real's shirt.

A strange expression flickered across Real's face for a fraction of a second. Rivas couldn't be sure, but if he'd been a betting man he would have wagered the face reflected jealousy. The expression disappeared, however, even faster than it had come.

Real tapped the pocket holding the phone. "They were preparing to enter the jungle when I last spoke with them," he answered. "They have already met with Sergeant Lopez. He is planning to lead them to the spot."

Rivas had looked down at the floor, but suddenly his eyes shot up. "Lopez and other Peruvian troops?" he asked with a trace of anxiety in his voice.

Real smiled and shook his head. "No."

"You asked? Specifically?"

"I did," Real said. "The sergeant has taken a short leave. He is alone, and in civilian clothing."

Rivas breathed a short sigh of relief. He had informants

throughout the various branches of the Peruvian armed forces, and if he had learned one thing it was that they couldn't be trusted to use good judgment. The army, air force—all of them— were good at what they did. But the ones who sold out to him tended to be not only untrustworthy but often lacking common sense. And it would hardly do for his men to be seen with a Peruvian regular at this point. Tension was running high, and Lopez would immediately be arrested. Everything he knew would be beaten out of him. If he didn't volunteer it willingly, which he might very well do in order to cut a deal.

"Good," Rivas said, nodding. He lifted his arms and rubbed both eyes with the back of his fists. He remembered what he had been thinking about before he drifted off. Yes, he was satisfied with the way things were going overall. He was doing limited damage with the bombings and machine-gun massacres and assassinations, but each one was strategic. Each strike made headlines, and each pointed a Peruvian finger of accusation north and an Ecuadoran finger south. A few more strikes in both countries and one, or both, of the old enemies would finally have had enough.

The war would begin.

And perhaps there would be a new Inca empire as Relámpago raved about. With a new Inca king to rule both countries.

Of course, this Inca king would be half Japanese.

6

A fight in the jungle was unlike a fight anywhere else on Earth.

The Executioner raised the H&K MP-5, pulling the trigger and sending a blind stream of fire into the direction from where most of the rounds seemed to be originating. He hadn't identified his attackers, and he prayed that when he did they wouldn't be Peruvian regulars. He had no desire to kill troops who were doing no more than carrying out orders. The soldiers were good men who had been told they were guarding emergency rations buried in the jungle, and were more than likely completely ignorant of what the canisters actually contained.

On the other hand, Bolan couldn't let them kill him. It wasn't just his life that was at stake. If he went down now before he had a chance to destroy the chemical warfare agents buried nearby, thousands would also die. He had faced death too many times in the past for the man with the hood and sickle to hold any terror for him. But the thought of a horrible death for the civilians, simple people in both Peru and Ecuador who were blameless in the age-old disputes between the two nations, sent a cold anger through his soul. He would die, willingly, if it would save them. But in this case, he had to live so they could live as well.

He was at least fifteen yards from the edge of the jungle where he'd emerged onto the pile of debris in the clearing. Too far to risk turning and trying to make it back over the springy, unsure footing to the cover and concealment of the trees. Each step he had taken before the gunfire erupted had been like a man walking across a loosely stuffed bed mattress, and the fact that he still didn't provide a stationary target might well account for the fact that he hadn't yet been hit. But even a bad shot could get lucky.

With nowhere else to go, Bolan dived down into the pile of leaves, twigs, branches and vines, burrowing out of sight. For a moment, the gunfire stopped.

Bolan remained motionless, breathing shallowly, assessing the situation. One of the two men behind him had taken at least one bullet; he had heard the scream and then the moan. Had it been Scarberry or Richards? He didn't know.

A new volley of fire struck the pile ten feet to his left, then more bullets scattered leaves five feet away. What the gunmen were doing was obvious. Since they could no longer see their target, they intended to shoot holes through every inch of the pile until they got him. Using his arms almost like a man swimming, Bolan burrowed deeper into the pile. Through the tangled mess he could see the damp dark earth below, two feet away. Twisting his head, he looked up and saw that the leaves and limbs had closed over the hole he'd made when he dived into the pile. A burst of fire shot over his head, through the cut foliage where he had hidden only seconds before. The next burst had moved past him, to his right. For the time being, he was safe. The men were shooting over him into the mound. But they would change their angle of trajectory sooner or later. He would have to move again. Where he'd go next, he wasn't sure. He felt somewhat like an animal suddenly trapped in its own den.

The gunfire above died once more, and Bolan heard excited voices whispering. He guessed that his attackers had seen the futility of wasting further rounds until they could locate him once more. For all they knew, he might already be dead. The Executioner took the opportunity to make a quick check of his weapons. He had slung the Heckler & Koch over his shoulder, and it was still in place on its sling. The H&K MP-5 submachine gun was the finest weapon of its type in the world. With a choice of full-auto, semiauto and burst modes, it fired from a closed bolt that eliminated the wasted first round, which often came from weapons that began with the bolt open. The carriage held a 30-round magazine, and Bolan carried four more box mags. When they were gone, he would trade the subgun for one or both of his pistols. A quick pat down told him they were both still holstered beneath his vest.

The voices continued to whisper. Bolan listened, slowly shrugging out of the subgun sling and bringing the weapon around him. He had used the H&K many times in the past, and for him there was nothing new about it. What was new, however, was the ammunition loaded in the magazines. The new bullets, with a weight of only sixty grains, were only half as heavy as the more common 115-grain 9 mm rounds. But they traveled at an almost unbelievable 2000 feet per second and hit their target with a whopping 535 foot-pounds of energy. What made them even more unique was the fact that they weren't hollowpoints but totally fragmenting soft points. They didn't, however, fragment until they hit a water-soluble substance—such as a human body. They penetrated glass, heavy clothing and wood in one piece, but exploded shortly after entering flesh.

After thousands upon thousands of rounds of test-firing all calibers of the ammo, John "Cowboy" Kissinger, Stony Man Farm's chief armorer, had judged them fit for field carry by Bolan, Able Team and Phoenix Force. But they were about to see their first actual use in combat.

The voices suddenly stopped talking and the jungle grew quiet overhead. Bolan wondered again who had been hit, Scarberry or Richards. The same voice had uttered both the scream and subsequent moan, but he hadn't been able to pinpoint it to either of the two men. All he knew was that one of them was hurt, maybe dead by now. The other one could be, too. A bullet through the brain stem would have killed before any noise or protest was made. He might be in this battle alone, but there was no way of knowing. If he was, so be it. It would hardly be the first time he had faced stacked odds by himself.

Through the thick pile of trashed trees and overgrowth, Bolan heard the voices begin to whisper again. He couldn't make out the words, nor even the language that was being spoken. But the tone and inflection sounded as if a disagreement of some kind was at hand. If so, he suspected they were trying to decide which of them would crawl onto the pile to inspect the hole through which they'd seen him burrow.

The Executioner's jaw tightened as he considered his options. He could wait where he was and then shoot the first man whose face showed above him. That would be no problem—action was always faster than reaction. But after one or two men had died like that, and his position had been confirmed, the bullets would come in hordes. They would saturate the area where they knew him to be, and with his limited mobility in the debris he would surely die.

A rustling sound just below him caused Bolan to look downward. A few feet ahead of him, about knee level where he stood, he saw a pair of eyes glowing through the branches in the semidarkness. Then the animal moved, turning sideways, and hurried out of sight.

Pakka. A jungle rodent as big as a medium-sized dog. They were killed and eaten by the natives of Peru and surrounding countries. But hunger wasn't what now caught the soldier's attention in regard to the big rat. It had apparently been trapped inside the pile when the gunfight started. But it was moving, and apparently leaving.

Bolan was many times the size of a *pakka,* but if the animal had found a pathway through the tangled undergrowth, perhaps he could, too.

The Executioner heard the snaps and crunches of twigs overhead. One—or more—of the men was making his way across the pile to the site where they had last seen him. Bolan waited, the

MP-5 aimed upward. A few seconds later, hands parted the leaves and branches that had closed in over him and a bearded face peeked timidly down.

Bolan squeezed the trigger, and three rounds of the super-speed 60-grain soft-point slugs decapitated the man. By the time he fell to his side on the piled branches, his body had little more than a neck above the shoulders.

Quickly, the Executioner slung the H&K over his shoulder again. Fighting his way through the brambles the rest of the way to the ground, he dropped to the spot where he'd seen the *pakka* moments before. A narrow tunnel showed him the path the animal had taken when fleeing him, and he squirmed into it on his belly. It had been gloomy within the pile where he had burrowed. But now, on the ground with all of the pile blocking the sun, all light faded into darkness. He stopped long enough to reach for his flashlight, then crawled on beneath the debris.

With the flashlight, Bolan could see the narrow tunnel the *pakka* had rooted out through the freshly cut tangles. Far too small for him, he would have to enlarge it as he went. And he would have to do so as quietly as possible to avoid detection. If the men surrounding the pile heard him, they would fire indiscriminately at the sounds. He'd be riddled with rifle rounds and buried there forever.

Holding the tiny flashlight in his teeth, Bolan crawled forward. The smallest crackling of drying leaf, the mildest snap of twigs, sounded like explosions in his ears. In the soft earth of the jungle floor he could occasionally see tracks as he cleared away the loose leaves. He followed those tracks. The *pakka* had to have entered the pile somewhere. And it was there that the Executioner would exit.

By now, the men in the clearing knew he was on the move. Above, he could hear their trampling feet as they bounced across the springy branches in search of him. Occasionally, one of them fired a burst of rounds down into the branches, vines and leaves.

Bolan wondered briefly if the *pakka* would survive. It might well be him that the men were hearing as, like the Executioner himself, the big rat did his best to escape death. He wondered once more about Scarberry and Richards. Where were they now? Which one of them was hurt? Then, pushing such thoughts from his mind, he tunneled on. He couldn't help either man until he helped himself.

Bolan soon lost all sense of direction in the underground labyrinth the *pakka* had created. All he knew was that the animal had twisted and turned his way through the pile and now he was twisting and turning the pathway in reverse. Five minutes of painfully slow crawling became ten, then ten became fifteen. Finally, Bolan looked at the luminous hands of his watch and saw that he'd been inside the maze for nearly half an hour. All the while, the overhead trampling and the occasional bursts of fire had continued.

The MP-5 slung over his shoulder had been an impediment to his progress in the narrow confines, and several times he had been tempted to discard it inside the pile. When he finally emerged, he planned to rely on the sound-suppressed Beretta for as long as surprise was his ally. But after that, Bolan knew he would be vastly outnumbered. And the greater firepower of the H&K would provide an advantage he couldn't afford to give up.

It would be the only advantage he had.

He had been below the surface of the pile for nearly forty-five minutes when streams of light began to show ahead. Killing the flashlight, the soldier stuffed it back into his pocket. Drawing the Beretta, he flipped the selector switch to semiauto, then transferred the machine pistol to his left hand. With his right, he drew the machete. The chopping tool's twelve-inch blackened blade reflected no light. In fact, it seemed to suck up the beams coming in like some deadly and mysterious razor-sharp "black hole."

Using his elbows to pull himself forward, Bolan scooted toward the edge of the pile. He stopped suddenly when he saw a pair of ragged work boots walk past, gave it ten seconds, then resumed his crawl. Eternity seemed to have come and gone by the time he reached the opening at the edge of the foliage. Slowly, he stuck his head out until he could see both ways. He pulled back as soon as he saw the man walking toward him.

Many things registered in the Executioner's brain in a microsecond. First, the man carried an AK-47. That was nothing unexpected. It was that Soviet weapon's distinctive sound signature that he had heard since the first shots when he'd stepped up onto the pile of jungle growth. But second, the man didn't wear the uniform of any of the Peruvian military forces. He did have on faded camouflage pants. But above them was a soiled and torn shirt which, unless Bolan had read it incorrectly, read Hard Rock Café, Phoenix, Arizona. His boots hadn't been military issue, either.

He could be wrong—soldiers within economically depressed nations sometimes wore anything they could get their hands on—but Bolan didn't think this man represented the Peruvian government. Or any other government for that matter. Which meant none of the other men did, either.

So who were they?

The man in the work boots came closer, and Bolan rose to a squatting position within the pile. He glanced at the machete in his right hand, then the Beretta in his left. The sound-suppressed 93-R was quiet. But the big blade was even more so.

Bolan watched as the man drew even with him, let him take one more step, then suddenly rose from the leaves. The machete came up over his shoulder before slashing violently down and across. By the time it stopped in front of the Executioner's left thigh, the head of the man in the Hard Rock T-shirt was tumbling to the jungle floor.

Moving swiftly, Bolan stuffed the body inside the pile of jungle debris and rolled the head in after it. Dropping to all fours, he took up hiding within the branches once again. He had barely resumed his position when he heard the sounds of another man approaching. Evidently, some of the men were searching the top of the pile for him while others performed a revolving patrol around the perimeter in case he tried to exit.

Again, Bolan waited until the man passed, then stood behind him. This man's neck was thicker, and the machete didn't totally decapitate him. But it did enough—more than enough. The Executioner felt the thick heavy blade crunch through the spine and stop three-quarters of the way to the other side of the man's neck. The carotid artery parted, sending a flood of crimson shooting out as the man toppled to the ground.

Bolan stuffed him in next to his comrade and resumed his hiding place once more. He knew he couldn't keep this plan of attack going much longer. For one thing, the ground just outside his exit hole was now soaked in crimson and would almost certainly be noticed soon. For another, he had used up every square inch of space inside the enlarged hole where he'd been exiting the pile. He could barely squeeze into hiding again himself, let alone fit more dead men inside.

No, it was almost time to change strategy. But as long as he could still secrete himself there, he would try it one more time.

Above and behind him, he could still hear the trampling feet of the men bouncing across the springboard surface. And he could not only hear their voices now but the words. That didn't mean he could understand them, however. They were in neither English or Spanish, both of which the Executioner spoke. Bolan frowned in concentration as he listened. The language was some native Indian tongue. Quechua—both the language of, and the collective name for, the tribes that had made up the ancient Inca empire—was the Executioner's guess.

More footsteps padded his way, and Bolan risked a quick glance out of his hole. As he knew it eventually would, his luck had run out. This time, instead of a solitary roving sentry, three men walked abreast around the perimeter of the clearing. He had proved he could silently take out one man at a time with the machete. And he suspected that with the element of surprise he could manage two. But three—that was pushing things. He'd give it a try, but he didn't plan to get his hopes up.

Making sure the MP-5 was ready on the sling, Bolan waited. As soon as the men were past him, he rose as he had done before. The machete sliced cleanly through the neck of the man nearest him. Bolan kept the heavy blade's momentum moving, reversing its direction in a figure-eight motion and sending it backhand toward the man in the middle as he took a short half step that way. But the man moved slightly at the last instant, turning to see what had happened at his side. Instead of the throat where Bolan had aimed, the blade's edge caught the man full in the face—precisely on the bridge of the nose. Bone crunched and shattered beneath the heavy steel as the edge cut its way through flesh into brain but wedged itself firmly in the skull.

Bolan had no time to pry the machete loose. The third man, farthest from him, had been at such an angle that he had seen everything that had happened. And he was over the surprise and beginning to react. The barrel of his AK-47 rose, settling on the Executioner.

Letting the machete fall to the ground with the man whose skull had claimed it, Bolan raised the Beretta 93-R in his left hand. Extending it as if he were pointing his finger, he squeezed the trigger and a lone 9 mm hollowpoint round shot forth. It wasn't one of the fragmenting 60-grains but rather a slow-moving 123-grain hollowpoint slug. In order for the sound-suppressed Beretta to operate as quietly as possible, only subsonic rounds could be used.

The jacketed hollowpoint bullet, however, did its job. A third eye appeared in the man's face. Blood poured out the hole like red wine from a decanter. The man stared with all three eyes wide in confusion, then toppled forward onto his face.

The voices Bolan had heard above now stopped suddenly. When they resumed, they were far more excited.

The element of surprise was over.

The Executioner dropped the Beretta and reached for the MP-5.

THERE WAS a wide line between killing and murder, Hal Brognola knew well. In both his overt role as a high-ranking official within the U.S. Department of Justice, as well as his more clandestine function as director of the Sensitive Operations Group at Stony Man Farm, Brognola had taken lives. But they had all been killings rather than murders. The fact was, he had never in all his years even considered murdering a man.

Until now.

Brognola sat behind his desk in the Justice Building as two of his agents brought Steve Mackey through the door. Two hours ago, Mackey had been *carrying* the handcuffs he now wore, as well as a SIG-Sauer pistol, a badge and Justice Department credentials. Those items had been taken away from him as soon as what he'd done became apparent. Now, as the two other agents slammed him down into the straight-backed chair in front of Brognola's desk, the G-man felt the anger flood through him like a fast-moving cancer.

Yes, he wanted to kill this man. But that would be murder. So he wouldn't. Besides, Steve Mackey had information that Brognola needed.

The big Fed nodded the two agents toward the door.

One of them—Wilson was his name—frowned. "But sir," he stammered awkwardly. "This guy—"

"I'll be fine," Brognola assured him. "And I want to talk to him alone."

The two agents looked at each other with concern in their eyes, and Brognola had to smile. Mackey was a desperate man at this point who might be capable of anything, and his two subordinates were worried about Brognola's safety. They needn't be.

"Get out of here," he ordered the two men with feigned jocularity. "Or do you think I'm too old to take care of myself?"

"No sir," Wilson said quickly, shaking his head. "I didn't mean—"

"Of course you did," Brognola interrupted him. "And I appreciate your concern, however ungrounded it may be. Now...get out of here."

Without further words, the two men left the office and closed the door behind them. But unless Brognola missed his guess, they weren't more than two steps from the door. Which was okay. The door, like the rest of the office, was soundproofed with several layers of insulation.

What he was about to discuss with former U.S. Department of Justice agent Steve Mackey wasn't for their ears. Outside of the rest of the staff at Stony Man Farm, the President of the United States would be the only person to ever learn what was about to go on in this room.

Mackey's eyes were red. He'd been crying. Brognola was unable to work up any sympathy, however. Without preamble, he said, "I need to know exactly what you've done, all that you've done and who you've put at risk," he said.

Mackey looked down at the floor, unable to meet Brognola's eyes. "Sir, I can't tell you how sorry I am," he said. "Please, let me try to explain why."

Brognola had risen to his feet and started around the side of the desk as the man had started speaking. As soon as he was close enough, the big Fed backhanded the agent across the face. The slap echoed off the walls of the office and turned Mackey's left cheek crimson. "You're a traitor to me, your fellow agents and the people of this nation."

The Justice man took a step back, filled his lungs with a deep breath and leaned back against the edge of his desk. He pulled a half-chewed cigar from the breast pocket of his sport coat and stuck it in his mouth. "Start talking," he said. "I'm especially interested in what intel you passed on to your contact in South America."

Mackey looked absolutely pitiful as he sat in the chair before Brognola. He wore a gray pin-striped suit, white shirt and a silk tie. His shoes were expensive—so expensive that Brognola certainly didn't recognize the brand, just knew he didn't own any like them himself—and looked as if they still carried the original shine. But in spite of the clothing, Mackey didn't look much different than someone who had just rolled out of the gutter. The suit was badly in need of being pressed, and Brognola guessed that had come from some less-than-gentle handling by fellow Justice agents since what he had done had come to light. The man hadn't been beaten. But he hadn't been treated with kid gloves, either. And while the suit had probably fit him well when he donned it that morning, shame and fear seemed to have made Mackey shrink within the garment. It now looked two sizes too large.

"Sir, please," Mackey said in a whining voice. "I'll tell you everything."

Maybe the other Justice men hadn't beaten Mackey, but Brognola had been fully prepared to do so. This man had endangered the lives of countless agents within the Justice Department and the subagencies which fell under it, and through joint investigations probably fellow Americans employed by the Treasury Department, the CIA and others.

But what particularly worried Brognola was Stony Man Farm. His E-mails from Bolan had made it clear that the Executioner thought there was a traitor within their midst somewhere. Someone in Peru knew who he was, and that person had been trying to kill him since the moment Jack Grimaldi had left him in Iquitos. That meant the information had to have originated in Washington. And it had. With this miserable excuse for a man he now saw bleeding in the chair in front of him.

Brognola glared down into Mackey's frightened eyes and chomped down harder on the unlit cigar stub between his teeth. Although he ran as little of the Farm's business from this Justice office as possible, completely removing the hat of director of sensitive operations for Stony Man was impossible. Decisions had to be made from someone in his position at any time or place. The Farm's very purpose ensured that most problems that came up required an immediate solution, which in turn meant he didn't have time to run off to the Shenandoah Mountains where the top-secret installation was located.

Mackey had been a trusted agent working out of the Washington, D.C., office for almost two years now. And it had just come to light that morning that, at least during the past six months, he had been selling the details of ongoing Justice investigations to organized crime figures. During that time he might well have also stumbled across information that he assumed was another Justice case but which in reality concerned the work of Stony Man Farm. And it was only a short jump from selling classified intel to mobsters to selling it to terrorists. It was even possible that Mackey didn't even know exactly who he was selling to.

Leaning in once more, Brognola ignored the blood that dripped down the man's chin. "Let's try one more time," he growled around the cigar. "Without the preamble of excuses you keep wanting to give. Or, we can do this all day."

THE EXECUTIONER had been on awkward footing when trying to walk across the springy blanket of chopped limbs and vines piled high in the clearing, and so were the men who were on top of the pile now. Bolan watched them bend their knees, trying to keep their balance as they swung their AK-47 rifles toward him. The movement caused them to bounce up and down. Some of them even lost their footing completely and fell as they began to fire. In any case, their aim was off.

But there were a dozen of them, easy, and they were all within ten yards of him. Pinpoint accuracy wasn't vital to their cause. At that distance, with full-auto weapons, they could simply "spray and pray," and eventually they would accomplish their goal. Which was to shred the Executioner into little pieces with 7.62 mm rifle rounds.

Bolan didn't bother aiming either. He had long been a follower of the point-shooting school of thought, and knew that until the distance between the weapon and target grew much farther than the average shooter thought, accurately firing a gun—be it pistol, subgun, shotgun or rifle—was little different than pointing a finger. With a pistol, he could easily hit a table-tennis ball at twenty yards with his Beretta, Desert Eagle or any other handgun he picked up. With a rifle, using the same philosophy—which the U.S. Army had once taught as the "Quick Kill" method—the Executioner's range of instinctive accuracy extended to over 150 yards.

The MP-5 submachine gun was somewhere between the rifle and pistol when it came to point-shooting capability. But the distance to the farthest edge of the clearing was within easy pistol range. With the subgun stock pressed against his shoulder, and focusing on the target over the barrel, Bolan began mowing down men with a smooth, deadly accuracy.

The first man to feel his fire wore tattered blue jeans and a khaki shirt that had probably been lifted from a dead Peruvian soldier. But by now Bolan knew that the men in the clearing were not Peruvian regulars. That meant they were terrorists of some kind, terrorists who had to have come for the same reason he had—to find the buried chemical weapons. But they didn't intend to destroy them as Bolan did. He didn't know exactly how, but these men would use the terrifying weapons to achieve their own nefarious goals.

Exactly who they were, and what those professed goals might be, the soldier didn't know. But he intended to find out.

The Executioner's first pull of the trigger stitched a pattern of red dots across the khaki shirt. The man who had worn it toppled to the springy bed of leaves and limbs. He rose slightly up and down as the pile of debris tried to settle under his weight. He had fallen facedown onto his belly with his eyes closed but pointing toward the Executioner. Unlike the horror that froze into the features of many men who fell to violent death, an expressionless look covered his face. All in all, with the blood now matting his shirt hidden from sight, he looked no different than a man who had laid down and gone to sleep.

Bolan turned the MP-5 toward a younger man with a long unkempt beard. He had whirled as he heard the sudden gunfire and was still in process of bringing his own AK around. A burst of the 60-grain copper-jacketed 9 mm rounds exploded from the H&K. The almost nonexistent recoil of the lightweight exploding rounds kept the muzzle climb down, and all three fragmenting bullets struck within a half inch in the center of the man's chest. A red mist seemed to appear from the terrorist's chest, floating up to cover his face. The red cloud cleared as the man fell forward.

Bolan wondered briefly again where Scarberry and Richards were, and which one of them had been hit by the earlier fire. Both men were still out of sight, and he again had to assume they had disappeared back into the cover of the jungle surrounding the signal clearing. He had little time to contemplate the mystery, however, as a steady stream of 7.62 mm rounds buzzed past his head like a swarm of angry wasps. The assault came from his left, and he turned his submachine gun that way. His finger was pulling back on the trigger even before he had spotted his target.

Two targets, Bolan saw as his eyes focused on a pair of the terrorists standing side by side on top of the pile. Like the other men, their knees were bent in an attempt to keep their balance on the precarious footing. The Executioner focused on the chest of the man to the right even as his thumb flipped the selector switch of his weapon to full-auto. A string of 9 mm rounds fled the H&K's barrel and cut back and forth between the two men in a lethal figure eight. More red fog rose into the air. Both men fell.

Behind them, the Executioner saw another terrorist pitch to the top of the piled leaves. He frowned slightly. He hadn't aimed at that man but had seen the blood shoot from him just before he fell. Had one of his rounds gone wide and struck the terrorist? Maybe, but he didn't think so. He had been in so many gun battles over the years that he could "feel" missed shots the moment he pulled the trigger. Much like a baseball pitcher who recognized he had thrown a wild pitch the split second it left his hand, a missed shot registered in Bolan's mind long before he actually saw the inaccuracy. And he had gotten no such gut feeling during his burst of eight rounds.

Bolan fired another burst into the throat of a heavy man wearing a faded green hat and cutoff sweatshirt. But his mind was still on the mystery. Had one of the rounds penetrated its target and traveled on to strike this third man? That was equally unlikely. The totally frangible bullets were built to split inside water-based flesh. He supposed there was always the possibility that one was bad and had failed to perform as it should. But thousands and thousands of test rounds fired at Stony Man Farm had shown no such faulty loading on the part of the manufacturers.

Bolan had little time to further contemplate the situation as one of the Russian rifle rounds cut through the sleeve of his shirt, searing across the skin of his upper arm but failing to break the skin. Flames of pain, however, erupted near his shoulder as he pointed the H&K toward the shooter. Ignoring the discomfort, he pulled the trigger once again. A man in a khaki T-shirt went down.

Out of the corner of his eye, the Executioner saw yet another of the terrorists fall to the piled debris. This time, there was no chance that a missed or overpenetrating round had accounted for the hit.

Someone was helping him, joining the fight from another, unseen site. And that someone could only be Scarberry or Richards.

Dropping the nearly spent 30-round magazine, the Executioner dived to the ground beneath a flurry of lead that flew his way. He ripped a box mag from his vest as he rolled across the jungle floor, thankful that he was on solid ground rather then still on the bouncing pile where his enemies now stood. The ground was still soaked from the tropical downpour, and dirty brown water splashed up over his shoulders, neck and face as he continued to roll, shoving the fresh load into the carriage of the MP-5.

Bolan came up on one knee and fired again. The hot 9 mm slug that had still been in the chamber when he changed magazines shot forth, followed by an uncountable number of the new bullets. As another pair of terrorists dropped to death in the jungle, he saw that at least one or two more had been taken out while he rolled. His jaw set firmly, and he felt himself nodding imperceptibly even as he continued to fire. Yes, he was getting help. From at least one of the two men who had entered the jungle with him.

A stitch of four more of the super-speed exploding rounds nearly took off one side of the head of another terrorist. Suddenly, Bolan realized that only one man still stood on the shaky pile of foliage in the center of the clearing. At the same time the Executioner realized it, so did the man himself. Dropping his AK-47 as if it had suddenly turned white-hot, he raised his hands high over his head and shouted, *"¡Por favor, hombre! ¡Por favor!"*

The Executioner's finger had moved halfway back on the trigger. Now it stopped, perhaps a pound of pressure away from shooting the terrorist. His eyes fell to a 1911 Government Model pistol holstered on the man's belt. He kept the barrel of the MP-5 trained at the man's chest as he said, "Slowly. Walk forward to the edge of the pile and step down. If your hands even look like they're going to drop toward the side arm, I'll drop you."

The man had spoken Spanish. But he understood English. He nodded vigorously and tiptoed across the pile toward Bolan, bouncing slightly up and down the whole way.

When he reached the edge of the springy debris, Bolan said, "Step down. Easy."

The man stepped gingerly off the pile, but his ankle caught on a twisted green limb. He tumbled into the mud on his face where he froze, his hands still over his head but now on the ground. He was too frightened to even move his face out of the mud for fear of disobeying orders and getting shot.

"Sit up," the soldier said.

Slowly, still worried that he might take a bullet, the man tried to rise with his hands still over his head. It was an impossible maneuver with his arms full stretched and his legs straight out behind him. He succeeded only in rocking back and forth on his belly like some just-hooked fish who had been dropped on dry land.

"Lie flat again!" Bolan barked, and the man dived face-first into the mud once more.

The soldier stepped forward, around behind the man, and pressed the muzzle of the MP-5 into the back of the terrorist's neck. He jerked the pistol from its holster and shoved it into his belt. Quickly, he ran a hand around the man's waistband, then up and down his legs before reaching beneath him to check for neck knives and other weapons that might be hidden in front. Finding nothing else, he stepped back and said, "Okay, get up. And you can use your hands."

The man brought his hands back to shoulder level and shoved himself up to all fours as if doing a push-up. He was facing away from Bolan now, and the Executioner walked around in front of him.

The terrorist looked no less comical in this position than he had flopping around on the ground. His face was coated in brown mud like some minstrel performer.

"Sit back," Bolan told the man.

He did.

The Executioner heard a rustling in the jungle around the clearing and swung the MP-5 toward the sound. But a moment later, Harvey Scarberry stepped out of the leaves. The former DEA man held the Winchester pumpgun in one hand and was stuffing 12-gauge shells into the tubular magazine even as he walked forward.

Bolan glanced to the pile of debris next to him—which now contained a fair amount of human debris atop the chopped limbs and other foliage. One of the men, whose demise had seemed to come out of nowhere during the gunfight, lay on his side. The clear evidence of Scarberry's shotgun work could now be seen in his upper back. Bolan reflected on the battle. He hadn't noticed the blast of the shotgun rounds at the time but, that was hardly unusual. With the near-constant roar of H&K 9 mm rounds and the AK-47, the 12-gauge explosions had simply been drowned out.

Scarberry walked forward.

"Richards?" Bolan asked.

The former DEA man shook his head. "Round clipped his carotid. Bled to death. I pulled him back into the trees, but there was nothing more I could do."

The Executioner nodded. Such were the fortunes of war. He studied Scarberry's face for a moment. Richards and the former DEA man had hardly been friends. But Scarberry looked as if he had indeed lost a friend.

"What have we got here?" Scarberry asked, letting the barrel of his Winchester drift over to cover the mud-faced man on the ground.

"We're about to find out," the Executioner said. "Stand up."

The man with the mud on his face slowly rose to his feet, raising his hands high again.

"You can drop them."

The terrorist let his hands fall slowly to his side.

"What do they call you?" Bolan asked.

The man hesitated for a moment, as if trying to decide exactly what he should say. Beneath the mud mask, Bolan could see the indecision on his face as his mind worked overtime. A few seconds later, the face relaxed as if some gigantic burden had been lifted from him. The fact that he had made some inward decision of monumental importance was obvious.

"My name is Solari," the man said. "And I will tell you anything you wish to know if you spare my life."

Bolan stared into the terrorist's eyes. The man could be lying, running some hustle to stall for time. But that wasn't the feeling the Executioner got from him. Unless he was reading the man completely wrong, this was one terrorist who was more than willing to give up his comrades in order to save himself.

Jamming the barrel of the MP-5 into Solari's chest, Bolan pushed him back until his knees hit the pile, bent and he fell to a seat on the rubble.

"Then you better sit down," the Executioner said. "This is going to take a while." He paused, the H&K still pressed against the man's chest. "There's a lot I want to know."

7

Iquitos was a true frontier town. Unless the traveler wanted to undertake a jungle hike of hundreds of miles through the Amazon it was unreachable by land. The only practical way in and out was by air or river, which meant it was as isolated from the rest of Peru as it could get and still remain within the country's borders. As a city of nearly four hundred thousand people, and the capital of the district of Loreto, Iquitos had television, radio and newspapers of course. But news from the rest of the country and the world, more often than not, arrived late.

Mack Bolan was used to such places. He had fought evil all over the world, many times in remote places similar to Iquitos, areas that seemed more removed from the rest of the planet than the moon itself. So he wasn't particularly surprised when he returned to find out that terrorist strikes had been taking place in both Peru and Ecuador, not only during the day they had been in the jungle, but the day before that as well. The strikes were the talk of Iquitos and, he guessed, the rest of the cities in both nations.

The soldier, Scarberry and Solari had returned in William Richards's boat and had seen two Peruvian navy gunboats gliding up the Amazon toward the border with Ecuador. Now, as

Bolan sat behind the rickshaw driver who had taken them from the river into town, he saw activity gearing up at the large air force base. He knew the same thing would be going on at both ESSEL and the army base next to it.

War was even closer now than it had been before they'd followed Willie Richards into the jungle. The Peruvian troops were gearing up, and while the hostilities might begin with conventional guns, bullets and bombs, the use of chemical weaponry was inevitable.

The wind whipped through the soldier's hair as they raced along the streets toward the Plaza de Armas. Bolan and Scarberry had squeezed Solari between them in the back of the rickshaw. They passed several anti-Ecuadoran demonstrations attempting to get organized, with stern men carrying signs emblazoned with angry slogans. The demonstrations were small and would probably burn themselves out without violence. But in a day or two, if the bombs and other terrorist attacks continued and were still being blamed on the Ecuadoran government rather than terrorists, big problems would arise. People would gather in frustration. Adrenaline would mix with mob mentality to blend into a lethal cocktail of anger and retribution. Common sense would be pushed to the side, and the Peruvians might well become their own worst enemies and destroy themselves.

The rickshaw slowed as it reached the plaza, turning the corner at Ari's Burgers. What was equally frightening was that although he couldn't see them, Bolan knew similar potential riots were forming in Ecuador against the Peruvians. Both countries were at risk.

And neither was to blame.

The rickshaw slowed again as it drew up in front of the Internet café. Bolan had interrogated Solari as best he could on the trip back down the river and had learned much, if not all, of what the terrorist had to tell. Bolan needed to contact Stony Man Farm. Things were heating up, and soon the Peruvian army would be heading into the jungle for the chemicals. Solari had taken them to the spot where the canisters had been buried, but destroying them on site had been impossible. Such a job required delicate handling with specialized equipment—equipment Bolan didn't have. He had considered moving them to another hiding spot, but that would have taken a half day's work at best. Not to mention the fact that there was no way to move them without leaving tracks that would lead anyone looking directly to the new hiding place.

Such effort would be useless. So the Executioner had decided upon another plan.

Bolan paid the rickshaw driver and looked at Solari. The man had become as docile as a puppy. The Executioner turned back to the problem at hand. He had tried telephoning Brognola as soon as they got out of the jungle and met with the same problems he'd had with phones ever since arriving in Peru. At best, the connections were always fuzzy, scratchy links with a second or so delay between the time words were spoken and heard. It made for the two parties talking over each other, having to repeat things several times, wasted time and misinterpreted intelligence. And while the phones at Stony Man and one of the lines leading into Brognola's office were secure, there was no such guarantee on the South American end.

Bolan prepared to exit the rickshaw as the driver stopped. He could have used one of Stony Man Farm's cutting edge cell phones with satellite relays back to the Farm. But cell phone conversations could be intercepted. Even twenty-dollar walkie-talkies often accidentally picked up their waves. As strange as it had seemed, the Internet cafés with their primitive computers had become his most reliable method of contacting home.

The Executioner got out of the rickshaw and waited for Solari to follow. Scarberry pushed the terrorist out of the rickshaw, then got out himself. Using a hand hidden in the front pocket of this khaki safari vest, he prodded the prisoner toward the café door.

Bolan had spoken plainly to the man on the trip back down the river to Iquitos. He had put Solari in Scarberry's custody, and explained to the Peruvian that for all practical purposes the former DEA man owned him. Scarberry would be carrying the hammerless S&W .357 Magnum pistol out of sight in his pocket. His finger would be on the trigger, the barrel pointed at the Solari, at all times.

Harvey Scarberry had long years of experience working with informants, and he had proved himself to be a capable warrior time and time again during this mission. Bolan had no qualms about turning the custody of their prisoner over to the man so he could concentrate his own efforts on other tasks.

Bolan led the way into the building toward the computers. Scarberry nudged Solari to a row of chairs against the wall—a makeshift waiting area. The two men took seats as Bolan found an open computer. Quickly, he logged on-line and tapped in the code to Stony Man. Because of the communications problems he faced in Peru, the Farm was keeping one of its computers on-line twenty-four hours a day, with an auditory alert sounding anytime Bolan logged on. The Executioner set up a private chat room behind the Farm's state-of-the-art cybersecurity, and soon had contact with Barbara Price. Price was operating under one of several on-line identities she used: MC1. Mission Controller One.

The Executioner kept his messages short, as did Price.

jungleman307: Hello, Barb.
MC1: Striker.
jungleman307: Affirmative. Is hr there?
MC1: Negative, at JD.
jungleman307: You have contact?
MC1: Land phone, yes. Just spoke to him.
jungleman307: Get him back.

For a minute or so, there was no more exchange. The Executioner pictured the beautiful honey-blonde in his mind. She was on the phone, calling Brognola at the Justice Department. Finally, she came back:

MC1: Hal on-line, Striker.
jungleman307: Ascertain any new developments regarding leak
on my ID.
MC1: Stand by.

The was a pause of a few moments, during which time Bolan
again pictured her talking to Brognola over the phone.

The message box flashed again, and new words appeared.

MC1: Uncovered leak in JD. Still interrogating. No direct link
to you yet.
jungleman307: Affirmative. Have NFP terr in custody here.
Some interrogation, more to come.

Bolan hit the Send button and immediately began a new message while Price relayed the intel to Brognola, on the phone.

jungleman307: Chem-weapons found in jungle. Left by Peru but
discovered by NFP. 17 cans. Send for pickup.

With a handheld global positioning unit, the Executioner had
taken a reading at the site where the chemical weapons were
hidden. He typed in the coordinates before logging off. It
should be easy enough for a team of blacksuits—the regular
strike forces at Stony Man Farm—to find the location and haul
out the cans. They could come into nearby Colombia under the
guise of being DEA task force agents, fly across the border in
a helicopter and make the pickup before anyone in the Peruvian government even knew they'd been there. They could
even use the same landing zone the Peruvian army had chopped
out of the jungle when they brought the chemicals in. The
blacksuits would just have to come down on top of a few of
the dead NFP bodies the Executioner had left scattered across
it when he left.

THE LOVELY YOUNG prostitute—Marina—was back in the lobby of the Hotel Florentina when Bolan and Scarberry walked Solari up the steps. The Executioner remembered Alvarez asking him to say hello for him, which in turn reminded him that they had been expecting a message from the young man. He stopped at the front desk. "Anyone call for us?" he asked the desk clerk.

"Yes," the man said, reaching under the desk and coming out with a dirty yellow pad of paper. "Señor Alvarez." Bolan glanced down at the page the man tore off the pad as he took it from the desk clerk's hand.

"Señor Alvarez, he say he will call back," the clerk added.

Bolan nodded and turned back to the other two men. Scarberry still had his hand in his pocket. Solari hadn't forgotten why. He had given them no trouble and didn't appear inclined to do so. At least in the near future.

Which made the Executioner a little uneasy. The man was cooperating, which was good, but he was cooperating a little too well.

Bolan had transported the long guns from the hotel room to the jungle in a large duffel bag, and had returned them to Iquitos the same way. Now, he dropped the bag on one of the beds and turned. He thought briefly of Willie Richards as he sat next to the bed. Richards and Scarberry had hardly been friends. They were rivals in the jungle guide business and had been about a half step away from being all-out enemies. But Richards's death seemed to have had as deep an effect on Scarberry, as if he'd lost a brother. According to the former DEA man, Richards had no family; there had been no one who needed to be notified. So they had buried him in the jungle where Scarberry thought he'd want to spend eternity.

Scarberry and Solari took seats on the bed across from the Executioner. The former DEA man had picked up a copy of a local newspaper on the walk from the Internet café, and he was studying the front page. But Solari was staring anxiously at the soldier, waiting for whatever would happen next.

"Okay," Bolan said. "Let me make sure I've got this straight. Kenji Rivas is the head of New and Free Peru."

Solari nodded his head.

"And the NFP has hooked up with a faction of CONAIE in Ecuador—the Lightning Bolts. Led by—" He noticed Solari nodding vigorously again and found it slightly irritating. He had no respect for terrorists, and he had even less for a man like Solari. The NFP lieutenant had rolled over faster, and with less protest, than any man with whom the Executioner had ever dealt. He had changed sides without hesitation, which either meant the word *loyalty* held no meaning for him or he was up to something. Maybe both. In any case, Solari did not, and never had, believed in the ideology of New and Free Peru. But he had taken part in the atrocities the group had committed in the name of that ideology.

Bolan wasn't sure if a life-form lower than terrorist existed. But if it did, it had to be a terrorist who didn't even believe in what he was doing.

"You don't have to nod your head every time I say something, Solari," the soldier said. "I'm thinking out loud. Sorting things out in my mind. You just tell me if I've gotten anything wrong."

Solari shrank visibly, like a child who had been reprimanded. Then, without even realizing he'd done it, he nodded again.

"The Lightning Bolt faction leader is a man named Alejandro Carillo, but he is called Relámpago," Bolan went on. "He's been pulling off the strikes in Ecuador while Rivas has led them in Peru, and both men are making it look like the attacks are the direct work of the opposite militaries. They're planting false evidence at the scenes."

In his nervous condition Solari couldn't help himself. His head bobbed up and down uncontrollably.

Bolan ignored it. "Their objective is to ensure that the war gets started. Speed it up. And by doing so, speed up the use of the chemical weapons by both sides."

Scarberry looked up from the newspaper, then turned it around so Bolan could see the front page. "From the looks of things, they're doing a damn good job of it, too."

He stared at the headlines. In addition to a machine-gun rampage at one of the law schools in Ecuador, bombs had gone off in Cuenca and Guayaquil. One of the Peruvian president's top advisers had been assassinated near Cuzco, and snipers had opened fire in Lima and Quito. The story hinted that evidence linking military operatives from both nations had been found at several scenes, and the implication was that while open hostilities might not yet have broken out, a full-scale clandestine war was already in full swing between the two nations.

Bolan sat back and fell silent for a few seconds, thinking. His primary mission when he'd come to South America had been to locate and destroy the chemical agents in the possession of both Peru and Ecuador. He had known there was little time before war broke out, and that soon after it did these weapons of mass destruction were likely to be used. Now, it looked as if his mission needed to take a slightly different turn. If he was going to stop the chemical weapons from being used, he would first have to stop Kenji Rivas and Alejandro "Relámpago" Carillo. The alignment between the two terrorists meant his time had grown even shorter. The fact that Solari and the other NFP men had been at the site in the jungle proved that the terrorists were not only trying to get the war started but, if they could, get their hands on the chemical weapons themselves. The spread of the deadly agents was their ultimate goal to creating chaos, and if they could gain possession of a supply and do it themselves they could speed up their agenda considerably.

Bolan looked into Solari's frightened eyes. "Tell me how you knew where the canisters were," he demanded.

"Lopez," Solari said. "A sergeant at the army base."

"What's he look like?" the Executioner asked.

"Before, he was medium height, weight, with brown eyes and black hair."

He had just described ninety-five percent of the men in South America. But if a fake beard was added like Juan Torres suspected had been worn by the man who hired him to kill Bolan, he could fit the bill.

"You said 'before,'" Bolan said. "What did you mean by that?"

"That he now looks like death."

Bolan stated at the other man. "He was with you in the jungle?"

Solari's head bobbed up and down. "Rivas paid him to lead us there personally. He was not dressed in his uniform, of course."

The Executioner's brain kicked into high gear. Yes, he definitely had a hunch that it was this Lopez who was the mystery man hiring people to kill him. If that was the case, the man had contacts that went all the way back to Washington. He wished it had been Lopez who had survived the gunfight in the jungle rather than Solari. But if wishes really came true, he supposed he'd just be able to wish that all the chemical weapons in Peru and Ecuador evaporated into thin air. Without killing anyone.

Bolan crossed his legs as he continued to stare at Solari. The situation was beginning to become clear to him. But a few pieces of the puzzle pieces were still missing. For instance, it seemed almost ludicrous that Rivas thought he could create enough chaos to just waltz in and take over Peru, with Relámpago doing the same in Ecuador. Even in the aftermath of the deaths of thousands, even with the outrage against the current governments that would saturate the hearts of the survivors, it seemed a long shot. On the other hand, Bolan reminded himself that this was Latin America. Revolutions and coups had occurred against even greater odds. So it was not only conceivable that the NFP and Lightning Bolts might attempt such a takeover, it was quite possible they could even pull it off. But their success or failure wasn't really the issue, Bolan realized. The reality of the situation was that they were going to try, and that included ensuring that the upcoming war escalated to the point where thousands, if not hundreds of thousands, of people died.

Solari broke into his thoughts, speaking without being prompted. "Relámpago is a patriot," he said. "He is serious about returning the lands to the Quechua people." He stopped.

"What about Rivas?" Bolan asked.

"Oh," Solari said. "Kenji is serious about this, too. But he doesn't care about the native people of Peru. His mother was

Japanese, and he thinks of himself as Japanese even though his father was Peruvian." He paused to take a deep breath that seemed to settle his nerves somewhat. "Kenji only wants the power. And money."

Bolan studied the man's face and body language. Whenever he dealt with informants, he had to count on getting heavily shaded intelligence that had been spun to their own benefit. How much of what Solari was saying about Rivas and Relámpago was actually true? There was no way of knowing at this point.

The Executioner's eyes moved to Scarberry, who was still reading the paper. "You know either of these men?" he asked. "Rivas or Relámpago?"

Scarberry dropped the paper to his lap. "Never had the pleasure," he said. "But I've heard of them both." He glanced at Solari, then looked back at Bolan. "I'd say there's a better than even chance that what he just said is true. Relámpago, as far as I know, has never performed a criminal act that wasn't directly related to his cause. Don't get me wrong, I'm not justifying his actions, just pointing out the motive. He's what I would call a true believer." The former DEA agent cleared his throat before going on. "Rivas, he's another story."

He looked at Solari again. "Is this the same Kenji Rivas who used to be hooked into the Colombian cocaine trade?"

Solari nodded. "It is the same man."

Scarberry turned back to speak to Bolan but hooked a thumb at Solari. "Then I think our new best buddy here's on the mark again. We—DEA—had intel on Rivas as far back as ten years ago. He grew up in the jungle near Iquitos but took off for Bogotá as soon as he was grown. Worked his way up the ladder in the dope business. Not a kingpin, mind you, but a major player. We knew who he was, but we could never make a case on him."

"What do you think about this sudden career change? From drug dealer to revolutionary?" Bolan asked.

"I'd say if it's the same Rivas—" He stopped in midsentence and looked at Solari.

"I told you it was," Solari stated. He hadn't been beaten or killed yet and he was relaxing and getting bolder.

Scarberry went on as if Solari had not spoken. "Like I said, he was a player but never a top dog. My guess is that he was ambitious and saw an angle. If he hadn't, he'd have stayed in Colombia with the coke."

"You take over two countries, there's money in it," the Executioner said. "And that pretty much makes you a kingpin."

Scarberry agreed. "Right on both accounts. But what's your point? Why does it matter that Relámpago is in this for the cause and Rivas just wants power and money? The outcome is the same—they murder people."

"But the way you go after them isn't the same," Bolan said. He turned to Solari. "Where's Rivas now?"

Solari shrugged. "I do not know. He was planning to kill one of the president's advisers while I went after the chemicals."

The soldier gave the other man a hard look. The fact that a snitch appeared to be cooperating was never a reason to trust him. "According to the paper he's already done that. How were you supposed to contact him when you got out of the jungle?"

"He was to call me," Solari said.

"Where?"

"Here. Iquitos. The El Dorado hotel."

Bolan continued to look the other man in the eye. The El Dorado was an upscale hotel across from the Plaza de Armas, catty-corner from Ari's. A night in one of its air-conditioned rooms cost more than most Peruvians would make in a month. Most terrorist groups like the NFP couldn't afford such luxuries for their men. But Rivas could. He had money. Cocaine money. He had made it in Colombia and didn't mind spending it. Each dollar was an investment in his future.

Bolan nodded to himself. Things were coming clear. For all practical purposes, there was no New and Free Peru. It had been a sham from the beginning. A cover for what Rivas really had in mind.

The room grew silent and Bolan closed his eyes. A plan was forming. It was still a shapeless thing, more of a hint of a plan. But that was how all battle strategy began. He would let it grow, and gradually it would take shape on its own. Opening his eyes again, he looked at Scarberry. "Can you get the local DEA office file on Rivas?"

Scarberry shrugged. "Maybe. I still hang out with the guys now and then. Play darts every Wednesday night with them at a bar. Most of them wouldn't risk it—it'd be their ass if they got caught."

The Executioner could see the wheels turning behind Scarberry's eyes. And he didn't have to be psychic to know what they were turning around. "But there's somebody who will," Bolan said. "Somebody who doesn't spend his life worrying about pensions and promotions and getting in trouble with the boss. Somebody who got into this business to help people and still wants to and does the right thing instead of the bureaucratically correct thing."

Scarberry chuckled. "What makes you so sure of that?" he asked.

"Because no office of any agency can operate without at least one man like that," Bolan said. "One risk taker." He paused to let it sink in, then said, "So what's the guy's name?"

"Tony Loriega," Scarberry said. He stood. "I can call him from the lobby."

DRUG ENFORCEMENT Administration Special Agent Tony Loriega had been born in New York City and was a first generation American of Filipino heritage. When he walked in the open doorway an hour later, Bolan saw that he was barely five feet tall. He probably didn't tip the scales at 120 pounds, and could easily have qualified as a jockey. But when Bolan looked into the man's eyes he saw why Loriega had not chosen that, or any profession other than the one he had. The dark brown eyes set in Loriega's naturally tanned skin led to the soul of a warrior. And Bolan was reminded of an old saying that dynamite sometimes came in small packages.

Loriega stopped just inside the doorway and looked at Scarberry. "The things we young guys do to help out you old men," he said, shaking his head. "You're lucky I love you, Grandpa."

Scarberry held up the back of his hand with all of the fingers curled into a fist except the middle one.

Loriega laughed. "I'd make another crack about you and Anita," he said, "but I think I've pressed my luck already." Without being told, he moved across the room to take a seat next to Bolan. In one hand was a briefcase half as big as him, and after setting it in his lap, he extended that hand and introduced himself. "Tony Loriega."

"Mike Belasko," Bolan said.

Loriega grinned a boyish grin. "I don't know exactly who you are Belasko, and I'm pretty sure I don't even want to, but if this old man—" he hooked a thumb over his shoulder at Scarberry "—says you can be trusted, then I trust you." He coughed slightly, and through the confidence he exuded Bolan saw just a hint of hesitancy. "I'm sure it goes without saying that the less my superiors know about me being here, the better for me, too."

Bolan nodded. He couldn't blame the man for that. His job was at stake.

Loriega now turned his eyes to Solari, and the Executioner could see that he recognized the informant for what he was. "You I don't know and don't want to know." Solari started to speak, but Loriega's voice drowned him out. "My old buddy Scarberry here has his hand in his pocket, and unless I'm very mistaken it's curled around one of those old-fashioned cowboy six-shooters he and the other old-timers still swear by. It's pointed at you, and that tells me that even though you've agreed to help he doesn't trust you."

He gave Scarberry a pleasant smile. "Right so far?"

Scarberry smiled. "For a kid just out of diapers who hasn't started shaving yet, you're pretty smart."

"So I don't trust you, either," Loriega finished, turning back to Solari. "Keep in mind that I'll kill you, too, if I have to. You from around here?"

Solari's eyebrows raised at the seemingly out-of-place question. "I was born in the jungle," he said.

"Then you know there's no better place in the world to get rid of a body," Loriega said pleasantly. "Just dump your dead ass in the good old bush and a day later—poof! You're just gone."

Solari had grown braver since they'd arrived at the Florentina. And now, maybe it was the Filipino's diminutive size, or a sudden flash of shame that he had kowtowed to Bolan and Scarberry ever since meeting them. In any case, the terrorist suddenly snorted through his nose. "You talk very tough," he snarled. "But you are DEA, and you aren't even allowed to carry guns in my country."

Loriega's smile widened. He looked at Scarberry and said, "You haven't explained to him that we sometimes bend the rules a little?"

Then, almost too fast for the eye to follow, he moved. One moment he was sitting next to Bolan, and the next he was standing in front of Solari with the razor-honed edge of a Spanish Navajo knife held to the terrorist's throat. Somewhere in between, everyone in the room had heard the ratchet sound as the ten-inch blade came out of the handle.

Scarberry shook his head back and forth in mock regret. "I'm sorry, Solari," he said. "I forgot to tell you and Belasko both. Tony is an expert knife man. An expert at all the Filipino fighting arts."

"And don't kid yourself on the gun-carrying thing, either," Loriega said, still staring at the horrified man on the bed in front of him. Then, almost as quickly as he had moved toward Solari, Loriega returned to his seat next to the Executioner. The knife folded back into its handle and disappeared.

"Let's take a look at Rivas's file," Bolan said.

Loriega opened the briefcase and pulled out a bulging manila folder.

"I'm going to need a little time to study this," the Executioner said. "Scarberry, I want you to look at it, too. Refresh your memory on what you knew. Catch up on what Rivas has been up to since you retired."

Loriega stood. "Hope the Alzheimer's doesn't get in the way," he said good-naturedly. He looked to across to Solari. "How about I take your little friend here for a walk in the park?"

"Good idea," Bolan said. "Give us—" he glanced at his watch "—say, an hour and a half?"

"You got it."

Loriega back to Solari. "Let's go," he said.

Solari was now terrified of the small man he had tried to scorn, and didn't want to go anywhere with him. He shook his head.

Tony Loriega moved in, quickly again, but this time without the knife. Grasping the far larger man's wrist with one hand, he twisted slightly and Solari jerked to his feet. The pain from the nerve Loriega had pinched shot to Solari's face, and he gasped, almost screaming. The Filipino dropped his wrist and stepped back. "Be a good boy and come on," he said. "If not, I'll have to hold your hand the whole time."

A moment later they were gone.

"Damn good kid to work with," Scarberry said as he started to read a report. "Even if he is a bit of a smart-ass."

ALTHOUGH HE HAD a keen sense of human personalities, the Executioner was neither a psychologist nor psychiatrist. Nonetheless, one word kept popping into his mind as he read through the dozens of surveillance reports and a few transcripts of interrogations when the DEA and Peruvian authorities had gotten close enough to Kenji Rivas to warrant hauling him in for questioning.

That words was narcissist. The man had an ego the size of the entire South American continent.

Therefore, Bolan wasn't surprised when he came to the last document in the file and saw that it was a personality assessment worked up by an independent profiler who contracted his services to the DEA. In the last-paragraph summary of the admittedly "long-distance" diagnosis, the Executioner read "...subject exhibits extreme egocentric behavior and very possibly suffers from narcissism."

Bolan wasn't as sympathetic as the analyst. It didn't appear to him that Rivas was the one *suffering*. It looked to him more as if Rivas caused everyone else with whom he came in contact to suffer. And didn't mind if thousands more suffered—and died—in order for him to get what he wanted.

The Executioner had kept his seat across from Scarberry, reading each report and then handing it to the man on the bed opposite him. He had heard Scarberry grunt occasionally, and once the former DEA agent even said "I remember that" to himself under his breath. Finishing the psychological profile, Bolan stretched it out until it was taken from his hand. He dropped the empty manila file on top of Loriega's briefcase, scooted up against the wall to use it as a backrest and stared across the room in thought.

Okay, Relámpago was a terrorist who thought of himself as a freedom fighter. A "true believer" as Scarberry had said. But Rivas was a common, garden-variety, dope-peddling hoodlum who was masquerading as a terrorist. How could the knowledge of that difference be used?

Bolan crossed his legs. While Relámpago was just as much a murderer as Rivas, he worked toward what he believed was a "greater good" and believed his end justified his means. He rationalized what he did with the same practicality as a man who knew he had to "break eggs to cook an omelet." Even though at some level he had to know his methodology was abominable, he viewed himself as a good man working for the sake of others rather than for himself.

Rivas, on the other hand, had set up the New and Free Peru movement as nothing but a vehicle toward his own goals—power and money. He might profess a passionate need to help the oppressed and downtrodden, but he secretly laughed at the stupidity of those who believed him. They were, in his view, the most naive of children. And like any true narcissist, he would regard them as living only for his personal use.

Which meant the only reason he had hooked up with Relámpago and the Lightning Bolts was because they could be of use to him. And somewhere down the line, when Rivas didn't need his Ecuadoran partner anymore, Relámpago was going to find out that an NFP bullet had his name engraved on it. Why take over only Peru when he could have Ecuador in the bargain?

Yes, Rivas would be planning to kill Relámpago. Of that, the Executioner was certain.

But could the NFP man pull it off without alienating the rest of the Lightning Bolts? Solari had told the Executioner about the blood oath on the way back down the river, and Bolan had no doubt it had been concocted by Rivas simply to ensure that the Lightning Bolts became his upon Relámpago's demise. That would not, of course, be the case if Relámpago's men knew Rivas was behind their leader's death. But keeping suspicion off himself shouldn't be such a difficult task. Because Relámpago thought Rivas's intentions were as selfless as his own, and therefore trusted the man, he would be easy to set up. All Rivas had to do was make sure a third party carried out the task. Preferably, someone not part of the NFP.

Bolan felt a tight grin begin to form at the corners of his lips as he continued to let his mind drift. The plan that had begun to form earlier had taken further shape as he studied the file. Now he had many of the details—many of the flaws that were always present in the first draft of a strategy—ironed out. The fact was, he saw only one serious shortcoming in his battle plan, and he suspected Scarberry could provide the answer to that problem.

Scarberry tossed the pages into the open briefcase on the floor and said, "Man's got a big ego and doesn't care who he hurts. Surprise, surprise." He shook his head in disbelief. "How much you suppose the suits in Washington paid that quack of a doctor to put into ten-dollar words what any street cop could have told them?"

The question was rhetorical, and Bolan didn't answer. He

was about to ask his own question of Scarberry when there was a knock on the door. He guessed it would be Loriega and Solari returning. But just in case he was wrong he slipped his hand under his vest and curled his fingers around the butt of the Beretta 93-R as he walked to the door.

He *was* wrong. But his hand dropped away from the Beretta anyway when he opened the door to see the desk clerk. The man was in a slightly agitated state of mind as he said, "Sir, Señor Alvarez. He is on the phone again."

Bolan followed the man down the walk past the garden sitting area to the phone on the wall. The receiver hung from the steel cord connecting it to the ancient rotary device, and he pressed it to his ear. "Belasko," he said.

"Ah, my friend the journalist!" Alvarez chuckled as he spoke. "I have information for you." The Executioner glanced around the lobby. The desk clerk was watching him like an excited child who knew a movie star was on the other end of the line, and the good-looking prostitute was once again eyeing him, hoping he'd changed his mind. It was more of an audience than he wanted while receiving sensitive information.

Alvarez seemed to sense his situation. "Can you speak freely?" he asked.

"No. Not here."

"Do you still have the man you brought back from the jungle with you?" Alvarez asked.

Bolan was slightly surprised that Alvarez knew about Solari. Then again, they had made no attempt at cloaking their movements once they returned to Iquitos. They had been seen in the rickshaws, at the Internet café, and walking back to the Florentina. It just proved that Alvarez had eyes everywhere in Iquitos.

"Still got him," Bolan said. "I suppose you know his name, too."

That brought another laugh from Alvarez. "No, but I can find it out quickly if you need me to."

"No, I already know it," he said.

"The reason I asked," Alvarez went on, "is that it will be easier for me to come to you than for you to come to me. Since you have him, I mean. I will be there in five minutes."

The line went dead.

The desk clerk beamed at the Executioner as if he had a true celebrity staying at the Florentina. The prostitute looked up with hope in her eyes that said that, even if he wasn't a celebrity, he had money, and she wanted some of it.

Bolan walked back to the room and resumed his seat on the bed. He began running down his plan to Scarberry as they waited. Ten minutes later, another knock sounded on the door. Scarberry answered it this time, and Bolan looked through the opening to see Alvarez and his bodyguards. As usual, the men looked nervous.

"Stay out here," Alvarez ordered them, then slammed the door in their faces. He walked across the room and shook hands with Bolan and Scarberry, then took a seat next to the former DEA man. With a wave of exasperation at the closed door, he said, "They have guarded me since I was a child, and they will always think of me as a child. Plus they have grown lazy in later years, more accustomed to protecting my father who rarely went out because of his illness. Now they must work for a living once again, and they don't like it."

"You'll whip them into shape, I'm sure," Scarberry said.

Alvarez nodded, his face serious. "Or replace them."

Bolan was about to ask him what he'd learned when yet another knock came. This time it was Loriega and Solari returning. When Bolan opened the door, two of the bodyguards had Solari against the wall. It was apparent that they had been about to shake him down for weapons when their attention had been diverted.

The diversion had come from Loriega who had the largest of the three men in an arm bar with the tip of his knife pressed into the man's throat.

Before anyone started bleeding, Bolan said, "It's okay. They're with us."

"Let them go," Alvarez called out from the bed.

The two men holding Solari stepped back from the wall. Loriega let the big man go and started into the room. The bodyguard said, "I will take the knife," and grabbed the DEA man's arm.

Loriega spun his wrist out of the man's grip and let the edge of the blade sweep across the other man's hairy forearm. The bodyguard jerked his arm back in fright. For a moment, everyone froze. Then the bodyguard held his arm up to look at it. There was no blood, but the forearm had been shaved clean.

The small DEA agent smiled good-naturedly and wiped the hair off his knife on the big man's shirt. "No, I think I will keep it," he said.

Before any guns could be drawn, Alvarez called out, "Carlos! You and the other men sit in the courtyard. Do not bother us again until I come out."

"But Señor Arturo," the giant protested, "with the knife he could—"

"Kill *you*, Carlos," Alvarez said. "He has already proved that. Now go sit down."

Bolan closed the door. Loriega motioned Solari to the room's lone chair and took a seat next to Bolan on the bed.

The Executioner let his eyes fall on Alvarez. "What did you learn?" he asked.

"The man behind the attacks was a sergeant at the local army base. Next to ESSEL," Alvarez said.

"Sergeant Lopez," Bolan said.

Alvarez was surprised. "You know this already?"

Bolan nodded. "He was the one who led this man," he hooked a thumb toward Solari's chair, "into the jungle."

Alvarez nodded. "To show him where the canisters of chemical agents were buried."

"Shit," Scarberry said, shaking his head. "Is there anything you don't know?"

Alvarez gave the DEA man a wry smile and said, "I didn't know that your friend already knew the sergeant's name." He shrugged innocently.

"So Lopez hired the street vendor at Ari's as well as the gunman at the airport?"

"Yes," Alvarez answered. "As well as Juan Torres, the man who attacked you with the machete after you left me yesterday."

Scarberry looked up. "You know about that?"

"Of course," Alvarez said.

He turned back to Bolan. "Torres was incompetent, and the man at the airport was also a poor choice, in my opinion. He worked loosely with the cartels but was for hire. Definitely small-time."

Now that everyone was there, the Executioner began to explain his plan from the beginning once more. "What I've got in mind is to have Solari check into the El Dorado just as Rivas ordered him to. There will be a few hours missing—a small hole in his time clock. But those hours can be explained by the next part."

The Executioner went on to explain the plan he had refined in his mind, a plan that at first had the other men's jaws dropping for its sheer boldness, then smiling at the utter genius within the strategy.

"As I see it," Bolan concluded, "there's only one major problem left."

Solari and Alvarez frowned, but both Scarberry and Loriega nodded their heads in comprehension.

"The link between you and Solari," Loriega said. "Somehow, we need a logical way he ended up dealing with you, and 'old friend' just ain't gonna hack it. Rivas would smell something wrong."

"Right," Bolan said. "What we need is a middleman, someone who it would be reasonable for Solari to know and would also be likely to know a few nefarious Americans."

Scarberry snorted. "Men like that wouldn't be hard to find," he said. "But we have to be able to trust whoever steps into this role, too."

"I would volunteer," Alvarez said. "And I would be the most likely candidate. But my father's and my feelings about the drug trade are widely known. Rivas knows I would never help him."

Bolan held up a hand before any of the others could explain their situation. "You'd all volunteer—I know that. But none of you fit the bill." He paused, took a deep breath, then let it out. His mind drifted back to Ari's Burgers, and a man he had briefly seen the first night he had been in Iquitos. "The fact is, there's only one man I know of who's in the right position to help us. A man who could step right into this role and already has the right background and training, and who I'd guess we could trust, too. The problem is that I don't know whether or not he'll be willing."

"Well," Scarberry said, "who is it?"

"Lee Kinelli."

For a few moments, Scarberry, Solari, Alvarez and Loriega all sat there with their mouths as wide open as they'd been when Bolan first started to lay out his plan. Then, one by one the mouths closed and smiles appeared.

"You're right about being able to trust him," Scarberry said. "At least that's my take, too."

"But you're also right about the fact that he may not want to help," Loriega added.

The Executioner rose to his feet. "There's only one way to find out."

8

The difference between the Hotel Florentina and the El Dorado was like the difference between the Equator and the Arctic. After several days of living in heat that ranged from the high eighties to more than a hundred, and humidity that rarely dropped below ninety-five percent, entering the new hotel felt like walking into a meat locker.

Scarberry, Loriega, Alvarez and his bodyguards all headed into the El Dorado's lounge as Bolan followed Solari though the doors to the hotel registration desk. Solari carried a small soft-sided bag packed with various odds and ends that Bolan had given him. Rivas had ordered his lieutenant to check in and await Rivas's call. Solari should have been there several hours earlier, so Bolan wasn't surprised to hear the desk clerk say, "Ah, Señor Solari. We have been waiting. Someone has been trying to reach you." He glanced at the telephone on the counter.

A lump seemed to form in Solari's throat. But he forced a smile, and when he spoke his voice was steady. "Did he leave a name?"

The clerk shook his head. "No, he said he would call back."

Solari began filling out a registration card.

"Two of you?" the clerk asked.

Bolan shook his head. "I'm just visiting."

The clerk nodded. He waited until the card had been completed, then handed Solari a key. "You gentlemen will enjoy both the restaurant and lounge, I believe," he said. "Shall I call for a porter?"

Solari shook his head. "I can manage," he said. "I have only this." He held up the suitcase.

Bolan followed the man back out of the registration area and into the lounge where the rest of the men were seated at a long table drinking cold beer. All but Scarberry. The former DEA agent was on the pay phone in the corner, speaking in a low voice. He grinned when he saw the soldier and waved him that way. Bolan pointed Solari toward the table and walked over to the phone. As soon as Bolan was next to Scarberry, the man handed him the receiver. "Say hello to the next Mrs. Scarberry," he said. "I asked her and she said yes."

Bolan took the phone, said, "Congratulations," and handed it back to Scarberry. "I hate to ruin the engagement party," he stated, "but we've got work to do."

Scarberry nodded, said goodbye to Anita and hung up. He and the other men followed Bolan to the elevators.

A few minutes later, they were in the upscale room and finding seats on the bed, chairs and divan to await the next call.

Solari had protested the plan from the beginning, which hadn't surprised Bolan. But his objections had been mild compared to what one would have expected out of an informant in his situation. Now, he began to protest again, but his words seemed to hold no more conviction than they had before. It was as if he simply didn't care one way or the other whether Bolan and the others were successful.

"What you have planned will never work," Solari said, half whining. "Rivas will—"

Bolan started to cut him off but Loriega beat him to it. "Solari?" he said in a calm voice.

Solari looked at him. "Yes?"

Loriega pulled out his knife and opened it. "Shut the fuck up or I'll cut your throat."

Solari had seen all he wanted of the big folding knife. He did as he'd been told.

Right before leaving the Hotel Florentina, Scarberry had placed a call to the man Bolan had suggested play the part of the middleman between him and Solari. Scarberry had said only that they needed his help, that it could be dangerous and they'd like to meet with him. Without giving them either a yes or no before he heard more, the mobster turned missionary, Lee Kinelli, had agreed to meet them at the El Dorado. Now, a knock came at the door.

Bolan rose from the chair he had taken by the desk and opened it.

Kinelli stood in the hall wearing what looked like the same well-worn T-shirt he'd had on that night at Ari's. He was whistling softly and appeared on the surface not to have a care in the world. But Bolan didn't miss the fact that as soon Kinelli had given him the once-over, the minister's eyes shot behind him to see what he might face once he stepped through the door. Nor did Bolan miss seeing that Kinelli's hands were shoved deep into the pockets of his baggy pants.

The Executioner remembered the small revolver he had seen under the table the night the street vendor had tried to shoot him. Kinelli might have given up murder, but he still seemed to believe in self-defense.

"Come in, Reverend," Bolan said, stepping back. Kinelli walked through the door and into the room, still whistling. All of the men except Solari seemed to know him at least on a "hello" basis, and greeted him. Kinelli smiled back at them pleasantly but seriously. All but gone was the joking man who had teased Scarberry about church attendance a few nights earlier. Kinelli might not have heard the whole story from Scarberry on the phone, but he had heard enough to understand that the matter was serious.

As soon as he'd found a seat, Bolan laid things out for him. Kinelli saw the role the Executioner wanted him to play without having to be told. "So you'd like me to be the link between you and Solari," he said. "I'm to play the part of a man who had the connections to set him up quickly with mercenaries, or criminals of some kind, who could sweep in with a helicopter and grab the chemicals before the army found out they'd been stolen and went out to reclaim them."

"That's right," Bolan said. "We didn't move them when we were there because it was too big of a job. We didn't have time to do it effectively—we'd have left tracks or taken two days trying to cover them."

Kinelli frowned. "So the chemical weapons are still out there? Waiting to be used?"

Bolan glanced at his watch as he thought of the blacksuits Stony Man Farm was sending to pick up the chemicals. By now they should have come and gone. "Shouldn't be," he said. "If they are, they won't be much longer."

Across the room, both Alvarez and Loriega looked at Scarberry. None of the men knew about Stony Man Farm or the blacksuits. Scarberry just shrugged. "He sends a lot of E-mails is all I know," he said under his breath.

"But the chemicals are no longer within the grasp of anyone who could use them?" Kinelli seemed to want to be sure of this. "Terrorists or the Peruvian government?"

"No, they aren't," Bolan said. "At least not *these* chemical weapons. But there are more and we don't know where they are. If the war breaks out, there'll still be massive casualties of people who don't even know what it's all about."

"So why did you pick me, specifically, for this job?" Kinelli asked, staring into the Executioner's eyes.

Bolan met the gaze. "I think you know the answer to that question as well as I do."

The two men stayed in eye-lock for a few more seconds, then Kinelli looked away. "I don't know who you are, Mr. Belasko, but you're some kind of cop. I never liked cops very much. Now I try to love everybody. It isn't always easy, but I try. I've changed my ways. I'm not like I used to be. I didn't do it myself. Jesus Christ did it for me."

Bolan waited.

Kinelli looked back at the soldier, and there was just the hint of a tear in one eye. "You're asking me to make it look like everything I've done since I came to Iquitos was a masquerade. Just a cover for whatever criminal behavior I was really up to."

"No one except the men in this room and the terrorists are going to know about your involvement," Bolan said.

"Can you assure me of that?" Kinelli asked. He didn't wait for an answer. "No, of course you can't. And if word gets out, the rumors will fly." He paused, then reached up unashamedly and wiped his eye. "I'm not concerned about my own reputation," he said. "The good Lord knows I deserve any humiliation that comes my way. What I am concerned about is what such misinformation might do to my ministry. What will it do to the man or woman who might be sitting on the fence right now, about to accept Christ, and then finds out they've been listening to a complete charlatan? Someone who was just here preaching in order to cover his tracks in criminal endeavors? What will it do to this person who was close to being saved but was just dragging their feet a little?"

"I can't answer that any more than I can give you a hundred percent assurance that word will never leak out," Bolan said. "All I can do is tell you we'll do our best to keep it within this group." He drew in a deep breath as he watched the conflict on the minister's face. "What you've got to do, Reverend Kinelli, is weigh the chances of this adversely affecting your ministry against the thousand of lives will be lost to chemical warfare. Did it ever occur to you that some of them might be dragging their feet a little in the religion department, too? What happens to them if they die before they make their decision?"

Kinelli looked down at the floor, his face a mask of misery. He closed his eyes, and while his lips didn't move and no sounds came from his mouth, the Executioner had no doubt about what he was doing. Praying.

Bolan gave him a few seconds, then said. "We need to know

your answer, Reverend, and I'm afraid we need to know now. Will you help us?"

For several more seconds, Lee Kinelli continued to look down, his eyes closed tightly. The room grew silent as the other men waited. Then, suddenly, the pain left Kinelli's face. His eyes opened and he looked up at Bolan. Rather than the distress Bolan had seen in the man's features only moments before, his face now almost glowed as if he had just received divine guidance.

Kinelli smiled at the Executioner, then reached into his pocket and pulled out the same small revolver Bolan had seen that night at Ari's. Bolan recognized it now as an old, blue-worn, Colt Detective Special. "I assume you've got other weapons," Kinelli said. "All I've got is this little .38."

Bolan breathed a silent sigh of relief. He was about to assure Kinelli that he would provide adequate firepower.

But before he could speak the phone rang.

KENJI RIVAS LET the waiter lead him through the Palace Hotel's restaurant to a table against the wall. He took a seat and glanced around. It was late, and only one table was occupied besides his own. Two men and two women, all wearing ridiculous straw hats that pegged them as tourists were laughing, drinking and speaking what he guessed was Hebrew. There had been a large bus of Israelis parked outside when he checked in earlier, and he had seen many of them in the lobby.

Rivas ordered a drink from the waiter and watched him relay the message to the bartender in the next room. He settled into his chair, happy to be out of the jungle and taking a brief reprieve from the bombings, shootings and other strikes he and the other NFP men had carried off during the past two days. He opened the newspaper he had picked up in the lobby and scanned the headlines. They made him smile. All of his and Relámpago's missions had been successful, and there was a even a follow-up story on the Trujillo bombings that mentioned that Ecuadoran dog tags had been found at the scene. It was only a matter of time now before word of the other evidence that had been planted would leak out and then things would really get interesting. Marches and protests had already begun in several cities in Peru and Ecuador, and a few had even turned violent. Rivas chuckled to himself as he scanned more headlines. Shakespeare had said that the world was a stage. But it was really a giant chessboard, and right now he felt like the greatest chess master of all time.

An editorial speculated that war with Ecuador was inevitable, and another story spoke of things already heating up along the border. Shots had been fired by both sides earlier in the day, and two Ecuadoran soldiers and three Peruvians had been hit before the skirmish ended. One of the NATO soldiers—a Swede by this account—had also been killed. Rivas closed the paper as the waiter brought his drink. It wouldn't be long now under any circumstances. He and Relámpago would continue to strike. And if Solari had been successful in getting his hands on the chemicals to which Lopez was leading him, it would be a very short time indeed until all-out chaos ruled both countries.

Sipping his drink, Rivas thought about Relámpago and smiled. The tall Indian was carrying out his tasks with the enthusiasm of the true zealot, and for a moment the former cocaine dealer wondered what it would be like to have a cause other than money and power. Some said it made a person happier, but he could hardly imagine that. It made no sense that one could gain more happiness helping others rather than one's self. Ludicrous. Turning from Relámpago's motivation, Rivas considered the man's fate. They had already sworn a blood oath to the fact that if one of them were killed his men would follow the other. So the only thing that remained now was the timing. He would use the Quechua as long as he was useful, then have him killed and have his men finish the takeover of Ecuador. He would send someone—either Solari or Paco Real—to take command north of the border. He hadn't yet worked out the details of Relámpago's upcoming death, but it was vital to his plan that the other

Lightning Bolts had no reason to suspect him. Rivas shrugged at his own thoughts. It was no problem. Something would come up. Some opportunity would arise, and he would take advantage of it.

The waiter arrived, and Rivas ordered fish and another drink. His mind returned to Solari as we waited. Where was the man? He should have been back in Iquitos several hours ago, but the hotel had told him Solari hadn't checked in. This worried him. He didn't like loose ends. But there were hundreds of possible delays once one entered the jungle, and there was no reason to get excited at this point.

The waiter returned with his dinner and the other drink, set it down and walked away. Rivas would have liked to have taken his time but no matter what he told himself, Solari's tardiness had him concerned. So he downed the drink, hurriedly ate the fish and signed the bill.

In his room on the third floor, he placed the call again.

"Ah, Señor," the same desk clerk who had answered earlier said. "Yes, I am happy to say that your friends are now here."

Friends? Rivas thought. The man had said "friends" not "friend." He had ordered Solari to go to the El Dorado alone. "Put me through," he said quickly.

A moment later the phone was ringing. Then Solari's voice said, "Yes?"

"Who is with you and why are you late?" Rivas demanded. "And were you successful?"

Solari's voice was strained, fearful, as he spoke. "It is a long story," he said. "I will try to make it brief. An American—actually several Americans—are with me. I am late because—" Rivas heard noise in the background, as if the phone were being wrenched from Solari's hand.

A moment later, a voice with a deep American accent said, "Are you in charge?"

"Who is this?" Rivas demanded.

"My name is Belasko," the voice said. "But since we're going to be doing business, we might as well be friends. Call me Mike."

Rivas's head was swimming. He waited, then finally said, "What is going on there?"

"Okay, long story short," the American said. "Your men here met up with Sergeant Lopez, and he took them to the site where the army had buried some chemical weapons. Of course we— my men and I—didn't know jack about it then. The first we heard about it was when we got the call that there was something in the jungle that needed to be picked up and moved. Fast. So we made our way to a spot to meet your buddy here, Solari."

Rivas listened quietly as his stomach began to grow nauseous.

"Tell you what," the man said. "I'll let your man explain the rest to you himself. Then we'll talk again about where we're all going from here."

Solari came back on a moment later. "I am sorry," he said quietly.

"We will walk about your sorrow later," Rivas said curtly. "Right now, I want to know the rest. Why did you call for these men?"

"When Lopez led us to the site we were ambushed by soldiers. From his own base! They didn't know of his involvement with us. He wasn't in uniform, of course. And he was wearing that false beard. They didn't recognize him and opened fire."

"Go on."

"They killed everyone but me and two others," Solari said. "Lopez was killed by his own comrades but they didn't even know it. I escaped. Our other two men were taken prisoner."

"You have not answered my question," Rivas said, his voice rising in anger. "Why did you call for these men? Who are they?"

"Please," Solari said. "It is very complicated. I am getting to that."

Rivas forced himself to remain quiet. His hand reached into his pocket and grasped the tiny North American Arms .32 autopistol. Had Solari been telling him this in person, he suspected he would have shot the man.

"Many of the soldiers were also killed. Only four remained. I knew they would contact the base, so I shot their radio and took off through the jungle. As soon as I reached the nearest village with a phone, I realized I couldn't call you. You were in Cuzco."

Rivas took a deep breath. It was true. He had been killing the president's adviser. "Continue," he said.

"I knew that without radio contact they would have to send a man on foot to report what had happened. So we still had a chance to secure the chemicals before reinforcements arrived from the base. But I had to act fast. Unable to reach you, I called the only other man I knew who might have the right contacts to men who could get there in time. Lee Kinelli."

Rivas's hand tightened around the receiver. Lee Kinelli. Rivas had seen him once or twice but didn't know the man. Evidently Solari did, however. And everyone in the Amazon had heard that the preacher had once been tied to the Mob in the United States. Now, it not only looked as if the rumors had been true but as if Kinelli were still connected.

The nausea in Rivas's stomach grew, and he wished he hadn't eaten the fish so quickly. He could imagine what had happened then. Kinelli had called upon cutthroats within his own organization to go pick up the chemicals. When they'd realized what they had, they had to have decided they wanted more money than whatever Solari had offered them. They had to have killed both the soldiers and their NFP prisoners at the site, taken control of the chemical weapons and for all practical purposes kidnapped Solari.

As soon as he said, "Go on" again, Rivas learned that his guess was correct. The gringos now wanted to sell the chemicals to them.

"Put this Belasko back on," the NFP man ordered Solari.

A moment later, Rivas heard the Americans irritating accent. "You're welcome to the chemicals, Rivas," he said. "We have no use for them. But they're going to cost you a hundred thousand."

"I do not have that kind of money," Rivas said. "I am a freedom fighter who—"

"Cut it right there, Rivas," the American said, interrupting. "You think I'm stupid? You think I don't know where you were and what you were before you got onto this New and Free Peru hustle? You've got the money, my friend. And if you want to see those nasty little cans we picked up for you again, you're going to give it to us." He paused, and when he came back on his voice was even lower and more menacing. "You insult my intelligence again by telling me you can't afford it and the price will double."

"Is Lee Kinelli there?" Rivas demanded. "Put him on."

"My pleasure."

A moment later another unfamiliar voice said, "Lee Kinelli."

"So, padre," Rivas said, almost spitting out the last word. "You are not what you appear to be."

Kinelli laughed in his ear. "Are you, Rivas? No. None of us are what we appear to be. And that includes me." His voice took on a tone as if he were speaking from behind a pulpit. "But I can help you just the same, my son," he said sarcastically. "You see the Lord works in mysterious ways."

Rivas was trying to think, and with all the sudden new developments it wasn't easy. "How do I know that you are really Lee Kinelli?" he said. "How do I know any of you are who you say?" he said. "I think it is more likely that you are government agents setting a trap." Rivas didn't really believe that was the case. But it was possible, and only a fool wouldn't require some kind of proof that it were not so.

Particularly when an opportunity to solve two problems at the same time had just presented itself.

"Good questions," Kinelli said. "You want proof?"

"I demand proof," Rivas said with as much dignity as he could muster.

"You know what I look like?" Kinelli asked.

"I have seen you. You have been pointed out."

"Then we'll meet face-to-face? Will that convince you?"

"Not entirely," Rivas said. "If this is a trap, you would still be happy to meet me. No, I think you and your men must prove to me that you are not from the government in a more satisfactory way. And until that is done, I will speak no more of chemicals."

"Just exactly what kind of proof do you want?" Kinelli asked.

"I want you to kill a man for me," Rivas said. "This will prove that you are not from the police or military."

Kinelli laughed into the phone again. "I'm getting a little old for such stuff," he said. "Talk to Belasko again."

Rivas heard whispers in the background and then Belasko's voice came on again. "Consider it done, Rivas. But if I have to kill somebody for you, it's going to cost you another fifty thousands on top of the hundred."

"Meet me in Lima tomorrow," Rivas said. "Be at the Inca Market by three o'clock. Bring only Solari and Kinelli with you. I will find you."

"Be there with bells on," the American said. "We'll keep your little cans safe for you in the meantime." Rivas heard the line click dead in his ear as the man hung up on the other end.

The NFP leader placed the receiver back in the cradle and sat looking at the wall. The nausea was still in his stomach. But the situation would work out. He had the money, and a hundred and fifty thousand dollars was nothing compared to what the investment would make him.

THINGS WERE about to get tricky.

Bolan knew he would have to play this rest of this mission close to the vest as he turned the rental car onto Avenue La Marina. He had rented the vehicle, and two others to carry the rest of the men, as soon as Jack Grimaldi had touched down at the Lima airport an hour earlier. As he neared the Inca Market, he glanced into the rearview mirror. Behind him, he could see Tony Loriega driving one of the other cars. He was officially on sick leave from his DEA position in Iquitos. Harvey Scarberry sat beside him. As the soldier watched in the mirror, the former DEA man yawned. After the phone call from Rivas, Bolan had gotten the first decent night's sleep he'd had since coming to Peru.

Scarberry, however, had gone to celebrate his engagement to Anita. With Anita. And he didn't look as if he'd slept a wink.

Somewhere behind them, in the third car, one of Alvarez's bodyguards was driving his partners and boss. Against all protests from his bodyguards, Alvarez had insisted on coming. The young man was ready to step into his father's shoes, and he wanted in on the action. Bolan had hesitated at first, then consented. If he could make use of a former Mafia hit man, he supposed he could utilize the efforts of someone who sold a few illegal pre-Columbian artifacts. Rivas couldn't afford to kill Bolan and Kinelli before he got his hands on the chemicals. But he was likely to try to pull something, and having the extra guns of Alvarez and his men along couldn't hurt. Their presence might even stop a potential outbreak of violence—something the Executioner was all in favor of. While Rivas couldn't afford to kill him yet, neither could he afford to kill Rivas. Not if he wanted the NFP man to lead him to Relámpago.

Bolan saw the market ahead and slowed. Yes, he thought, there was a definite order in which each step had to be taken during the rest of this mission, and to take it out of that order could prove disastrous, not only to him but to the people of two nations. He was about to meet Kenji Rivas. Bolan would have to continue the illusion he had created that he and the other men were Americans in the employ of Lee Kinelli so Rivas could lead them to Relámpago. It simply wouldn't work the other way around. The key to it all was the blood oath between Relámpago and Rivas. Rivas, according to Solari's speculation, had seen the oath as merely a manipulative tool. But Relámpago's misguided sense of responsibility to his cause meant that if Rivas died first, the Quechua would fight on, probably turning Rivas into a martyr. He would double his efforts to instigate the war between Ecuador and Peru as some perverse memorial to the man he had considered his brother.

A brother who, even now, was plotting his death.

A space in the dirt outside the Inca Market was open and

Bolan pulled in, parking parallel to the open front of the mall-like building. He watched the other two cars pass and find spots farther down the block, then turned to Kinelli beside him. "You ready, Reverend?" he asked.

Kinelli nodded, his face blank. Since making his decision, he seemed to have had no further qualms about what he was doing. He had done an expert job on the phone to Rivas, and, all in all, seemed to have reverted to the calm, calculating man he had to have been when he'd been associated with organized crime in the States. Bolan just hoped that his newfound morality hadn't been left behind with his pacifism. Just in case, he said, "Reverend, I don't expect any trouble here. At least no shooting—that wouldn't be good for either us or Rivas." He watched the other man's face. There was no change. "As soon as Rivas has seen you, and you legitimized our position, you're free to go."

Kinelli nodded. "I appreciate your concern," he said. "But there are two things I've got to make clear. First, I don't know if you believe in prayer or not, Belasko, but I do. And I've come to the conclusion that I'm doing the right thing by helping you. Why? God told me so. Simple as that. But He didn't tell me to get off the boat halfway across the river. I'll be with you until this is over, you kick me out, or I get killed."

Bolan nodded. "What's the second thing?"

The deadpan expression on Kinelli's face finally broke. A hard smile curled his lips. "It was going to be that you quit calling me 'Reverend' until this is over. But I just changed my mind. I'm convinced I'm doing God's work. It's just a different kind of ministry."

The soldier nodded, then turned and rested one arm over the back seat where Solari sat. "Solari," he said, "you've cooperated well so far. Almost too well. It makes me wonder if you're up to something. Are you?"

"No, no," the man in the back seat said quickly. "I am just wanting to get out of this alive."

"Let's hope so," Bolan said. "Because the first hint I get of you trying to double-cross us, I'll shoot you." For emphasis, he pulled the Desert Eagle out of his holster and held it above the seat for a second. "And this will put a much bigger hole in you than the revolver Scarberry had on you earlier."

Solari's dark brown skin turned a sickly gray.

"One other thing," Bolan said. "If you get out of my sight for any reason, you better get that bug in your pocket switched on fast. If it isn't working, for even a second, I'll kill you."

Solari looked even sicker. "I have already promised to turn it on and keep it on." He barely breathed. "But what if the battery runs out of power?"

"Then so do you."

Bolan turned back to Kinelli. In addition to the Detective Special in his pocket, Bolan had given him the 9 mm SIG-Sauer 9 mm he had taken from the street vendor at Ari's. The minister had it hidden beneath his T-shirt.

"Ready?" Bolan asked.

"Let's do it," Kinelli said.

The three men got out of the car in time to see Scarberry enter the marketplace. Twenty feet behind him was Loriega, and farther back, Alvarez had talked all of his bodyguards, except Carlos, into fanning out so it wouldn't appear they were together. Carlos was sticking to his young boss like glue. But it wouldn't matter. One set of two hard-looking men together should draw no undue attention.

The Inca Market was a filled with shops and stalls that dispensed everything from top quality jewelry to inexpensive native crafts. Bolan let Kinelli lead the way with Solari right behind him. The Executioner kept an eye on the man in the middle as he brought up the rear.

Solari was another aspect of the final game plan that could be difficult. While Bolan played Rivas, he would have to keep a close eye on Solari. It would be better if the traitorous NFP man was never allowed to speak to his leader alone. But that was an impractical idea and one the Executioner knew he could never in reality pull off. Solari was Rivas's man. It would only be natural that they might want to confer privately after all that had happened, and Bolan could come up with no reasonable argument to use against such a conference. The Executioner's warning just now had not been given lightly. He had a bad feeling about the man.

Luckily, Tony Loriega had brought a transmitter and receiver in his briefcase. So Bolan had dropped the transmitter into Solari's pocket and had the receiver in his. It was small—like a hearing aid—and he could surreptitiously stick it in his ear at a moment's notice.

Kinelli led them into a large shop just to the left of the entryway and the three men began looking at the gold, silver and copper jewelry in the glass cases along one wall. Kinelli was good. He even asked the attendant to see a thick silver and gold Inca warrior's bracelet. Bolan glanced at his watch. It was still a few minutes until three o'clock. And he suspected Rivas would watch them for a while before making contact, anyway.

The trio left the shop and moved on through the mall, occasionally seeing Scarberry, Loriega and the Alvarez troop as they went. Bolan stopped Solari in front of a leather craft shop, where they began looking at briefcases and other goods. The other thing Bolan couldn't forget was the leak. His cover had been compromised even before he got to Peru, which meant the leak had to come from Washington. He had picked up an E-mail from Brognola right before they left Iquitos informing him that they had an agent from the Washington office in custody. And it looked as if Sergeant Lopez had been the man who had kept hiring people to kill him in Iquitos. Alvarez thought so too, and Bolan suspected the young man's intelligence network was efficient. And the attempts on his life seemed to have stopped since Lopez's death in the jungle. But that only meant they had found the two ends of the leak—not the middle.

The Executioner moved his party on through the mall, stopping at various shops and stalls. He kept a wary eye out for anyone who might glance his way a little too long but saw no such signs. Americans were hardly abnormal here. It was close to the airport, and therefore a common shopping place for gifts and souvenirs before flying home. Moving to the rear of the marketplace, they entered a store with rack after rack of sweaters and other angora products from Peru's Andes region. Bolan passed a table filled with stuffed llamas and other animals, then began pretending to be interested in the sweaters and jackets. Gradually, they worked their way through the store to the stone walls at the rear.

The soldier was getting ready to round the rack of sweaters at the back of the store when he felt the gun barrel jab into his ribs from behind. "Don't move," a voice whispered in Spanish. On the other side of the rack, the Executioner could see that a man was standing right behind Lee Kinelli in a similar position. Solari had been standing next to the Executioner, and Bolan now heard the man let out a long sigh of relief.

The soldier froze where he was. He had expected something like this. "Okay, I'm not moving," the Executioner whispered back. "You Rivas?"

There was a long silence, then the voice said, "Yes."

Bolan nodded, then said, "Then I guess you know if you kill me you'll never find what you're looking for."

"Perhaps I will just take you out of here at gunpoint and force you to take me to the chemicals," the voice said. But even the man's tone didn't sound convinced.

No, Bolan thought. This was all for show. Rivas had ordered him and Kinelli to bring Solari and no one else. But he was far too smart to think they'd have obeyed that order. It was too easy to have other men stationed in the market, and he'd know that.

A half dozen more NFP men appeared at the front of the store, walking their way. Bolan saw one of them hand money to the shopkeeper and her two employees. The three women glanced nervously toward the back, then hurriedly left the store, closing the door behind them. One of the men turned the sign around so that the Spanish word for open now faced inward. One man stayed by the door while the rest drew guns as they walked toward Bolan, Kinelli, Solari and the two men holding them at gunpoint. A moment later, they were surrounded by the new men.

The Executioner got his first sight of Kenji Rivas as the man moved out and around to his front. He was tall for either a Peruvian or Japanese—almost six feet. He had the straight black hair of both his mother and father, but it was clipped short. Rivas wore a lightweight sport coat of expensive cotton and coordinated slacks. He might not look like the stereotype South American cocaine dealer, but he favored that image more than the revolutionary he was masquerading as. In his hand, he held an Argentine-made Government Model .45-caliber pistol.

Before he could speak again, the front door opened and Tony Loriega walked in, looking around as if he were lost. "Hey, you guys open?" he asked.

"No," the man at the front door said. "Get out."

"But I need a sweater for my mother," Loriega said. He had held the door half open behind him, but now he swung it the rest of the way back. His other hand shot forward in a short punch to the NFP man's chin. The DEA agent's fist hit the button, and the man dropped to the ground and Scarberry, Alvarez and his bodyguards all rushed in, guns drawn. Loriega's own hand now held a Glock 21. Quickly, the men who had covered Bolan and Kinelli spread out across the room and took up positions with their weapons trained toward the back of the store.

Rivas and all the other NFP men had turned their weapons toward the door when it opened, but none had fired. Obviously, Rivas had ordered them not to in the event something like this happening. Now, every man in the room found himself both aiming a gun and looking into one.

"Back home we'd call this a Mexican standoff," Tony Loriega said. "Down here, I suppose it's Peruvian."

Rivas smiled. "You can't blame a man for trying," he said.

"There was always the chance that you would be stupid enough to follow my order to come alone."

"I suppose so," Bolan said. "Now, why doesn't everybody put up their toys? Then we can go somewhere and talk about getting you what you want."

Rivas shoved his pistol into his belt and let his coattail cover it. The rest of his men followed his lead. "A fine idea," he said. "Shall we adjourn to the parking lot? We can talk this over in my car."

Bolan nodded. "It shouldn't be hard to work out. You get us the money, and we get you your little steel cans."

"You are forgetting something," Rivas said. "First, you must prove to me that you are not from the police or military."

"Oh, yeah," Bolan said as they all started to the front door. "Somebody you wanted killed, wasn't it?"

9

Bolan pressed the tiny radio receiver in his ear and crossed his legs. He was in the last row of seats in the rear of the plane, his eyes looking straight ahead. Down the aisle, he could see Jack Grimaldi behind the controls. Scattered throughout the passenger area were Scarberry, Loriega, Kinelli, Alvarez and his men. But Bolan's attention was glued to the instrument in his ear as he did his best to pick up the impossible. Once in a while, the plane flown by Grimaldi got into range of the other aircraft and he could hear Solari's and Rivas's voices. But most of the time there was simply too much distance and too much other interference. Grimaldi was sticking as close to them as possible, but even his superb air gymnastics weren't good enough.

The transmitter and receiver Loriega had provided were state-of-the-art. But they hadn't been designed to work between two airborne aircraft, and the Executioner had not been able to hear even half of what had been said between Solari and Rivas in the other plane.

Bolan set his jaw. He had threatened to kill Solari if the receiver didn't work, but he could hardly blame the man for this new development. As they so often did in clandestine missions, unforeseen events had just happened. The plane flew on through the air as Bolan strained to pick up any words he could.

The situation had not taken long to resolve once Bolan and Rivas had entered the Executioner's rental car in the market's parking lot. In order to prove that they weren't government agents setting Rivas up for a fall, the former Colombian cocaine dealer demanded that they kill a man. The plan involved flying with him to Quito, Ecuador, where the target was located. The man Rivas wanted killed, of course, was Alejandro Carillo. He went by the nickname Relámpago.

The receiver in Bolan's ear buzzed momentarily and he heard voices. But he couldn't make out any of the words. He wondered how much Solari knew about electronic surveillance equipment. The man might think the Executioner was picking up every word. If that was the case, he would keep his mouth shut. But Solari had another reason to keep Rivas in the dark if he was smart. The NFP leader wasn't likely to look kindly on a subordinate who had cooperated with the enemy. Solari's reward for tipping off Rivas might well be death.

Okay, Bolan thought as he ripped the receiver from his ear and dropped it into his pocket. He could play "what if" like this all day and not get anywhere. The bottom line was that there had been more than ample opportunity for Solari to give them up if he was going to. He either had, or he hadn't, and there was no way to know at this point. The Executioner would simply have to let things unfold and play it by ear.

Bolan stared at the back of the seat in front of him, reviewing the other aspects of this final leg of the mission in his mind. Rivas had to accompany them to Quito to set up Relámpago for the kill. The problem had come when the NFP man insisted on taking several of his own men with him. It wasn't a demand that was out of place under the circumstances. Bolan had men with him, and it was only logical that Rivas should have protection along, too. But when he combined Rivas's men with Bolan's crew, there were simply too many to fit into the craft Jack Grimaldi was flying or the plane the NFP had at their disposal. So both planes had been called into service, and Rivas had wanted Solari with him. The Executioner had come up with no good argument against this that wouldn't have made Rivas suspicious. He had the chemicals that Rivas wanted, and he had no reason to keep Solari with him.

A few rows up, Bolan saw Scarberry unbuckle his seat belt. The former DEA man walked forward and conversed with Grimaldi for a few seconds, then turned and went to the back of the plane. "Any luck?" he asked, pointing at Bolan's ear.

Bolan shook his head. "No," he said. "I picked up some of it but not much. The voices I did hear weren't excited, and there was no other indication that Solari had sold us out. But that doesn't mean anything."

Scarberry nodded and dropped into the seat next to the Executioner. "What were they talking about when you heard them?"

"Soccer." Bolan nodded toward Grimaldi. "Where are we now?"

"According to your pilot, about ten miles from the border."

"We under radar?"

Scarberry shivered his shoulders and blew air through his lips, making them flutter. "So close to the ground I wanted to piss just looking out the window."

"Jack still in touch with Rivas's pilot?"

Scarberry nodded. "Yeah, they talk back and forth now and then. Their pilot's not as good as yours, but he's good. Flying low and knows the way." The former DEA man's eyes were bloodshot and now he closed them.

"How's everybody feeling?" the soldier asked. He really meant Scarberry. The man looked exhausted.

But Scarberry wasn't so tired that he didn't pick up on Bolan's intent. "I'm okay," he said. "Just having a little sinking spell. The others, Alvarez and his men, Kinelli, they're all fine. Slept well. And Loriega is young—like he loves to keep reminding me." He grinned weakly, and said, "I'll be okay. I know what you're thinking, but I did get a few winks in last night."

"Grab a few more while you still can," he said. "If all goes well, we'll take out Relámpago and then hit Rivas before he knows what's happened. By tomorrow it'll all be history and you'll be back with Anita. You two can start picking out towels and place settings."

"Oh, shit," Scarberry scowled. "I forgot about all that crap." He settled back into his seat and closed his eyes.

Bolan quietly stepped over the man and moved down the aisle to the front of the craft. They were still flying low to the ground. "How much farther, Jack?" he said.

"We crossed the border maybe five minutes ago," the pilot said.

"Any problems?"

Grimaldi shook his head. "Nah, we were maybe fifty miles away from the Cordillera where the NATO troops are," he said. "I don't think anybody even saw us. If they did, they'll chalk it up to just another couple of drug planes coming home."

"Let me know five minutes before we land."

"You got it, big guy."

Bolan turned to leave but Grimaldi shot out a hand, stopping him. The Executioner turned back.

"This guy Kinelli," the pilot began.

"Yeah?"

"I never ran into him back in my old days flying for the bad guys. But I remember the name. Heavy dude."

Bolan nodded. "So I've heard. Something else on your mind about him?"

Grimaldi shrugged. "Just thought I'd tell you I've been talking to him. For what it's worth, I think he's for real. The change of heart, all that."

"Well," Bolan said, "if he's not sincere about it he's fooled me, too." He returned to his seat.

When Grimaldi sent word back with Loriega that they were nearing Quito, Bolan got up and stood in the aisle. Getting the men's attention, he said, "According to what Rivas told me, we'll be coming down on a short landing strip outside the city. He's arranged for Relámpago to send vehicles to pick us up. If Relámpago is with them, we kill him and all his men right there." He paused a moment, then added, "Rivas knows all that. What he doesn't know is that just as soon as that's over, we kill him and his men, too."

The Executioner's eyes fell on one of Alvarez's bodyguards. The man's face had gone pale. "If that bothers anybody," Bolan went on, "keep in mind that these men are responsible for the murders of several dozen law students a few days ago. Keep in mind that they've bombed hundreds of innocent men, women and children. And don't forget they're trying to get chemical weapons so they can take out many, many more." He cleared his throat. "These animals can call themselves whatever they want. They can hide behind whatever cause they want to. But the bottom line is that they are terrorists, gentlemen. Mass murderers. And if we don't stop them now, they'll murder more until someone does kill them."

Bolan waited a moment, then continued. "You've got your personal arms, and I'm going to pass out long guns in a minute." He took a breath. "Any questions?"

Alvarez spoke up. "Suppose Relámpago is not with the men who pick us up?"

"Then we play it by ear," Bolan said. "We get in the car and go with them until we finally hook up with the man. I was in the car with Rivas when he called Relámpago and told him when and where to meet us. The story is that we've been hired to help step up the number of strikes and bring on the war."

Alvarez wasn't finished. "How do we know Solari didn't tell Rivas everything while they were on the other plane?"

"We don't," Bolan said. "So everything may have changed since we got on board."

Loriega had turned to kneel in his seat, facing the Executioner. "Even if he's burned us," the DEA agent said, "Rivas still wants Relámpago dead. My guess is he's going to pretend he doesn't know. At least until we kill the man. And he still wants the chemicals. He may still think he can work an angle on that, too."

"That's possible," the Executioner said. "But he also might just decide to cut his losses on the chemicals. Sooner or later, he's going to get the war started anyway and accomplish his goal even without them. The governments will do it for him. So he may decide to keep it simple." Bolan reached up and rubbed his chin, thinking. "They're ahead of us, so they'll be landing first. That means they can be out of their plane before we hit the ground. So it's also possible that the second we step off this plane, Rivas and his men will open fire on us. He can always go back to his original plan of killing Relámpago later."

A solemn look came over the faces in the aircraft as that possibility sank in.

Bolan walked back to the lockers at the rear of the plane and opened them, letting the men arm themselves with rifles, machine guns and ammo. As they did, he thought about the situation. He was, primarily and at heart, a soldier. But he had done his fair share of undercover work over the years, and one thing he had learned was that much of the time the clandestine operative moved in this gray area of not knowing whether his cover was still holding up or not. It was different than what the uniformed cop or military man faced. When they saw bad guys with guns, they started shooting. But now, he and the other men were about to get off this plane and face killers who would be every bit as well armed as they. And they wouldn't know whether to fire until the other side started it. This put them as quite a disadvantage, to say the least.

"Striker!" Grimaldi's voice came back from the front of the plane.

Bolan walked forward. Through the windshield he could see the tall snowcapped volcano Mount Pichincha set amid the other peaks of the Andes. "Yeah, Jack?"

Grimaldi was frowning. "The other pilot just radioed me," he said. "Told me he'd lead me in, but that I was to land first."

Bolan frowned. "Did he say why?"

"Something about their landing gear. I couldn't make it all out. Lots of interference."

The Executioner looked back out though the glass. In the distance he could see the green-terraced slopes leading down from the mountains to Quitos. In the city below, the sun glistened off what looked like hundreds of church domes, spires and the blood-red rooftops of the houses and buildings. "Try him again, Jack," Bolan said. "That doesn't make any sense."

The pilot did. But again, the only the words which came back completely clear were the instructions that they should land first.

"Something's not right," Bolan said. "That interference could be artificially induced. What are the odds that both times it's his excuse, not our instructions, that gets covered?"

"Not high," Grimaldi said. "What to you want me to do?"

"Keep following him for now," Bolan said. "I don't see that we have any other choice."

Grimaldi followed the other plane over the city. Again, there was no radio traffic to indicate that air traffic controllers were paying a bit of attention. The two planes banked sharply, then flew up and over Panecillo Hill, where the ancient Incas had once worshiped their sun god. They flew on until finally, in another valley higher in the mountains, the Executioner saw the landing strip. It looked like a perfect site for drug runners and others bent on landing clandestinely. Perhaps a quarter mile off the major road he had seen winding through the mountains, it was totally secluded from view except from the air.

Bolan stared down at the road. Four vehicles were headed in the general direction of the landing strip and appeared to be in convoy. It had to be Relámpago, or at least his men, on their way to what they thought was a simple task of picking up hired mercenaries to assist them in creating havoc throughout Ecuador.

Bolan hurried back to where the other men now sat with their rifles across their laps as Grimaldi made his final descent toward the ground. "They've got us landing first," he said.

Alvarez smiled. "Then I don't think they plan to ambush us as we get off the plane."

"No. But that doesn't mean Rivas doesn't have something else in mind," Bolan said. "It stinks to high heaven. I want everybody on their feet. The second we touch ground, open the exits. As soon as the plane is slow enough to keep from killing yourselves, jump."

ALEJANDRO "RELÁMPAGO" Carillo had devoted his life to his Quechua people. Deep in his heart, he knew many of the things he had done were questionable. No, not questionable. They were reprehensible. But long ago he had perfected the skill of pushing such uncomfortable thoughts from his mind. The trick was to tell himself over and over that the deaths of innocents was often unavoidable. Then he had to dehumanize those who fell in his wake as he fought for the Quechua's freedom. A man in his position could not afford to look down at a female arm blown from the rest of its body by one of his bombs. He might notice that the bloody hand wore a wedding ring, and if he did he would have to acknowledge the fact that the severed arm had once been part of a wife. He could not afford to look too long at the lifeless form of a man sprawled on the sidewalk, put there by the bullets from his machine gun. To do so would conjure up thoughts that the corpse might have been married to the arm he had just seen. That would personalize the deaths and make them real.

And he never looked a child in the eye, living or dead.

But such thoughts were not bothering Relámpago as he coaxed the Ford Bronco up the steep mountain highway. Rivas had called him several hours ago to told him to be at the landing strip to pick up mercenaries who would assist them until the war started. But then, only a half hour ago, he had received a second emergency call. He didn't know exactly what had happened but, somehow, the mercs had tricked Rivas. They were not who they had claimed to be.

Relámpago knew only that two planes were coming in, and the first one to land would be carrying the mercs. He was to kill them as soon as he saw them. Rivas would be on the second airplane. He and his men would land and join in the fight, and

Rivas would explain it all to Relámpago as soon as it was over.

Now, as he chugged up the mountain road at nine thousand feet above sea level, he wondered what kind of trick these men had played. What had their story been? What had made Rivas agree to hire them? Did they, perhaps, have the chemical weaponry Rivas's men were supposed to retrieve near Iquitos? The thought made Relámpago shudder. He didn't like such weapons. They killed indiscriminately.

The Quechua held the accelerator closer to the floorboard. Next to him sat Freire. In the back seat was Renaldo. Three more cars followed them, empty except for the drivers. They had left most of the men behind in order to have room to transport the newcomers. Now that they were to kill them, he wished the others were along.

Relámpago breathed deeply as he turned off the asphalt roadway onto hard-packed dirt that led to the landing strip. It had been used for years by drug runners, some of whom had been friends of his. Some were Quechua, who had used the money they made selling cocaine to the decadent Americans to further the cause. Of course many had given in to the temptation of the luxury that could come with the same money, and had forgotten their people. Some of those he had killed. The rest who had forsaken the cause would die when he and Rivas took over the two governments.

The Lighting Bolt leader needed both hands to steer the Ford Bronco as it bumped its way over the pitted road. He smiled inwardly, thinking of helping his NFP friend. He had needed a man such as Kenji Rivas for some time. Rivas thought on a much bigger scale than he did. By himself, he knew he would never rise above being a small-time jungle pest to the Ecuadoran government or the American oil companies who had stolen the Quechua land. But together, he knew they could indeed take over both Ecuador and Peru and return the land to the people.

Ahead, Relámpago saw the open area where the grass and weeds had been forced down by the tires of countless airplanes. Foothills ringed the valley, and on every side of the landing strip the vegetation grew up through the rocks and boulders. Beyond the valley, in the sky, he could see two planes flying toward him, just above the mountains. As he watched, the plane in the lead rose slightly and circled back the way it had come. The other plane came forward, preparing to drop to the landing strip.

Relámpago pulled the Bronco to a halt at the side of the landing strip. He grabbed his Calico M-950 and started to get out of the vehicle. He was stopped when the cellular phone on the seat next to him rang. "Hello," he said into the instrument.

Rivas's voice was calm as he spoke. "I have called to wish you luck, my brother. We will land as soon as possible and assist you."

"Who are these men?" Relámpago asked. "How did they trick you?"

"They are government spies," Rivas said. "But there is no time to explain more now. Kill them, my Quechua brother! And should I die, remember our oath and take care of my men."

"Do they know that I know who they are?" the Lightning Bolt leader asked. "Do they expect an attack?"

"No. Let them get out of the plane and assemble before you begin to fire."

For a brief moment, Relámpago wondered why Rivas didn't land his plane first so they could all ambush the men as they got off the plane. But he pushed the thought from his mind as he did all uncomfortable ideas. There was a reason—there had to be. Rivas didn't have time to explain now, but he would when this battle was over. His chest swelled with pride. "I will do it," he said into the phone. "As you would for me." He hung up and dropped the phone back on the seat.

The Lightning Bolt leader checked the Calico's bolt to make sure a round was chambered, and watched the plane rushing toward him as it neared the ground. Freire and Renaldo knew of the change in plans. They had been in the car with him when Rivas called earlier. But the drivers of the other vehicles still thought they were picking up allies. "Freire," Relámpago said. "Come with me." He opened the door. "Renaldo. Go tell the drivers of the other cars to arm themselves and join us. As soon as these men get off the plane, we kill them."

Renaldo left to inform the other men, and Relámpago and Freire took up positions behind the Bronco. The other men soon joined them. All had rifles.

He waited, watching, as the plane's tires hit the ground and it began to slow. He was surprised when he saw the first man jump from the still-moving craft. He was even more surprised when the second hit the ground and the plane continued to roll toward him.

"AS SOON AS I hit the ground," Bolan shouted into Jack Grimaldi's ear, "take off again."

Grimaldi nodded. He didn't need to be told why. If the plane was disabled by gunfire, they'd be stranded. Although he had proved many times in the past that he could hold his own in a gunfight, his first and foremost responsibility was the plane.

The Executioner waited until Scarberry had jumped from the rolling plane before diving through the door himself. He hit the ground on his shoulder, hearing a long blast of 9 mm fire as he rolled. The gun firing the blast was easy to identify—Calico M-950. Which meant the gunner had at least a 50-round hexagonal drum mounted on top of the piece, and more likely one hundred rounds at his disposal. Bolan filed the information in his brain in case it was needed.

Rolling to a stop on one knee, the Executioner raised the Heckler & Koch MP-5. To the side of the runway, perhaps fifty yards away, he saw a Ford Bronco parked in front of three other vehicles. He couldn't be sure, but it looked as if six men were scattered behind the cars, using them for cover. Actually, he thought, as he pressed the trigger back on the MP-5, they had the Lightning Bolt terrorists outnumbered. He had Kinelli, Scarberry, Loriega, Alvarez and the bodyguards. But there was one major difference which outweighed the man-to-man ratio.

The men that were firing at them had cover, while Bolan and

the others were in the wide-open landing strip, like ducks in a shooting gallery.

The Executioner's first burst of fire shattered the Bronco's windshield, sending sharp shards of glass sparkling up into the air. Behind him, scattered up and down the strip where they had exited the plane, the other men opened up and more rounds peppered the vehicles. But Bolan saw no one fall behind the cars and return fire forced him to drop to the ground once more and roll. He heard a scream behind him but he had no time to look back and see which of his team had been hit.

Dust and dirt blew around Bolan's face as he came to a halt once more, this time in the prone position. He had to rise slightly to allow for the long 30-round magazine extending beneath the subgun, and rounds from an AK-47 zipped past his face as he did. But he had sighted on the head of the man who had picked him as a target, and his aim was more true than that of his opponent. A quick burst of the 60-grain RBCD rounds burst from the Executioner's MP-5, each one leaving the barrel at 2000 feet per second. At least one of the total fragmenting rounds caught the corner of the shooter's head, just above the eye socket. An explosion of crimson burst from his skull, and he fell out and away from cover.

More rounds flew toward Bolan as he rolled again. He hit on his shoulder and attempted to come around prone once more but his knee struck a rock, spun him and he found himself seated, facing the assault. For a moment he thought he'd been hit by one of the big 7.62 mm rifle rounds as needles of pain shot through his leg. Then he saw the rock to his side.

Throwing the H&K's collapsible stock against his shoulder once more, he peppered the grille of a Chevy Blazer just behind the Bronco. A rainbow of colors began to drop from under the hood as oil and other automotive fluids dripped from the exploded engine parts. In his peripheral vision, Bolan saw another man fall from behind the Bronco. One of this own men, behind him, had scored a hit. But at almost the same time, he heard another groan of pain come from his rear, and knew it had been a trade. Another of his people was down.

Diving forward under a new barrage of bullets aimed his way, the Executioner went prone again. Beneath the Blazer, he could see two pairs of boots. Holding the submachine gun sideways, he carpeted the ground between the rocky soil and bottom of the car with a steady stream of the 9 mm rounds. Shrieks of both surprise and alarm came from behind the Blazer as the supersonic rounds took the men in the feet and ankles. One of the men dropped his AK-47 and hopped to the side of the car. The other fell straight down behind the vehicle. Bolan could see him on his side, clutching both feet with his hands.

The Executioner sent another burst of fire beneath the vehicle, and this time his rounds found more vital targets. The familiar red mist clouded the area beneath the vehicle. He turned the MP-5 toward the gunman hopping at the side, but the man was already dancing in death from rounds fired from behind the Executioner.

Directly above him, Bolan heard the engine of the other plane. He looked up to see it flying slowly overhead. Rivas. The man was watching the action below.

Bolan's jaw tightened as he continued to fire, roll, fire and roll. Twice, he dropped the empty magazines from the H&K and inserted full ones. It was clear now what had happened. Solari had told his boss that Bolan and the other men were not what they appeared to be. So Rivas had made a second call to Relámpago from the plane, changing the "pick up" order to instructions to assassinate. It was a situation that had no downside for Rivas—either Bolan or Relámpago would be dead before the gunfire ceased. If he was lucky, he might get rid of them both. Yes, Rivas had decided to just cut his losses. He would abandon the idea of seizing the chemical weapons himself and just continue the terrorist strikes he had already started.

The war would start on its own and then the governments of Peru and Ecuador would use the chemicals for him.

Bolan fired a burst into the air, knowing even as he did there was little chance of hitting the plane. He had no idea what story the NFP leader had used on Relámpago to cover himself, but he had no doubt it had been a great one. Kenji Rivas had proved nothing in his life so much as the fact that he could lie, and lie well.

Another scream behind him told the Executioner that yet another of his men was down. He rolled again, falling prone once more as yet another burst of fire came his way. But the rounds from the Lightning Bolts behind the vehicles had slowed as their manpower steadily decreased. If he had counted correctly, four of the six men he'd seen were dead. But the two who remained were trying to make up the difference.

Another two rounds flew from the MP-5, then the bolt locked back on an empty weapon. The Executioner rolled again, switching magazines and releasing the bolt to chamber the first round. He scanned the ground beneath the cars for more feet, but the two men who remained had seen what happened to the other pair. They were keeping their boots, and well as the rest of their bodies, out of sight.

Movement to his side caused the Executioner to glance that way, and he saw Scarberry crawling forward. The former DEA man's face was coated in sweat and dirt, and his shirt had been ripped along the side. A trickle of red followed him on the ground as he made his way toward Bolan.

"You hit?" the Executioner yelled over the gunfire.

Scarberry shook his head. "A scratch!" he shouted back. "Barely broke the skin. Loriega took one in the shoulder. He's still up, though. But two of Alvarez's men—history."

Bolan fired another burst toward the Bronco, which he knew provided cover for one of the two remaining men. The odds had shifted now that so many of their comrades bit the dust, and the Executioner and his party had them pinned down.

Scarberry had stuck with his Remington 12-gauge but was firing slugs as he pumped the weapon. Bolan had seen several of the huge single holes appear in the vehicles. They were effective, and the Executioner guessed that they had been responsible for at least one of the dead men he hadn't killed himself. But the shotgun wasn't what he wanted in Scarberry's hands now. Not for what he had planned.

Rolling to a position next to the former DEA man, the Executioner fired another burst of rounds to keep the men behind the vehicles down. "You know how to fire this MP-5?" he asked Scarberry.

"I know *how* to shoot them," Scarberry said as he sent another deer slug into the Blazer. "I just don't *like* shooting the damn things."

Bolan jerked the sling off his shoulder and shoved the weapon into the man's hand. "Life's full of things we don't want to," he said. "Cover me." He dropped two more 30-round mags onto the ground next to Scarberry.

The Executioner rolled again, but this time he kept rolling until he had reached the edge of the landing strip. The cover and concealment was not what he'd have liked. But it was better than the open-air shooting gallery of the landing strip. At least some vegetation and a rock formation here and there would break up his path as he made his way toward the Bronco.

Rising to his knees, Bolan drew the Beretta with one hand, the Desert Eagle with the other. Slowly, as the gunfire continued, he made his way forward, moving from one meager refuge to the next. But the men behind the Bronco had seen him move, and some of their fire now turned his way. He was forced to move slowly, hitting the ground each time rounds ricocheted off the rocks and tore the leaves from the vines around him.

From this new angle, the Executioner could see the battlefield that had been behind him before. As Scarberry had said, two of Alvarez's bodyguards lay dead on the landing strip. Loriega was kneeling, still firing with a pistol but his other arm hung lifelessly at his side. Kinelli had taken an M-16 from the plane, and he was sending short, controlled bursts of fire into the cars. The minister appeared unhurt, as did Alvarez and his other two men.

As Bolan dodged bullets on his way from boulder to boulder, first on his knees, then his belly, he heard Kinelli switch to full-auto. A steady stream of 5.56 mm rounds shot from the rifle and into the body of the car. At the same time, Scarberry continued a steady assault with the MP-5 and Alvarez and his men—all toting more M-16s—blasted away, as well. By now, the vehicle had been shot hundreds of times, and large holes had opened up in the doors, frame and everything not made of solid steel.

Bolan heard a moan escape the lips of one of the men behind the Bronco. A second later, a short stocky man with long black hair took a step back from the vehicle. He dropped his AK-47 to his side, holding it with one hand as his other tried to pry a jagged piece of the car body from his stomach.

The Executioner was twenty yards away. As the man continued to claw at the shrapnel in his belly, Bolan lifted the Beretta in his left hand and dropped the sights on the man's head. A quiet subsonic 9 mm slug hissed from the barrel, and the terrorist dropped to the ground.

The round had been quiet, but it hadn't gone unnoticed. The other man behind the Bronco suddenly stopped firing. His head shot up over the back of the vehicle, and Bolan saw the sharp Indian features covered in dark sun-dried skin. This man, too, had long black hair. But it was tied in place with a black headband.

Before Bolan could fire, the man dropped out of sight. But he didn't stay hidden long.

A loud, eerie scream came from the back of the Bronco. Then, stepping out from behind the car, the tall Indian charged the Executioner. Bolan watched from behind the rock where he was kneeling. In the man's hand he saw the Calico he had heard since he'd exited the plane.

Wild 9 mm rounds roared from the weapon as the man sprinted toward him. Bolan saw that he was tall and lean and wore faded blue jeans and a printed Andes shirt. His face was contorted in hatred and anger as he ran forward, holding the Calico's trigger back in a continuous spray of bullets. He was screaming something, over and over, but the endless explosions drowned out his words.

The Executioner rose to his feet as the wild rounds blew past him. He knew who this man was. When Relámpago was still ten yards away, Bolan raised the Desert Eagle and took aim. With the Lightning Bolt leader still screaming his incoherent chant, the Executioner pressed the trigger. The Eagle roared, sending a 240-grain .44 Magnum hollowpoint round dead center into the terrorist's chest.

Relámpago's finger fell back off the trigger as he stumbled forward. The Calico hit the ground and clattered across the rocks. His eyes opened wide as he dropped to his knees. Then his momentum threw him toward Bolan. The tall Quechua hit the ground on his side at Bolan's feet.

His lips were still moving, reciting the chant he had screamed since his kamikaze attack had first begun. But now, even though his words had been reduced to a whisper, the Executioner could make them out.

"For...my...people..." came out of Relámpago's mouth along with a froth of blood.

Bolan aimed the barrel of the Desert Eagle down at the man's ear. "For *all* people," he said and pulled the trigger again.

"Belasko!" Scarberry yelled from the landing strip.

Bolan turned toward the former DEA agent and saw him staring skyward. Following his gaze, the Executioner saw Rivas's plane flying slowly overhead again. But now, something was falling through the air below it. As the object came closer, it took human shape and shrieks of terror could be heard. Finally, it was close enough that Bolan could see that it was Solari.

By the time the Executioner got to the spot where Solari hit the ground fifty yards away, the man was no longer recognizable.

Scarberry, Kinelli, Alvarez and two of his men, and a wounded-but-walking Tony Loriega joined Bolan around the body. Slightly extended from the right front pocket of Solari's pants, barely visible through the blood that covered much of the mangled corpse, the Executioner could see the corner of a white piece of paper.

10

The room at the El Dorado was waiting for them when they returned to Iquitos. So was another note that the desk clerk handed them in a white envelope. *Go up to the room and wait for my call,* it read. It wasn't signed.

Bolan led Scarberry and Kinelli to the elevator. Loriega had gone from the airport to the hospital. They had patched up his shoulder wound well enough to get him back to Peru. He'd be okay, and Bolan didn't think any of the tendons or vital nerve endings had been seriously damaged. But he needed better medical care than they could provide.

Alvarez and his surviving bodyguards had also parted ways with the others right after Grimaldi had landed. Two of their own were dead, and arrangements for their burials had to be made.

As they rode the elevator up to the third floor, Bolan wondered exactly what Rivas had up his sleeve. Solari had told him that the Executioner and the other men were not what they appeared to be. And, as Bolan had suspected might happen, Solari had paid a heavy price for openness. Evidently Rivas didn't think his current honesty made up for the past sins of cooperating with the enemy. In any case, Rivas knew who they were. Bolan was not some American mercenary or gangster in Kinelli's employee.

Rivas knew Bolan represented the good guys in one way or another, and that meant the deal on the chemical weapons was off.

So why did Rivas still want to contact him at the El Dorado? What made the NFP leader think the Executioner was going to do anything but kill him if they met again? It didn't make sense. The smartest thing Rivas could do was stay as far away from him as possible. Further contact with the Executioner was not only useless, it was dangerous.

The elevator stopped and the doors rolled back. Bolan led the other men into the hallway. No, Rivas had something else in mind. Something Bolan couldn't have thought of. The note Solari had as he fell though the sky instructed the Executioner to go directly back to the El Dorado hotel in Iquitos. Rivas was behaving as if the deal for the chemicals was still on.

Bolan stuck the key in the door, twisted the knob and opened it. The phone began ringing the moment he stepped through the door. Which meant someone—maybe Rivas himself—was watching the hotel. The man was in Iquitos.

Bolan picked up the phone. "Go ahead," he said.

"Ah, Mr. Belasko," Rivas said. "Tsk, tsk, tsk. What dirty little lies you tell."

"Yeah, and you're the last bastion of truth aren't you, Rivas?" Bolan said. "Any particular reason you're calling? You've got to know I'm coming after you. And that when I find you I'm going to kill you. I'd think I'd be the last person you'd want to call."

The man on the other end of the line chuckled. "Kill me?" he said in a voice of mock surprise. "Why would you do that? We still have business to conduct." There was a pause. "The chemicals."

Bolan could barely believe his ears. "Sure," he said. "Be happy to sell them to you. Half-price sale today, as a matter of fact. Come on up to the room."

"Now, Mr. Belasko," Rivas said, "you are being sarcastic and it does not become you. I don't know exactly who you are or what agency of your government you represent. My guess would be the CIA, but that is neither here nor there. In any case, yes, I know you are not going to sell me the chemicals at any price." Another chuckle came over the phone. "I have, however, learned that your friend Mr. Scarberry was once with the DEA here in Iquitos. Funny I never ran into him. But I don't think you are with the DEA, or that coming after me was a DEA operation."

"You're very wise, Rivas," the Executioner said. "No wonder you've gotten so far in life."

"Thank you," the NFP man said. "Anyway, since you won't sell me what I want, I have arranged a trade." Silence came over the line. A moment later, Rivas said, "Are you still there?"

"Of course I am. I'm just waiting to hear whatever insanity you plan to spout out next. You've got nothing I want to trade for."

"No," the NFP man said. "You are correct. I have nothing you would want to trade for. But perhaps Mr. Scarberry will be more cooperative. Would you put him on the line, please?"

Bolan frowned, wondering that this was all about, as he handed the phone to Scarberry. The former DEA man took it and pressed it against his ear. "Rivas, what makes you think—" Suddenly, his face turned white and he stopped speaking. He grasped the receiver so tightly Bolan thought it might snap in two. Finally, in a whisper so low he could hardly be heard, he said. "Okay. I'll put him back on." He handed the phone to Bolan again and stared at the wall like a zombie.

The soldier took the phone. Rivas began speaking again. A few moments later, Bolan said "Okay" into the receiver and hung up.

Turning toward Scarberry, he said, "I'm supposed to come alone. Rivas is going to call us back in half an hour with further instructions. I told him I'd do it."

Scarberry came out of his stupor. "What do you mean, you told him you'd do it? You can't do it. You don't have the chemicals anymore. I heard you tell Kinelli so."

Bolan shook his head. "No, I don't have them anymore. By now they're safe in the U.S."

"Then how in hell do you think you can pull this off?" Scarberry almost screamed.

Lee Kinelli had sat quietly on the bed since they'd arrived, but now he cut in. "Excuse me, gentlemen, but did I miss something? It almost sounds like you're talking about actually trading the chemical weapons to Rivas."

Bolan started to explain but Scarberry beat him to it. The former DEA man's eyes were wild with fear as he turned to the minister. "Rivas has Anita," he said. "I just talked to her myself."

HE WENT ALONE, as he'd been ordered to go.

The rickshaw stopped under a streetlight. Bolan got out and paid the driver before walking through the shadows down to the dock. He had racked his brain trying to come up with a plan to get Anita back. The obvious answer was to have Stony Man Farm hurry down with a set of fake chemical weapon canisters and plant them in the jungle where they'd removed the real ones. But that would take hours, and all attempts he had made to stall Rivas when he called back with instructions had fallen on deaf ears. The NFP man wasn't taking any chances this time. Bolan would play the game his way, on his time chart, or Anita would die.

So he had come up with another plan. Not as good, perhaps, but all he had.

The rowboat came out of the darkness into the faint glow of the lights along the dock. It was manned by a lone rower. "Señor Belasko?" the man said, giving the Executioner a giant, gaping smile.

Bolan didn't answer. He just got in.

The oarsman took them away from land and the lights of the dock into the darkness of the Amazon. Bolan watched the shore fade in the distance under the full moon overhead. It took a good fifteen minutes to reach the large luxury cabin cruiser, and Bolan was reminded again that the NFP wasn't the typical "pay as you go" terrorist outfit This craft had cost money. And that money had come from cocaine dollars.

A ladder came down over the side and the soldier climbed to the deck where a half-dozen armed men awaited. Rivas was nowhere in sight. He waited while two of the NFP men shook him down. He had known that would happen and left the Desert Eagle, Beretta and all other weapons with Scarberry and Kinelli. There was no sense in carrying them down to the boat only to have them taken.

When the two men were satisfied that he was unarmed, they stepped back and pointed to the ladder leading belowdeck. Bolan followed one of the men down while another prodded him along with the barrel of an AK-47. He could hear the feet of the other four behind them. They walked down a short hallway and turned into the master cabin, where Rivas lay half-reclining on the bed. His back rested against several pillows, and he was talking in a soft voice to the girl tied, hand and foot, next to him. He looked up when Bolan walked in.

"Ah, my friend Mike Belasko," he said. "I am so happy you could make it."

Bolan ignored him as he walked toward Anita. The girl still wore the Inca skirt and top from Ari's, and the headband announcing the café was wrapped around her forehead. She looked up at the Executioner with fearful eyes but didn't speak.

There were no visible signs of abuse, but Bolan asked her anyway. "Has anyone hurt you?"

Anita knew what he meant. She closed her eyes and shook her head. The fear in her face told him that even if she hadn't been abused, the threat had hung in the air ever since they'd kidnapped her. He looked over at Rivas, who was grinning at him. "You're a lucky man," he said.

"Ah? How so?"

"You didn't hurt her. I promised Scarberry I'd kill you on sight if you had."

Rivas laughed. "You Americans," he said, shaking his head. "You always talk as if you were in a John Wayne movie." He nodded toward the men with the rifles in the doorway. "You have no weapon, and they would kill you before you reached me."

The Executioner smiled back at him, but his face was hard. He held up his hands. "I have these," he said.

"Perhaps we should tie your hands then," Rivas said. "Carlos?"

One of the men with the AK-47s handed his rifle to another and stepped forward. He pulled a short piece of rope from the pocket of his ragged pants and started to tie Bolan's hands in front of him.

"No, Carlos," Rivas said. "Behind."

Bolan smiled again. "I'm still going to kill you," he said. "That's a promise."

"Yes, Belasko, of course you are," Rivas said in a bored voice. Above them, the engine sounded and then the craft began to pull away and head down the Amazon.

Bolan was taken to a chair against the wall. He sat silently, staring straight ahead but covertly watching the movements of the men in his peripheral vision. When they had become used to him, and no longer stared his way as if he might get loose any moment and carry out the threat to kill with his hands, he let his hands rise slightly to belt level. Slowly, he ran a finger along the top of his belt until he felt the short slit at the top of the leather. It was centered in the small of his back. His finger probed gently inside the slit, then came out again.

It was still there. But it was too soon to make use of it. Way too soon.

The smells of the river came through the portals as the cruiser sailed into the night. Bolan waited. Rivas would pull the boat into shore as close to the helicopter clearing as possible. Probably the same spot where Bolan, Scarberry and Willie Richards had docked Richards's fishing boat two days before. Rivas knew the army had hidden the chemicals close by, and he thought that Bolan had rehidden them somewhere in the same vicinity. Just not the exact spot. And he didn't want to dig up the entire jungle looking when war was about to start. The Peruvian military might come to retrieve the canisters themselves while he was still looking.

Bolan watched the man on the bed. Rivas was still lying there, talking to Anita in a low voice. Occasionally, he reached out to brush back a lock of hair that fell over her forehead each time the craft dipped in the waves. Whenever he did, he looked over at Bolan and smiled, trying to get a reaction.

Bolan didn't give him the satisfaction of letting on that he even noticed.

The Executioner's job was to accompany them to the helicopter landing site, then lead them to the spot where the chemicals were hidden. As soon as the canisters were safely stored on the boat, the NFP man had assured him that he and Anita were free to go. He would even give them a ride back to Iquitos if they liked.

Right. What Rivas actually meant to do was to kill them as soon as he had his hands on the chemical weapons.

Bolan thought of the leak that had burned his cover even before he'd arrived in Peru. Brognola had finished interrogating the dirty Justice agent in Washington but still didn't know the exact pipeline between him and Rivas. The sergeant at the army base was part of it, but there had to be more. Bolan looked across the room at Rivas and suddenly saw the possibility of killing two birds with one stone.

"Hey, Rivas," he said.

The NFP man looked up from whispering to Anita.

"Too bad about Lopez."

Rivas shrugged and sat up on the bed. "There are many others willing to take his place," he said.

"Like who? Suarez?"

Rivas hooted out loud. "Ramon? No, he is like you. A fool who doesn't want money. He can't be bought. I've tried already."

Bolan nodded. At least he had learned Scarberry's old friend wasn't part of the traitorous group. "Well, that's nothing to worry about," he said, taking a gamble. "Imenez outranks him anyway."

Rivas's eyes came back to him. "Perhaps," he said but his eyes told Bolan "yes." He glanced back at Anita on the bed.

"No perhaps about it," the Executioner said. "Unless Mackey was lying."

This time Rivas's head shot up at the sound of the name. "Who?" he demanded.

"Come on," Bolan said. "Don't act like you don't recognize the name. Mackey. Steve Mackey in Washington. You didn't know my people busted him?" The Executioner was gambling. But so far his gambles had been paying off. And when a gambler was on a streak that was no time to stop.

"I knew immediately," Rivas said. "Before you, I am sure. But Mackey is out on bond. My bond. And he has been assured that all legal fees will be taken care of and that he will have a very nice job waiting for him in Lima if he keeps his mouth shut."

"Yeah, well," Bolan said. "Too bad he didn't. According to what my man in Washington got out of him, he was leaking information to both Lopez and Colonel Imenez. But you're right—not Suarez."

Rivas stared Bolan in the eye, and his own eyes were angry black orbs. "On the phone you told me I was a wise man," he said. "You were being sarcastic. But now, I will tell you in all candor, you are very perceptive."

Bolan met the stare. His gamble had paid off, and he had indeed killed the two birds he'd set out to get. First, he had learned that Colonel Imenez was the missing link in the pipeline from Washington to Rivas. And second, any shadow of a doubt that Rivas planned to kill him and Anita was gone. The NFP man would have never given up that information if he planned on letting them live.

The moon was high in the sky when the cruiser's engine slowed and they pulled into shore. The waters had receded even farther from where they'd been the day that Bolan, Scarberry and Richards had gone into the jungle. Rivas's cabin cruiser rode lower in the water as well, and they had been forced to bypass the shortcut and take the long route along the Amazon to the Napo River. But the Executioner recognized the area where the men on deck had anchored off as he was prodded on deck with an AK-47.

Anita had been untied from the bed, then had her hands bound behind her back like Bolan. The way she was dressed the jungle was going to be tough on her. The four men who had stayed on deck to operate the boat now joined Rivas and the six guards. Two took charge of Bolan and Anita, one on each side. With flashlight leading the way, they took off into the jungle along the same path to the clearing the Executioner had traveled two days earlier. The men at their sides guided Bolan and Anita, helping them over the rickety jungle bridges and other rough areas. Rivas walked just in front of them. The going was hard, but Anita didn't complain. Several times, she looked up at him, her deep brown eyes shining in the moonlight. In them, Bolan saw fear. But he also saw hope.

A drizzle began soon after they entered the jungle, and an hour later it turned to rain. Soon, they were all covered in mud. Twice during the trek, when he was sure no one was watching him, Bolan checked the slit in the back of his belt. Everything was still in place.

When the flashlights finally shone through the rain to illuminate the clearing, Bolan took a final look at Rivas and the other men. None of them were watching. They were too excited to see that they had reached their goal. Careful not to fumble it, the Executioner pried out the single-edged razor blade that he had inserted into the slit in his belt. Silently, as they took the final steps along the jungle path, he went to work on the cord binding his wrists. By the time they reached the clearing, the ties had been severed.

The Executioner kept his hands in place, holding on to the cords as he stopped with the other men at the edge of the clearing. The remains of the men the Executioner had killed still lay across the pile of foliage. The stench of two day-old corpses, rotting in the high humidity, assaulted their senses but it wasn't as bad as if could have been; much of the dead flesh had been eaten by insects and other scavengers.

Rivas stopped and turned toward him. "We know they must be close by," he said. "The army is too lazy to take them far and you didn't have the manpower."

The Executioner nodded. "You're nearly on top of them," he said.

"What?" Rivas asked. In the moonlight, Bolan could see him scowling.

"Didn't Solari tell you how I kept from getting shot out here that day?" Bolan said.

Rivas turned back to the pile of debris in the middle of the clearing and suddenly let out a laugh that echoed through the dark jungle night. "The chemicals are right there? Under the pile?"

Bolan shrugged. "Seemed like as good a place to hide them as any."

Rivas grabbed Bolan by the arm. "Where, exactly?"

The Executioner moved to the hole where he had finally emerged after tunneling his way through the pile. Still holding his hands behind him as if they were bound, he kicked a foot at the dark opening. "Send some men in there," he said. "Tell them to follow the tunnel. They'll find them."

Rivas cast a suspicious look at him, but he turned to two of the men and barked out the order. The men dropped onto their bellies and started to crawl into the hole. Several curses came from beneath the debris, then a moment later they dragged the remains of the men the Executioner had silently dispatched with the big RTAK jungle knife out of the opening. A second later, they disappeared again.

The sounds of the two men struggling through the opening could be heard for several minutes. Then all sound went dead.

Rivas waited, gradually growing impatient. Finally, he called out, "Have you found the canisters?" When he got no response he turned irritably to two more of his followers. "The fools have probably gotten lost. Go find them."

Another pair of NFP men disappeared into the hole. Several more minutes went by, then suddenly there was a rustling within the pile of vines, branches and leaves. Rivas stared at the sounds, then suddenly realized what was happening.

Bolan let the severed cord fall from his hands, grabbed Anita and threw her back into the jungle to one side of the clearing. As he turned back, Lee Kinelli rolled out of the tunnel where the NFP men had disappeared. The minister gripped the MP-5 in his hands and begun shooting. At almost the same instant, Tony Loriega's head came straight up out of the foliage less than a yard inside the edge of the pile. The DEA man's left arm was in a sling, but his right hand held a Glock 19 with an extended magazine. Barely tall enough to see over the mound of vines and leaves from which he'd emerged, he had to raise the pistol high in the air and fire downward. Both men began taking out the terrorists holding the AK-47s.

Rivas had frozen for an instant when he saw Kinelli, but then his hand fell to the .45-caliber pistol holstered on his belt. Bolan dived forward in a flying tackle, wrapping his arms around the NFP man and trapping his gun hand at his side. The two men hit the muddy ground, gritty brown water splashing up and over them. They rolled onto their sides, both struggling for the gun still in Rivas's holster.

The New and Free Peru leader's left hand clawed for the Executioner's face. Bolan closed his eyelids tight against the attack and rolled over on top of the man, bringing a big fist high over his head. He drove it straight down into Rivas's face, flattening his nose against his skull and sending bursts of blood shooting from both nostrils. The clawing fingers fell away.

Behind him and over his head, the soldier could hear the roars of the MP-5, Loriega's Glock and the terrorists' AK-47s. Scarberry emerged from the pile and swung up the Remington 12-gauge. The former DEA man fired, then pumped, fired, then pumped again, sending patterns of 12-gauge buckshot into the faces and bodies of the NFP men.

Below him, Rivas had finally worked the pistol out of his holster. But before he could turn it toward Bolan the Executioner brought his fist up over his head again, then slammed it down with every ounce of strength in his arm and shoulder. He felt Rivas's already broken nose give way further with a crackling sound and then the NFP leader jerked spasmodically as splintered shards of bone drive deep within his brain. A second later, he went limp.

Three of the remaining six New and Free Peru men were still standing when Bolan rolled off Rivas and grabbed a fallen AK-47. Still on his knees in the mud, he up brought the rifle and stitched a figure eight between the two men nearest him. The pair fell to the ground, and the Executioner saw the last man take off down the jungle path. Slowly, deliberately, he raised the rifle to his shoulder and sighted down the barrel. Flipping the selector switch to semiauto, he gently squeezed the trigger. The Soviet-made rifle bounced slightly against his shoulder and the last of the New and Free Peru men man did a back flip in the air as the 7.62 mm rifle round split his spine between the shoulder blades.

The roar of the guns died, but the insects and other life seemed still afraid to be heard. So a deathly stillness fell over the jungle.

Bolan rose to his feet as Loriega tore his way out of the debris pile with his good arm. Lee Kinelli got up off the ground at the mouth of the tunnel. "If I was Catholic," the minister said, "I'd be crossing myself right now."

Bolan turned, looking for Scarberry. He found him a moment later at the edge of the jungle. The former DEA man and Anita were locked in an embrace.

Epilogue

Dawn had broken over the Amazon River by the time Bolan and the others returned the cabin cruiser to Iquitos. The ever-ready rickshaw drivers waited on shore, and the group took the two-wheeled taxis into town. Ari's had just opened for the breakfast trade, and the smell of frying eggs, meat, tortillas, corn and onions filled the open-air café as they took seats at a long table next to the sidewalk.

Scarberry and Anita had not taken their hands off of each other since being reunited, and that didn't change now. They sat next to each other at the table, across from Bolan, their chairs pulled close and their arms wrapped around each other's waist. Bolan was happy for them. It might be a May-December romance, and it might or might not last because of the difference in their cultures and a language barrier that was only partially overcome by Scarberry's command of Spanish. But for now, they were happy, and the Executioner wished them well.

Bolan could not, however, comply with the wish they had expressed first in the jungle, then pestered him about all the way back on the boat. Both Scarberry and Anita wanted him to stick around for the wedding. Anita had announced she was pregnant, and in his excitement Scarberry moved up the wedding date. They insisted that Bolan play the part of best man.

"You saved my life," Anita had told him in her heavily accented and broken English.

"Hell," Scarberry had said, putting it in far plainer terms, "you are the best man. At least the best I've ever met."

Time after time, Bolan had respectfully declined their request. A laptop had been on board Rivas's boat, and he had contacted Brognola to report the success of the mission and told him about Colonel Imenez. He had learned from Stony Man Farm's director that they would take care of Imenez and that the diplomatic overtures of the U.S. President to the heads of state of both Peru and Ecuador had been agreed to. The man in the White House was flying to Rio de Janeiro to moderate new peace talks that would, with any luck, end the hostilities. The Man had been semisuccessful in convincing both of his South American counterparts that the strikes against their countries had been the work of terrorists, not each other.

As soon as Bolan grabbed a final bite at Ari's Burgers, he was off to the airport to meet Grimaldi.

The Executioner's war was waiting, wherever he touched down.

Outlanders brings
you a bold new look
in May 2002!
Different look…
same exciting
adventures with
Kane, Brigid, Lakesh,
Grant and Domi!

James Axler
Outlanders®

The first of a brand-new two-book story arc—
The Dragon Kings:

DEVIL IN THE MOON

As the ruling oligarchy of nine barons
rebuild what was once the United States
after an internecine war for power, a
mysterious entity is attempting to impose
a dark destiny on Earth. But the tides of
battle turn with the discovery of a
functional pre-dark moon base, whose
human defenders are all that stand
between Earth and its obliteration.

*In the Outlands, the shocking truth
is humanity's last hope.*

**Watch for the second book
of The Dragon Kings series,
Dragoneye coming in August 2002.**